Praise for Lina Bengtsdotter's debut thriller, *For The Missing*

'This smash hit Swedish debut breathes new life into a few well-worn det-fic themes to create a thriller that lingers in the memory' – *Sunday Times Crime Club*

'A powerful Scandi Noir debut by a promising new author . . . Atmospheric, evocative and with a heroine who overcomes some of the genre's clichés, this is a first-class procedural with all shades of grey unveiled like onion peel as the narrative progresses. With various parallel story strands deepening the mystery before they all come together in a flurry of unwelcome truths, this makes for an altogether excellent thriller' – *Crime Time*

'This debut novel is intelligent and arresting. And grim' – *Morning Star*

'This debut novel upholds the recent tradition of dark Nordic noir. A girl goes missing on her way home from the party in the forested village of Gullspång. Enter a Stockholm detective with a secret of her own' – *i Newspaper*

'A brilliant, dense crime novel' – *Dagens Nyheter*

'The next big Swedish crime sensation' – *Dagbladet*

'A wonderful debut' – *Dziennik Zachodni*

Lina Bengtsdotter grew up in Gullspång, Sweden. She is a teacher in Swedish and Psychology and has published a number of short stories in various newspapers and magazines in Sweden and the Nordic countries. She has lived in the UK and in Italy and today resides outside of Stockholm with her three children.

Agnes Broomé is a literary translator and Preceptor in Scandinavian at Harvard University. With a PhD in Translation Studies, her translations include August Prize winner *The Expedition* by Bea Uusma.

FOR THE
LOST

LINA BENGTSDOTTER

Translated from the Swedish by
AGNES BROOMÉ

ORION

First published in Great Britain in 2022 by Orion Fiction,
an imprint of The Orion Publishing Group Ltd,
Carmelite House, 50 Victoria Embankment
London EC4Y 0DZ

An Hachette UK company

1 3 5 7 9 10 8 6 4 2

Copyright © Lina Bengtsdotter 2020
First published as *Beatrice* by Bokförlaget Forum, Sweden in 2020
Published by agreement with Bonnier Rights, Sweden
English translation © Agnes Broomé

A CIP catalogue record for this book
is available from the British Library.

ISBN (Mass Market Paperback) 978 1 4091 7941 2
ISBN (eBook) 978 1 4091 7942 9

Typeset by Deltatype Ltd, Birkenhead, Merseyside

Printed in Great Britain by Clays Ltd, Elcograf S.p.A.

www.orionbooks.co.uk

To Enna and Elmira. Hold on.

Prologue

They were sitting in a circle on the floor, in their nightgowns, slippers, and Thorazine hats. For a split second, I thought they were asylum patients who had lingered on the wrong side of life. Unhappy souls who had failed to find peace after being subjected to treatments like rotation therapy, surprise baths, and lobotomies.

'Who's there?' a voice said. 'Step into the light, stranger.'

'It's me.'

'Come in, Sara,' Lo said. 'We were just about to have story time.'

I entered the room. Candles in bottles burned in the middle of the circle. Their flickering flames cast long shadows across the girls' pale faces under the wide brims of their straw hats.

'What happens if we get caught?' I asked.

'We're not going to get caught,' Lo replied and made room next to her. She accepted a bottle from Nicki.

Heart's-ease, Dad used to call spirits. *A bottle of heart's-ease.* And he was spot on, I thought to myself as the burning liquid trickled down my throat and the pressure in my chest eased.

'Go on, Nicki,' Lo said.

Nicki bowed her head and went on: 'Once upon a time,

there was a girl ...' She looked up and asked us to close our eyes.

I closed my eyes and wished I was a girl who believed in fairy tales and sunshine stories. I wanted there to be hope for us somewhere, wanted us to leave the asylum strong, healthy people, capable of building normal lives for ourselves. Nothing fancy. Just regular lives.

I

The decibel level in the bar had risen. Charlie's head was spinning. She should have gone home hours ago, but then a man in a suit with no ring on his finger had sat down next to her, giving her hope the evening might still end the way she wanted.

They'd been talking for a while when the man, whose name was Jack, asked her where she was from.

'Stockholm,' Charlie replied.

'I meant originally. Isn't that a hint of dialect I detect?'

'It's been a long time since anyone commented on my dialect,' Charlie said. 'I thought it was gone.'

'It's not. Are you from Östergötland?'

'No, I grew up right on the border between Västergötland and Värmland.'

'In which town?'

'It's a tiny place. You don't know it.'

'Try me.'

'Gullspång.'

Jack frowned. 'You're right,' he said. 'I don't know it. Sorry.'

'No need to apologise.'

'So, tell me about it, then,' Jack said. 'Tell me about Gullspång.'

Charlie was just about to say there was nothing to tell, but with four pints in her, she was feeling unexpectedly talkative.

'I lived in a small cottage pretty far outside the town proper.' She paused and took a sip of her beer. 'There was a cherry grove and a woodshed and a sparkling lake.'

Jack smiled and said it sounded like a fairy tale.

'Lyckebo,' Charlie said.

'Pardon?'

'That was its name, the house I grew up in. Lyckebo.'

'Were you happy there?'

'I was,' Charlie replied. 'I really was.'

She'd read somewhere it was never too late to have had a happy childhood. Maybe this was how you made it happen. By exaggerating the good and erasing the bad, by lying and beautifying until you believed it yourself.

Jack asked if she had any siblings and Charlie thought about the boy's room that was never completed, about the cars Betty had painted on the walls, the bed that was going to be a bespoke built-in.

'Yes,' she said. 'A brother. We are very close.'

Were, she corrected herself inwardly. We *are* nothing anymore. She pictured Johan's face, the worry in his eyes when suspicions had surfaced about them being related by blood.

I really hope I'm not your brother.

And her response: *I thought you'd always wished for a family.*

Johan. For a while after he died, she'd been unable to turn off the slideshow of images playing on a loop in her head: his eyes when she came out of the lake with no clothes on, the motel bed, the cherry wine in Lyckebo. And then: all the things that never came to be.

'I have a sister,' Jack said, 'but I hardly ever see her. We

4

didn't even play together as children, despite being only two years apart. Maybe because we didn't like doing the same things.'

'For me and Johan, it was the opposite. We always liked doing the same things. We built forts in the woods behind our house and played down by the lake.'

'Your house was on a lake?'

Charlie nodded. It was practically true. 'We used to row out on the lake in our own little boat,' she went on, 'and we had a pet fox. It was as tame as a dog.'

'Is that even possible?' Jack said. 'Taming a fox?'

Charlie thought about the bloodbath in the chicken coop, about Betty telling her you can't take the wildness out of a wild animal: *They may seem as tame as anything, but sooner or later, their animal instincts will take over.* And later, when the disaster was a fact: *I told you so. Didn't I tell you it would end badly? Now look what happened.*

'It is,' Charlie said. 'Our fox was as meek as a lamb.'

Jack leaned closer. 'It sounds idyllic.'

'It was idyllic. A proper fairy-tale existence. Want another?' She nodded towards his empty pint glass.

'I'll get it,' he said, stood up, and began to push his way towards the bar.

Charlie watched him walk away. He was tall and nicely built, but that wasn't what had caught her interest. There was something about the confident way he walked, the way he looked at her like he was curious about her, the balance between possibility and resistance.

'Now you tell me a bit about you,' she said when he came back with fresh pints. 'Tell me about your job.' She'd already forgotten what he did for a living.

'There's not much to say,' Jack replied. 'Being an economist isn't particularly exciting. I actually wanted to be an actor. But my parents said that wasn't a real job, so ... And I suppose I might not have made it, but ...'

'But what?'

'Sometimes I wish I'd given it a go. I mean, what's the harm in trying? Now, I'll never know if it might have been for me.'

'It's never too late, though, is it?' Charlie said, thinking she was probably full of it, that it probably was exactly that, too late.

'I'll drink to that,' Jack said and raised his glass. 'Here's to it never being too late.'

'It just makes me sad,' Charlie added. 'Parents limiting their children.'

'Did yours?'

'Definitely not. My mum always said I could be anything I wanted – anything except a dancer.'

'So, what did you become?' Jack asked.

'A dancer,' Charlie replied. 'I became a dancer.'

It was quarter to one. The place was about to close.

'What do we do now?' Charlie asked.

'I'm ... married,' Jack said. 'I'm sorry if I—'

'Don't worry about it,' Charlie replied, trying to hide her disappointment. She felt duped. Why didn't he wear a ring? If he wasn't going to let the women he sat down next to by his volition pick him up, he should at least have the decency of wearing a ring.

'Wait,' Jack said when she got up. 'I mean, can't we—'

'I have to go home,' Charlie said. 'I have work tomorrow.'

'Dancing?'

'What?'

'I was asking if you're dancing?'

'Yes.'

'Can I walk you part of the way?'

'I'll be fine.'

'I'd like to walk with you, though, if that's OK?'

She shrugged. Her flat was less than five hundred yards away and she didn't mind him walking along if it was that important to him.

It was mid-April. The smell of gravel and dry asphalt made Charlie feel free, happy, and sad all at once. She wished time would stop when spring came, that she wouldn't have to listen to her colleagues go on and on about their summer holiday plans and then face the feeling of emptiness that always over-whelmed her whenever she had time off work.

'This is me,' she said when they reached her building. 'This is where I live. Thanks for a lovely evening.'

'Thank you,' Jack replied. 'You're interesting to talk to. You're ... different.'

But I hope you aren't, Charlie thought when he seemed to struggle with himself.

'I wouldn't mind coming upstairs with you for a bit ...' he continued. 'I'm ... not really the type to do something like this, but ...'

I know, Charlie thought as they walked up the stairs. No one thinks they're that type, and yet there are so bloody many of you.

She missed the keyhole and made a small dent in the door. Soon enough, it would look like the one to her last flat, like someone had tried to hack their way in.

*

'Nice place,' Jack said as they entered. He looked up at the ceiling as if trying to gauge how high it was.

Charlie had used part of the inheritance from her father to buy the flat on Östermalm. At first, she had refused to take even so much as a penny from Rikard Mild, but a stubborn lawyer had counselled her to swallow her pride, or it would all go to his other children and his widow. That had made Charlie consider her half-sister's enormous villa in one of Stockholm's poshest suburbs and decide to accept what she had a legal right to.

Anders had been the one who convinced her to invest in a new home. Charlie had put up a fight at first. There was nothing wrong with where she lived. And Anders had explained that he hadn't meant to imply there was, but that maybe she should plan for the future, just a little. Even if she didn't care for her own sake, it might come in handy if she ever wanted to start a family.

I won't, Charlie had replied.

But then she had started going with Anders to open houses because he was looking for a place to move after his divorce. And there was something about this loft conversion she'd fallen for. Maybe it was the fireplace and the beamed ceiling, or the big balcony that made her stomach flip when she looked down from it. It was out there she'd heard one prospective buyer whisper to another that the previous owner had hanged himself in the flat. Afterwards, Anders said that was probably just a trick to turn off other buyers. Some people were willing to go to pretty sick lengths to keep prices down.

For Charlie, the effect was the opposite. She didn't believe in signs, but something about the alleged hanging had made her more emotionally invested in the property. She'd thought about what Betty used to tell her about Lyckebo, about how she'd been able to buy it cheaply on account of the previous owner's suicide. *One man's trash is another's treasure...*

A week later, she'd won the bidding war and the flat on Grev Turegatan was hers.

'What a painting!' Jack exclaimed, pointing to the big artwork in the butler's pantry. 'Who's it by?'

'Susanne,' Charlie said. 'Susanne Sander. She's a friend. She's ... unknown.'

'She shouldn't be,' Jack said. He walked closer to the painting. 'I love the details.'

Charlie nodded and thought about how happy it had made her when Susanne gave her the painting. She loved everything about it: the swirling black water, the flowering cherry grove, and the old red house, the woman in a dress and clogs on the porch, the girl in her arms, a mother with her daughter. Betty and her.

'She's really talented,' Jack went on. 'I like the contrasts. Darkness and light, depth and surface. It's two different seasons.' He pointed to the corners of the painting, done in more muted colours. 'They're dressed warmer,' he said, referring to the two backs that belonged to a grown man and a little boy. Mattias and Johan.

Charlie thought to herself that Jack had missed the saddest part of the painting: the little children to the left of the house, a baby girl and a slightly older boy, both with their eyes closed. She hadn't noticed them herself at first, because their clothes were the same colours as the flowers and grass around them; you had to look really closely to make out their bodies and faces.

'Want a beer?' Charlie asked, turning to Jack.

Jack nodded.

'I didn't realise dancing was so ... lucrative,' he said when they stepped into the spacious, newly renovated kitchen.

Charlie made no reply. She just stopped, turned around, pulled off her top in one smooth motion, and kissed him.

'How do you want me?' he whispered as she pulled him into the living room.

They stumbled and ended up on the plush rug.

'Do you like this?' he said, after they'd pulled off all their clothes and he was kissing the inside of her thigh.

It tickled, but Charlie still whispered yes and hoped he would cut to the chase soon. She dug her fingers into his hair and slid down to hurry things along.

'Wow, so you're keen,' he mumbled. 'You're the keen type.'

2

When they were done, Charlie wriggled out of Jack's embrace. As much as she had yearned for closeness thirty minutes ago, she now wanted nothing more than for him to leave. But Jack wasn't the perspicacious type, she thought as he put his arm back around her.

'You haven't lived here long, have you?' he asked.

'No, why?'

'I was just thinking you don't have curtains, or a lot of stuff in general, really.'

'I don't like curtains or stuff,' she said, and thought about what Betty had always said.

No heavy baggage for me. I travel light.

But in the end, Betty's baggage had grown too heavy after all, and it had pulled her under.

'Would you mind ... going home now?' Charlie said, pushing his arm off her chest.

'Are you having me on?' Jack sat up.

'No. I have work tomorrow and aren't you ... married?'

'My wife's out of town. I'm not in a hurry. But sure. I'll leave if that's what you want.'

'It's OK,' Charlie said. 'You can sleep on the sofa.'

'Are you serious?'

Charlie thought to herself that this was the problem with bringing men home; you had no control of how long they stayed.

'I just prefer to sleep alone,' she said. 'It's nothing personal.'

'It feels bloody personal.'

Jack got up and started gathering up his clothes with quick, hostile movements.

'You want to know what I think?' he said once he was fully dressed.

Charlie figured she was about to find out whether she wanted to or not.

'I don't think your childhood was as amazing as you make out. You're … You seem kind of damaged.'

'Isn't that a bit of a leap, just because I like to sleep alone?' She sat up.

'It's not just that. It's something else, too. Something's off with you. I can feel it.'

Charlie lay back down and closed her eyes. It was just her luck that the man she brought home was a thin-skinned amateur psychologist. She had never given much thought to the fact that she couldn't bear to sleep with another person. The few short periods when she'd been in any kind of relationship, she'd avoided overnights as much as possible because the inevitable lack of sleep left her exhausted.

Charlie thought about the parties in Lyckebo, about Betty falling asleep anywhere but her bed and being impossible to rouse, the feeling of waking up in her room with stinky alcohol breath all over her. *Are you asleep? Are you asleep, sweetheart?*

'You're wrong,' Charlie called after Jack as he walked towards the front door. 'I'm no more damaged than anyone else.'

'I don't believe you,' he said, adding before he slammed the door behind him, 'and I don't believe for a second that you're a dancer, either.'

Sara

'I don't understand why I have to go to this place,' I said, turning to Rita. She was sitting far too close to the steering wheel and revved the engine every time she shifted gears.

'That's scary to me,' Rita said. 'That you don't understand why. Don't you know what you've been like this past year?'

I said nothing.

'You've been acting like a crazy person,' Rita went on, 'like a mental patient. I don't know why you're smiling. I've barely had the energy to do my job, what with all the phone calls and rules around you. I have a life, too, you know, a family to look after. Do you understand?'

I nodded, even though I didn't understand, because all Rita had was a weird boyfriend she didn't live with and never seemed to see. We were each other's closest living relatives and it sucked that after everything that had happened, she would still say such awful things to me, her own niece. Which one of us was the mental patient?

'It's not all my fault,' I said.

'Stop blaming others,' Rita replied. 'You've put yourself in this situation. No?' she went on when I rolled my eyes.

I thought to myself that most aspects of my situation were

outside of my control. It wasn't my fault Dad was dead, or that Mum hadn't come back, or that Rita hadn't offered to let me stay with her.

'Open the glovebox,' Rita said.

I opened the glovebox.

'Take out the cigarettes.'

I dug around old first-aid kits and manuals but couldn't find any cigarettes.

'Damn it,' Rita said. 'That prick took my smokes again. That's why I can't live with him. He doesn't understand the difference between yours and mine.'

'I have some,' I said.

We pulled over at a rest stop.

'Aren't you cold?' Rita asked, nodding towards my top, which showed half my midriff. She had tried to persuade me to put something else on, anything that didn't make me look like a streetwalker, but they were going to have to take me as I was at this place. 'This isn't a summer holiday you're going on, you know,' Rita added.

I said I did know that. But her words made me think of Dad and all his holiday plans. He used to talk about taking me to white beaches and palm trees, to coconuts and crystal-clear water. I quickly learnt not to believe him, but I'd still loved to listen to him talking about it. He described places so vividly I almost felt I'd been there. *You and me under a palm tree. I'm drinking a cold beer and you ... something else. White sand and turquoise water and not a soul as far as the eye can see.*

'I'm selling the house,' Rita said and ground her cigarette out. 'Look, there's no reason to keep it. And I can probably find some German or Norwegian who's willing to pay far too much for it. But I need to clean it out first and that's going to take a while, what with all the rubbish he collected.'

I pictured Rita and her friends emptying out our house. How they would laugh at the old Christmas curtains that had hung in the windows for years, be revolted by the smell of urine in the bathroom, roll their eyes at all the rubbish Dad had refused to get rid of. *How do people live like this?* The thought made me seethe with rage.

'He was almost like one of those hoarders at the end,' Rita commented.

'He just had a hard time throwing things out,' I said and thought about the jars full of bottle caps, broken lighters, and old coins.

'Exactly,' Rita said. 'And now all of it is my problem.'

'I'm sorry his death is so inconvenient for you.'

'That's not what I meant,' Rita said.

I told her I just wanted to go back home, that I wanted to take care of myself. But that wasn't possible, Rita said. I couldn't keep living like some Pippi Longstocking. Someone had to look after me.

Why?

For two reasons. One: I was destructive. Two: I didn't own a suitcase full of gold coins.

3

Charlie woke up before her alarm. She was lying naked on the sofa with just a thin blanket over her. Her throat was dry and her airways tight. She got up, pulled a shirt she found on the floor over her head and went to the kitchen.

Her breathalyser was sitting on the shelf above the fan. She blew into it and felt relieved to see the 0.0 on the screen. A few months ago, she had been pulled over the morning after a night out and been lucky to avoid trouble. She was done taking chances.

She took down the jar of sertraline and washed down four pills with a big gulp of water. A year and a half ago, she had doubled her dose from one to two hundred milligrams and the world had retreated even further. She was on the maximum dose now, the doctor who'd written the prescription had informed her. If this didn't help ...

She hadn't asked, then what? Because she already knew what the methods of last resort were.

The side effects had been exacerbated by the increased dosage. She now perspired excessively, suffered from insomnia, and had trouble remembering things, but she didn't mind, so long as it took the edge off the anxiety.

She forced herself to down a drinking yoghurt she found in the fridge, to settle her stomach. It wasn't until she noticed the strange aftertaste that she thought to check the expiration date and realised it was almost a week past it.

Fifteen minutes later, she went down to the garage, thinking about how much easier life is when you have money. She no longer had to look for a parking spot on crowded city streets or scrape ice off windows in the winter. The satisfaction of having more than just the necessities was really all in the details.

'Charline?'

Damn it, Charlie thought when she heard the whiny voice. She turned to her neighbour. Dorothea was, despite the spring weather, dressed in a fur coat that reached all the way to her feet.

'If this is about the paper things I put outside my door, I've removed them,' Charlie said.

'It's not about that.'

'OK. Do you mind if we talk about whatever it is some other time?' Charlie said. 'I'm on my way to work.'

'This habit you have of ... bringing strange men home late at night,' Dorothea ploughed on. 'A lot of people in the building think it's a problem.'

Charlie turned cold, then hot. She was Betty. It didn't matter that the setting was different. She was Betty and Dorothea was the lookouts in town, the home visits by the school staff, the screeching of women with adulterous husbands.

We don't care about them, sweetheart. We don't see them, don't hear them. Chin up and look straight ahead.

'In what way?' Charlie asked, levelly meeting Dorothea's eyes. 'In what way is it a problem?'

'Well, I'm sure you can see how,' Dorothea replied. 'It just doesn't seem safe, having all kinds of loose people running up and down the stairs, being given the entry code to the building.'

'How do you know it's loose people, that they're not my friends?'

'I don't know about you, Charline, but I for my part find it inappropriate. Maybe you should consider socialising with these friends of yours during the day instead. I believe I speak on behalf of the homeowners' association.'

'Then maybe you can relay a message from me to the home-owners' association,' Charlie said.

Dorothea nodded.

'I will invite whomever I like, whenever I like. And I don't care what people who don't know me think about me. Literally couldn't care less. Can you tell them that?'

'Why don't you tell them yourself at the next meeting.'

'I can't make it,' Charlie said. 'I'm busy that day.'

'How can you know that? We haven't even set a date for it yet.'

Charlie thought back to the previous homeowners' association meeting. The hours of complaining about bikes in storage areas, entry codes, and the poor cleaning job the contracted company had done in the stairwell. There were overly shrill children in the courtyard, strangers had been seen lurking around the entrance to the building, and one of the shrubberies hadn't been watered properly.

'Everyone has to attend, Charline, we're a small association and—'

'Am I required to by law?' Charlie said. 'Would it be illegal for me to not be there?'

Dorothea gave her a look of distaste and said that in this

association, everyone came to the meetings, always had. Then she turned around and stomped off towards her car.

Charlie thought about Betty again.

We don't care. We don't see, don't hear. Chin up.

But Charlie had seen the looks and heard the whispers. Sometimes, she'd even felt she could read minds, hear people thinking that the daughter was going to turn out as crazy as the mother.

Charlie had tried to make Betty be more like other mothers, the kind that didn't throw parties and invite just anyone. Because it could be dangerous. But Betty had laughed at her. Said she couldn't understand how she had managed to conceive such a critical and suspicious little girl.

And then, when the cash and booze were gone and Betty's frenzied elation had morphed into gloominess and she was lying on the sofa, staring into space, she would call for Charlie and tell her she should have listened. She should have listened because Charlie was the world's smartest person and Betty was an idiot. *I'm afraid your mum's an idiot, Charline.*

Dorothea drove past, revving her engine slightly and giving her one last glare.

Charlie smiled. I'm impervious, she thought. I don't care. And there it was again, a tiny flash of gratitude at being Betty Lager's daughter.

4

Her car. It looked like someone had lived in it. A jumble of paper cups, jumpers, and post. Why didn't she just clean it out? Why did things that other people seemed to do automatically seem so impossible for her?

She didn't remember that she'd promised to pick Anders up until she emerged onto the street. He lived just two blocks away and his car was at the garage.

While she was waiting outside his building, a family came out: a mum, dad, and a girl of about three. The mum had an infant in a carrier. Charlie watched as they set off down the street. What was it like to live that way? Creating little versions of yourself? Going to ballet lessons, parent-teacher meetings, and family get-togethers? Is that what it would have been like for her and Johan if not for …?

Don't romanticise, Betty whispered in her head. *Coupledom isn't for us, and it always falls apart anyway. One way or another, it always does.*

And yet, there they were, the mum, the dad and their children, and Charlie suddenly felt a wave of grief that life, or whatever it was, had damaged her so badly she would never be able to feel that kind of joy or safety with another person. It didn't matter that it might be imagined, false, and ultimately doomed to end. She wanted to believe in it, at least for a little while.

'This is lovely,' Anders said and picked up a brown banana peel from the floor. 'How can you bear living like this?'

'I can't.'

'Then why don't you keep it tidier? All you have to do is clean it out, right?'

'I clean it out all the time,' Charlie said. 'Or at least occasionally, but it just gets messy again straight away. It's the same thing at home. I don't understand how people keep everything tidy all the time.'

'It's just a question of putting things back where they go, straight away,' Anders said, as though it were the easiest thing in the world. 'You should take this car for a complete interior clean. I have a place that—'

'Some other time,' Charlie broke in. 'I have a lot on right now.'

'I thought things were kind of quiet, actually.'

'Not everything's about work,' Charlie retorted.

'Oh no? Did I miss something? Have you met someone?'

'Oh, come off it.'

'I'm not judging. I'm just jealous.'

'Of what?'

'That you have such an easy time finding company.'

'You would, too, if you just put some effort in.'

'Maybe, but how do you even go about meeting someone?' Anders said. 'Whenever I don't have Sam, I'm working. Besides, even if I did go out and make an effort, there's not a

lot to choose from … What are the chances of finding someone who's single and for there to be mutual attraction? What?'
He turned to Charlie who had burst out laughing. 'What's so
funny?'

'It's just that you sound like an old man, *mutual attraction*.'

'So what's your suggestion, then? I mean, to find someone
things could work out with.'

'Are you joking?' Charlie said. 'Since when have I ever
met anyone things could work out with? At least the way you
mean it. It usually works out for me, though.' She thought
about the night before and a wave of pleasure crashed over her.
Once Jack had stopped talking and got down to business, it
had been very good. If he hadn't been so angry and accusatory
afterwards, she would have liked to see him again.

Just then, a car turned out right in front of them.

'Oh, stop,' Anders said when she honked. 'He had right of
way, you know.'

'Does that mean he has to throw himself out like that,
though?' Charlie said.

'No, but you don't have to be so aggressive. Zebra crossing,'
he added and pointed towards a lady with a dog who had
already stepped into the street.

'I see her,' Charlie said.

'Why are you so stressed?'

'I'm not.'

'You should relax and enjoy not having any emergency cases
for once.'

'I am relaxed,' Charlie replied, and thought about how
unsettling she found it not to have a case to focus her energies
on. They had spent the day before at forensics being brought
up to speed on the latest technology, and unless something

urgent came in today, they were supposed to engage in what Challe liked to call 'their own edification'. Charlie, for her part, intended to take a deep dive into the latest international research on criminal profiling. She was hoping that would keep her nagging restlessness at bay.

Anders and Charlie walked into the lobby of the National Operations Department and swiped their cards at the barriers. Charlie had worked at the NOD for four years and was the youngest member of a team that consisted of the country's most skilled detectives. Despite that, she had never fully experienced that feeling other people often referred to: of not really knowing what they were doing and worrying about being exposed as an impostor. For her, it was the other way around. She was often surprised at the shortcomings and gaps in knowledge exhibited by her colleagues. Challe was her boss, but that wasn't why she respected him the most. He was sharp and hard in a way that appealed to her because his mood and reactions were easy to predict. She was also grateful to him for giving her more and more responsibility and for believing in her even though she had often given him reason to doubt.

They had fifteen minutes before the morning meeting. Charlie quickly skimmed the big morning papers' websites and then moved on to the local paper she had bought a subscription to. She had gone from avoiding anything to do with Gullspång to following almost everything that happened there. From the football team that had advanced from division five to division four and the dairy farmer who had become a silversmith instead, to bike and boat motor thefts.

Kristina was setting up refreshments in the conference room.

'Lovely weather today,' she said and opened the curtains. 'It looks like spring has finally sprung.'

'Yes, amazing,' Charlie replied.

She took a coffee cup and filled it with water from a pitcher on the table. It was no secret she and Kristina didn't get along, but Charlie was slowly learning to simply limit their conversations to the weather. That way, she didn't have to waste energy on trivialities. It usually worked.

Hugo entered and then Anders and Challe and the rest of the team.

They had a new colleague, Greger Vincent. He was a transfer from the Stockholm CID and had only been at the NOD for a few weeks. They hadn't worked a case together yet, but Charlie looked forward to doing so because Greger had a good reputation and had already made her laugh several times. Now, he sat down at the conference table, dressed in a white shirt with a coffee stain on it, which Kristina naturally couldn't resist commenting on as she walked towards the door.

'These things happen,' Greger replied indifferently.

Charlie smiled at him. She liked when people weren't too anxious about their appearance. Greger smiled back at her and raised his cup in a toast.

Sunlight streamed into the room. It was a happy, relaxed meeting, but, as usual, Charlie spent every minute of it hoping it would end. She could never get used to talking about nothing and participating in conversations with no direction or purpose. When the subject of travel plans came up, she picked up a second cinnamon roll and zoned out.

'What about you, Charlie?' Challe suddenly said.

'I don't know,' Charlie said. 'I might go down to my house in Gullspång. What?' she asked when the others chuckled.

'We're talking about what we're planning to do today,' Challe said. 'Our edification.'

'Oh, right ... Well, I guess I ... There are some new German studies on criminal profiling. I was going to read up on that.'

'Great,' Challe said. 'Maybe you can share with the group later if you come across anything interesting.'

Charlie nodded.

Greger left the room right ahead of Charlie. He kind of ... sauntered, she noted, as though he were a young boy, even though he had in fact just turned forty. Some people were like that; they retained a childish quality as they aged, while others, such as herself, were born old. At least that's what Betty used to say. *I have the world's oldest daughter.*

5

The first thing Charlie did when she got home from work was light a fire. Not because it was cold but because she liked to stare into the flames and listen to the crackling of burning birch wood. She hoped it might help to settle her restlessness, which had grown more intense as the day wore on. She should read for a while. She went and fetched her book from the nightstand. She was halfway through *Will and Testament*, and she had loved it from the first page, but right now, even Vigdis Hjorth's captivating narrative wasn't enough to distract her. Maybe she should head out for a bit, just a short outing and then home. It was Friday, after all.

She started scrolling through the numbers in her phone. It was full of incomplete names of men that required a brief description. Tim, the guitar guy, Bartender Adam, Ludde J. They would all either be too much hassle or it had been too long since she last saw them.

She gave up and texted Anders: *A pint?*

Within seconds, he texted back: a picture of a dinner table. *Maybe later.*

She sighed and resigned herself to going out on her own. Anders wouldn't be done with that dinner for hours and by the time it was over, he might not have the energy to come out.

Of all the promises Charlie liked to make herself, the promise not to drink alone was the hardest to keep. She'd read somewhere that if you didn't want to become an alcoholic, that was what you should avoid at all costs, but it was hard. The only thing that sometimes kept her from doing it was the fear that she would become properly addicted and therefore be forced to cut out alcohol entirely, because a teetotal life ... She wasn't sure it would be worth living.

Ten minutes later, she left her flat and hurried past Dorothea's door.

She had walked a few blocks at random when she heard loud music from further down the street on her right. It was coming from a basement. Charlie stopped next to a group of women in their thirties who were smoking on the street outside and asked if there was a bar down there.

There was, one of the women said, and not just any bar, but the bar with the cheapest beer in all of Stockholm, despite being located in Östermalm.

Charlie walked down a flight of steps and was greeted by damp air and low ceilings. She sat down on a barstool and ordered a pint.

Sara

'Isn't this lovely?' Rita said when we turned into the forecourt of the enormous brick building. 'It looks like a palace. It's hard to believe it used to be a madhouse.'

We walked up the gravel path. The park around the building was so big I couldn't see where it ended. It was full of neatly raked paths, topiaries, trees, and benches.

'Why are you stopping?' Rita asked.

'What's that?' I said, pointing.

'A statue,' Rita replied. 'Of an angel.'

'Yeah, I can see that, but why doesn't she have a head?'

'I guess it fell off,' Rita said. 'Why are you getting hung up on details?'

'It's Nike of Samothrace,' a voice said, and then a girl stepped out from behind a shrubbery. She was as lightly dressed as me. 'And it's not just her head that's missing,' she went on, pointing to the statue. 'She doesn't have any arms, either, or feet. But she does have wings, for all the good it'll do her. I mean, what's the point of being able to fly if you can't see where you're going?'

When we entered the lobby, we were greeted by a woman who extended her hand and shook first mine, then Rita's. Her name was Marianne, and she was the manager of the residential care home. She said she was sure I would like it there and asked us to follow her down a long hallway with fossils in the stone floor.

We had sat in Marianne's office for several minutes before I noticed the tiny dog in the corner behind the desk. It suddenly stood up and came over to me. It looked like no other dog I'd ever seen. It was as though its parts didn't quite go together; the teeth in its underbite were too big and its ears pointed in different directions.

I quickly got tired of listening to Marianne monotonously droning on about rules, visiting days, restrictions, and times to keep.

Rita seemed as unfocused as me. She was probably just waiting to get out of this place, smoke a cigarette, and go back to that man who didn't know the difference between yours and mine.

Marianne left the room for a bit and when she came back, she had with her a nightgown, a robe, and a pair of flat, white slippers for me. The floors were cold at Rödminnet, she said, and robes were required at breakfast if you weren't dressed yet. Eating in one's nightgown or underwear was not allowed.

'And this is for you,' she went on and handed me a hard-bound notebook. The front cover was a photograph of a sun beaming down onto a summer meadow. I asked what it was for, and Marianne said I was supposed to write in it, that every girl at Rödminnet had one. Then she asked if I had any questions.

'I was wondering,' I said, pointing at the dog in the corner, 'what breed that is?'

'She's a mutt,' Marianne replied. 'I think there's miniature pinscher and chihuahua in her, but I'm not sure. I found her in Spain,' she went on. 'You should have seen her back then, she was all skin and bone, and fleas. But I told my husband: I'm not leaving without that dog. And so, here she is, our little Piccolo, a true sunshine story.'

After Rita left, Marianne showed me to my room. We walked down long stone hallways. On the walls were large black-and-white photographs of people with sad eyes and weird hats. I stopped to read the caption under a picture of four women in white on a bench, all with embroidery hoops in their laps. *Patients from pavilion two doing needlepoint in the sunshine.*

'Unique, aren't they?' Marianne said.

'What are those weird hats?'

'Thorazine hats.'

'Huh?'

'Thorazine is a drug that was used in the olden days to treat psychosis. It made the patients' skin very sensitive to sunlight. The hats shielded them from the sun.'

A woman and a man were walking towards us from the other end of the hallway.

'This is Emelie, my assistant, and Frans, who is a psychologist,' Marianne said. 'Come, say hello to Sara.'

They came over and shook my hand. Meeting so many new people was making me feel tired. I just wanted to go and lie down in a room somewhere.

'This is it,' Marianne said and knocked on a door as she opened it. 'Lo, come say hello to your new room-mate. But, why aren't you dressed?' she exclaimed, and a hoarse voice replied that she was fully dressed.

Marianne sighed and asked me to come in. It was a fairly small room with pine bunk beds along one side and a long desk with two chairs along the other. The girl named Lo watched us from the top bunk.

'This is Sara Larsson,' Marianne said. 'The new girl I told you about.'

'You never mentioned a new girl,' Lo said. She sat up and crossed her thin legs.

'Yes, I did,' Marianne said. 'And now I'll let the two of you get acquainted. You can show Sara around Rödminnet. Show her the garden, the new raised beds in the greenhouse, and—'

'Relax,' Lo interrupted. 'I'll show her everything.'

'What was your name again?' Lo asked after Marianne left.

'Sara.'

'Sara, Sara, Sara,' she sighed. 'Commonest bloody name in the world.' She yawned and raised her arms above her head. 'Lo Luna Moon is my name,' she went on. 'My full name. It's because I was born prematurely on a night with a full moon. Lo Luna, see?'

I looked around the room again. The tall window, the autumn sky outside. The desk and the stacks of books on the windowsill.

'Are those yours?' I said, nodding towards the books.

'Yes. Do you like to read?' Lo asked. And when I didn't answer straight away: 'Or are you the kind of loser who has never opened a book in your life?'

'I love to read,' I lied, because I didn't want her to have the upper hand right from the start. I walked over to the books and pulled one out. There was an old man on the cover.

'*The Divine Comedy*,' Lo said.

'Is it funny?' I asked.

Lo just laughed. 'So,' she said once she'd calmed down, 'do you have a boyfriend?'

'Why?'

'I just want to know if you're going to be sneaking out at night and stuff.'

I thought about Jonas Landell. I had spent the past few months practically living with him in his grandmother's old house by the fire station. I think it was mostly because I liked not being alone and he was a good cook.

'No,' I said. 'No boyfriend. You?'

Lo shook her head and asked what my restrictions were. 'The things you're not allowed to do,' she clarified when she realised I didn't understand.

'Aren't they the same for everyone?' I asked.

Lo said it all depended on the state you were in. Some of the girls weren't even allowed to leave the building by themselves. 'You're probably going to find your freedom slightly curtailed.' She nodded towards my arms, where cuts shone bright red.

'That's not what it looks like,' I said.

'Sure,' Lo replied. 'You should know though, Sara, that in here, there's no judgement. In here, what people outside think of as madness is completely normal. You're not the only one with arms like that in here.'

'They're from the wood,' I explained. 'They're from the factory where I used to work.'

'Oh sure,' Lo said. 'But OK, whatever.'

Lo asked which members of staff I'd met and when I said I'd been introduced to Frans and Emelie, she told me to watch myself around Emelie, because she was a nasty piece of work who'd had girls transferred to places that were much

33

worse than The Asylum. Yes, they'd renamed Rödminnet, The Asylum, funny, no?

'Would you like me to give you the grand tour now?' Lo went on. 'Would you like to see the garden and the raised beds in the greenhouse?' She mimicked Marianne's tone.

'Not right now. I'm tired.'

I went over to the bed and lay down with my clothes on and stared up at the bottom of the top bunk. It was sagging under Lo's weight.

Lo told me I had only myself to blame if I dozed off and missed dinner. Then she continued to ask questions. She wanted to know why I was at The Asylum, if it was the first care home I'd been placed in and how many foster families I'd had. Then she wanted to know why I wasn't answering. It was pretty rude, she thought, to lie there in dead silence when someone was just asking a few simple questions.

'I'm tired,' I said again. 'Too tired to talk.'

'Fine, then I'm too tired to show you around later,' Lo replied. 'You won't know where anything is.'

'I reckon I can probably find it on my own.'

'Good luck,' Lo retorted. 'Just don't blame me when you get lost.'

6

I'm an idiot, Charlie thought when she woke up on her bath-room floor the next day. What had happened? She tried to piece together the memory fragments from the night before; the women on the street, the basement bar, the cheapest beer in town and then ... nothing.

She got to her feet. Dizziness made her grab hold of the sink. She peered out into the hallway, where her clothes lay strewn on the floor. She slowly gathered them up while she looked for her phone. It was on the kitchen counter.

She had an unread text from Anders.

Where are you?

She scrolled down and realised to her horror that she had sent him an incoherent text about how he should come out four hours earlier.

Her phone dinged. A new message from Anders.

You all right?

Absolutely, she typed with trembling fingers, *I'm all right*.

But how was she supposed to know if she was? The number of hours she had no memory of was alarming. She often had gaps in her memory after she'd been out drinking, but never an entire evening, an entire night. Suddenly, she was overcome with nausea and sprinted back to the bathroom, threw open the toilet lid, and vomited. When she was done, she rinsed off in the sink. Her heart was racing. She opened the bathroom cabinet and popped an oxazepam. Then she dragged herself to the bedroom, collapsed on the bed, and went back to sleep.

When she next woke up, it was almost eleven. For a little while, she felt drowsy and calm, but then she remembered all the things she'd forgotten, and panic surged through her again. She picked up her phone to distract herself. A breaking news headline on *Dagens Nyheter*'s website made her sit up: *Baby girl missing near Karlstad. Intense search underway.* The article was short but informative. A mother had left her nine-month-old daughter sleeping in her pram on the veranda outside her house and when she came out an hour later, both the baby and the pram were gone.

Charlie checked the other big news outlets. The missing baby was the top story everywhere, but details were thin on the ground.

She called her boss. He picked up immediately.

'I was just about to call you,' Challe said, 'about the baby in Karlstad. They're working against the clock, and they need our help. I figured I'd send you and Anders. Would you mind coming in?'

Dorothea opened her door two seconds after Charlie stepped out onto the landing. She must have been standing by her peephole, just waiting to jump her.

Charlie nodded curtly and started down the stairs.

'Hold on, Charline,' Dorothea called after her.

Charlie heaved a sigh and stopped. 'I'm in a hurry,' she said.

'I just wanted to let you know that I will be bringing up the problem of strangers running in and out at all hours at the next meeting. You've given me no choice.'

'I don't know why you're so worked up,' Charlie said. 'We just talked about it yesterday.'

'Exactly,' Dorothea replied. 'We talked about it just yesterday, and then you went and did it again last night. Yes, my husband and I were both woken up by the racket in the stairwell and when we looked out to see what was going on, well ... you'd brought home another friend.'

Charlie's heart skipped a beat. She had to hold on to the banister to keep from falling.

'Charline?' Dorothea had reached the top of the steps and was looking down at her. 'Are you all right, Charline?'

Charlie made no reply. She took a deep breath and continued down the stairs.

7

They had gathered in the conference room: Challe, Charlie, and Anders. Charlie did her best to avoid Anders's searching eyes. She tried to focus on the case at hand, but not even a missing infant could take her mind off the previous night. A stranger had come home with her. Who was he? What had they done?

'At half past eight this morning, Frida Palmgren put her nine-month-old daughter, Beatrice, out on the veranda in her pram,' Challe said. 'The girl usually sleeps for an hour and a half, but when Frida went back outside at half past nine, the child was gone. And the pram, too.'

'Do we have any information that's not in the papers?' Charlie asked.

'I'll get to that,' Challe replied.

'I just figured since we're pressed for time.'

'It'll take longer if you keep interrupting,' Challe said with an annoyed frown. 'The family is exceedingly wealthy. The child's father recently sold one of his companies for almost three billion, so we think there'll be a ransom demand before long.'

Challe turned to Charlie who had stood up, giving her a

look that said she should sit back down. But Charlie ran to the bathroom and threw up again.

After wiping away all incriminating traces and flushing twice, she looked in the mirror. What had she had to drink? What the fuck had happened? Who had come back with her? Had they had sex? She probed inward, felt the tenderness between her legs. Had that been there the day before, after her night with Jack? She couldn't remember.

'Are you not feeling well, Charlie?' Challe asked when she came back.

'I'm fine.'

Challe looked at her as though he expected more, but when nothing came, he just said the only thing she'd missed was that the family had no known enemies and that the door-knocking operation launched in the neighbourhood hadn't yielded any results so far. The dogs had picked up a scent but lost it again almost immediately because of the wind and rain. Besides, there was no telling whose scent it had been; it could have belonged to anyone who had visited the house in recent days.

'Who has visited?' Charlie asked.

'I believe they have a number of employees,' Challe said, 'and I suppose they might have had friends over, too.'

'Is there a team on the scene who can help support the parents if there's a call from the kidnappers?'

'They were just setting that up when I talked to the lead investigator,' Challe replied.

'All right, then we might as well get going, I guess,' Anders said, standing up.

Challe stopped Charlie on the way out. 'Can I have a word with you?'

'Sure,' Charlie said with a growing sense of unease.

'Can I trust that you'll behave yourself?' Challe said once they were alone.

'Of course.'

'There's no need to get upset. I wouldn't be having this conversation with you if you didn't—'

'I'm not upset. But a baby is missing. If you don't trust me to do my job, you should send someone else.'

'I do trust you.'

'Good,' Charlie said, adding inwardly that that wasn't exactly the impression he'd given just a moment ago.

'So don't let me down, Lager.'

'I'll do my best.'

And that was the truth, she thought as she walked away. She always did her best with whatever cards life dealt her.

She's finally asleep. Her chest rises and falls with each shallow breath. Her hair is curling in the heat. From time to time, her lips twitch as though she's sucking on an invisible dummy. Then she smiles in her sleep and the dimple in her left cheek deepens. I stroke her forehead. Her skin is so soft. She screws up her face, then relaxes again. I gently lean over her and smell the formula on her breath.

She's perfect.

8

'What happened last night?' Anders asked once they were on the road to Karlstad. There had been no need to discuss who was driving.

'Just a few too many pints,' Charlie said. She switched on the radio and turned the volume up so Anders would get the hint that she didn't want to talk. It didn't work.

'Have you fallen off the wagon again?' Anders said.

'I'm fine.'

'Then maybe you shouldn't call me in the middle of the night and ... You don't remember?' he asked when their eyes briefly met. 'You don't remember calling me?'

'Of course I do,' Charlie lied as panic started to creep back in. She'd seen the texts she'd sent Anders, but apparently she had called as well. What the fuck had she said to him? She picked up her handbag, pulled out a blister pack of oxazepam, and swallowed one without water.

'Headache?' Anders said.

She nodded and resisted the impulse to ask what state she'd been in when she called, if he'd heard anyone in the background, what she'd said. Maybe she should have stayed in Stockholm and tried to get to the bottom of what had

42

happened. Someone might have slipped a roofie into her beer. But then she thought about the statistics, that most people who thought they'd been drugged just had a high blood alcohol level. And even if that was what had happened ... what could she possibly do about it? She had no idea who had come home with her. She could go back to the bar and ask the people who worked there, but then what? An official investigation could be the end of her career. Challe might suspend her for good.

It didn't happen, she thought. Last night never happened. And for the second time in as many days, she was grateful for the skills she'd learnt as a child; the ability to compartmentalise, at least while she needed her focus to be elsewhere. From now on, the only thing that existed was a missing little girl whom they needed to find.

They had left the city behind, and fields, horse pastures, and forests spread out on either side of the motorway. They should reach Karlstad around four, so long as traffic kept moving.

'I keep hoping they'll call and say they've found her,' Anders said. 'It must be absolutely horrible for the parents. It's my worst fear, something happening to Sam. Sometimes I miss life before he was born, miss the feeling of being afraid of nothing.'

'I'm afraid of things,' Charlie said, 'even though I don't have children.'

'What are you afraid of?' Anders asked. 'Aside from the obvious.'

'What's the obvious?'

'Intimacy, love, relationships.'

'I'm not afraid of those things.'

'Then what are you afraid of?'

There's no point talking about it, Charlie thought. He doesn't understand. People with normal childhoods and psyches don't; they don't understand the baggage the less fortunate lug around with them.

'So, nothing?' Anders said.

'Mental illness,' she admitted. 'I'm afraid of losing my mind.'

'Why are you afraid of that?'

'Shouldn't everyone be? Isn't that the worst thing that can happen to a person, losing yourself?'

'I guess, when you think about it,' Anders said.

'I almost lost my mind after the thing with Johan,' she added. 'Causing someone's death is—'

'For God's sake, Charlie, you didn't cause his death.'

'Sure. But if I hadn't started digging into that cold case ...'

'Johan was the one who found it originally, and wasn't it his idea to go down to Gullspång to help out? How is it your fault that some lunatic went berserk and beat him to death? You can't blame yourself.'

'I know all of that,' Charlie said, 'but it still feels like it's my fault.'

'It's just a feeling,' Anders said. 'It's not true.'

But there's no such thing as *just* a feeling, Charlie thought. Feelings can utterly destroy a person. They can pull people down into the abyss and never let them resurface.

I feel like I'm falling, sweetheart, like there's nothing to hold on to.

9

Charlie read aloud the information they'd been given about Mr and Mrs Palmgren. She was normally fine to read in the car, but now she could only manage a few sentences at a time before having to look up at the road. There was nothing about Frida's profession, but Gustav Palmgren was an economist and entrepreneur with companies in both Sweden and Russia. The couple had moved home from Moscow just six months earlier, taking up residence in the newly renovated house on Hammarö.

'Frida was born in 1986,' Charlie said. 'She's twelve years younger than her husband.'

'OK,' Anders said. 'Is that a bad thing?'

'I'm just telling you how old they are.'

A phone call was coming in from a number with a 054-dialling code. Anders answered and put the phone on speaker.

'Any news?' he asked, after the officer on the other end had introduced himself as Roy Elmer in a broad regional dialect.

Tell us you found her, Charlie thought, tell us we can turn around.

But that wasn't the case. Roy just wanted an ETA. Anders told him they'd just passed Västerås.

Charlie finished reading what little material they'd been given and moved on to Google. First, she searched Frida Palmgren. There was very little information about her. She was mentioned as a donor to a fund set up in memory of a child who had died of cancer and as Gustav's wife in a handful of articles about him, but other than that it was just the usual stuff about when her name day was and where she lived.

Charlie opened Instagram and searched for her name. Frida Palmgren had an open account with 1690 followers. The most recent picture was a selfie taken just a few days earlier. Water and sunlight in the background. Frida's blue eyes looking straight into the camera. She looked younger than her thirty-four years. Her skin was perfect, her cheeks glowed, and her hair was glossy. Charlie scrolled down. The pictures were almost all of little Beatrice and the captions were more creative than usual. There was no *I love you to the moon and back* or *Out for a walk with my* followed by a heart emoji. Instead, Frida had used phrases from famous poems. Charlie's eyes lingered on a picture showing a beaming Beatrice in the spring sunshine. *For the light is you!*

She went further back in time, to 11 July 2017. A tiny bundle in a pram. *I must have waited a million years ...*

Frida Palmgren seemed completely infatuated with her daughter, at least judging from the pictures. But it was beyond well-known, Charlie mused, that Instagram pictures were often nothing but a façade. She went back to the search bar and tried Gustav Palmgren instead.

That resulted in a lot more hits. The first one outlined his involvement in various companies and listed information about his property (the plot was larger than average for the area), and how the residents of his neighbourhood voted (centre-right), and then articles about local boys returning triumphant from foreign adventures, a picture of Gustav with his arm around a colleague, both wearing expensive suits and smiling happily.

They built a classified ad site in Russia, the headline said, and the first paragraph summarised the amazing deal the two had struck in Russia.

Charlie read the rest of the interview aloud to Anders. It was pretty much a paean to their entrepreneurship, courage, and billions.

'I don't understand,' Charlie said. 'Explain to me how you get rich copying something that already exists? I mean, it must have already existed, right?'

'No idea,' Anders replied. 'But given as how it seems someone paid them for their company, their site must have been better than the others. I suppose they adapted it to the Russian market and just made it big.'

In the next article Charlie found, there was a longer, more serious interview with just Gustav, in which he reflected on his journey to the top. When she got to the end of it, she went back to the search results and clicked something that had caught her attention.

'What does he mean by the journey to the top?' she said.

'Pardon?' Anders replied.

'I just read an interview with him where he talked about the long journey to the top and ... well, I just get the feeling the guy started out pretty darn close to the top.'

Charlie looked at the picture again. It was of three young men in swimming trunks next to a lake. In the background, she noticed a familiar white building: Adamsberg Boarding School. She thought about her half-sisters, who had spent almost their entire childhoods there, in social circles that merged with each other.

'What do you mean?' Anders asked.

'Gustav went to boarding school,' she said. 'He went to Adamsberg. But from what he said in the interview, it sounded like he started at the very bottom of society.'

'What difference does it make?' Anders said.

'I don't know, I'm just telling you what I find. Isn't that how it works in the early stages of an investigation, when you don't know what might be significant?'

'I thought you were maybe implying it said something about him as a person.'

'Doesn't it? Surely your upbringing affects who you become, your socioeconomic class, and—'

'Sure,' Anders broke in. 'But being privileged doesn't automatically make you a bad person.'

'When did I ever say it did?' Charlie snapped. Then she remembered the squabble they'd had in a bar a few weeks earlier when Anders had accused her of classism. She'd said it couldn't be called classism when it was directed at the upper class, that saying that was as idiotic as going on about reverse racism, but Anders had been drunk and refused to understand. She was prejudiced against a certain class, consequently, she was classist.

She had laughed it off at the time, assuming he wasn't being serious, but now she wasn't so sure.

'You're not suggesting I think everyone from the upper class is a bad person, are you?'

'Sometimes you give that impression, Lager, just so you know.'

Sara

My first dinner at Rödminnet felt more like an interrogation. How old was I? What had I done before? What did I like to do?

Nicki, the girl I'd said hi to in the park, wanted to know where I was from, so I told her about Gullspång. No one had heard of it.

'No, Picco, you little ninny!' Lo suddenly exclaimed. 'That's all I had.' She lifted up the tablecloth. 'Stare all you like, there's nothing left. Does anyone have any more sausage?'

'I do,' I said, nodding towards the sausage ends on my plate.

I bent under the table and fed the pieces to the dog. She wolfed them down and then licked my fingers.

'It's unbelievable how scrawny she is,' Nicki said, 'considering how much she eats.'

'That's stray dogs for you,' Lo weighed in. 'When you live on the streets, you never know when your next meal's coming. So you'd better eat when you have the chance.'

'It's been a long time since she lived on the street,' Nicki commented.

'It doesn't matter,' Lo replied. 'If you ever have, you never forget. You never forget the hunger. Do you, puppy?' she said to Picco, who had now jumped up on her lap.

'I'm not even sure it's a dog,' Nicki said. And we had to agree Picco didn't quite look like any other dog we'd seen, what with her tail and long, slender paws. No wonder there was talk of her possibly being a rodent, maybe a sewer rat.

Lo rolled her eyes. Then she grabbed the dog's tiny snout and bared her fangs.

'Maybe this will shut you up,' she said to Nicki, taking no notice of the dog's deep growling. 'These aren't rodent teeth. So you can stop talking nonsense.'

'Put her down,' Nicki said. 'Emelie's coming.'

Lo quickly put Picco back down.

'Are you feeding her from the table again?' asked Emelie, who seemed to have appeared out of nowhere.

'No,' Lo replied, 'I was just holding her for a minute.'

'People food gives her digestive problems, you know that.'

'Absolutely,' Lo said. 'We would never feed her from the table.'

Emelie gave her an unpleasant look before walking over to another table and sitting down.

'Fucking bitch,' Nicki whispered.

Lo told her to shut her mouth, that it wasn't worth getting RFAed for something so trivial.

'What's RFA?' I asked.

'Be happy you don't know,' Lo said. 'It stands for "removal from association", but it's mostly about being locked up, and if they're really horrible about it, they strap you down, too. My advice to you: avoid it.'

'And how do you avoid it?' I asked.

'You follow the rules,' replied a ginger girl with cuts on her hands.

'Or you break them in a smart way,' Lo added.

*

'Tell me your story,' Lo said when we were back in our room. She was lying on her bed with her feet up against the wall.

'I don't have one,' I replied.

I closed my eyes, hoping Lo would take the hint that I didn't want to talk. She didn't.

'Drug abuse?' Lo said. 'Domestic violence? Self-harm? A mix of all three?'

'Nothing like that.'

'Then why are you here?'

'It's my dad.'

'Incest?' Lo asked, as though that were her first association with the word 'dad'.

'No. He's dead.'

'Sad,' Lo said. 'And your mum?'

'Gone.'

'Also dead?'

'No, just gone.'

'I'll never understand,' Lo said, 'how a parent can just abandon their child.'

'It's hardly my dad's fault he died.'

'I was talking about your mum.'

'What about you?' I asked, so I wouldn't have to talk about me anymore. 'Why are you here?'

'A misunderstanding,' Lo replied. 'They just came and took me one day. Social services, I mean. They took me from my mum for no reason whatsoever and since then I've lived with various foster families and in places like this.'

I said it sounded like hell and Lo said it had been. But she would be free soon. She only had 247 days left until she turned eighteen and then her incarceration would end, and she was finally going to be able to be with her mum again.

'Come up here,' she said.

I climbed up to her bunk.

'Check this out.' Lo pointed to a picture of a beautiful young woman in a bikini. Later, I found out that it was Donna, her mother. Below the photo, the wallpaper was covered in lines and crosses. 'These are the days left before my birthday,' Lo said, pointing. 'Soon, I'll be able to do whatever I want. That's my first tip to you: have a plan for what you're going to do when you get out. Do you have one?'

I said I'd only just arrived, that I couldn't bear to think about it.

'Want to see something?' Lo asked. Then she climbed down from the bed, opened the closet, and took out a discoloured, big-eyed doll styling head. 'This is Mia,' she said. 'Mum gave her to me when I turned eight. At first, I only did make-up, but now I mostly do her hair.' She turned the head around and showed me something called a fishtail plait.

'Looks good,' I said.

'Want me to do one on you?'

Lo had already walked over to the desk and pulled out a chair.

'Mum's going to flip when she sees your hair,' Lo said when she'd combed it all out. 'She's just going to love it. But you have to take better care of it. You should plait it at night, so you don't get tangles.'

When I said I didn't know how, Lo burst out laughing. She had never met a girl who couldn't do a simple plait.

'The only thing I'm good at when it comes to hair is plucking it,' I said. It was true. Plucking my own and other people's hair was one of my favourite things to do. It made me feel calm.

'Maybe you should come work in our salon,' Lo said. She had begun to plait my hair. 'What do you think? How would you like being a moustache plucker in the salon I'm going to open with my mum?'

'Is that even a job?'

'Let's just say it is.'

'OK.'

'Is that a yes?'

'Yes.'

There was a scratching sound from the door. Lo told me to hold the plait and went over to open it.

'All right, puppy, you can come in,' she said.

Picco came over to me. Her tail was wagging so hard her whole body swayed from side to side.

'A little sunshine story,' Lo said after saving her doll head from Picco's attentions. One day, Lo hoped people would say that about her, too. No one would ever be able to guess she had grown up in institutions. They would leave her salon with beautiful hair and say *That girl is a true sunshine story*.

IO

They had passed all the roadworks around Örebro when Maria called. That was another complicated aspect of having children, Charlie thought to herself, the fact that you couldn't completely cut the other parent out of your life if you split up. Anders and Maria had been divorced for over a year, but Maria still called as often as ever. About runny noses, mittens, planning days. Charlie had long since seen through it and told Anders that all the phone contact was just a way for her to control him, that he should restrict their communication to email and text only. But he clearly hadn't taken her advice to heart because he answered straight away.

'What did she want?' Charlie asked after Anders had been on for five minutes, saying that he understood, that he would look into it, that maybe her mother could take Sam one or two afternoons.

'She wants more child support,' Anders replied.

'Don't you have joint custody?'

'Yes, but sometimes she has to fill in when I'm working, and since she's back at work now too ... babysitters and cleaners and that aren't exactly free, and ... What?' Anders said when Charlie accidentally sighed a little too loudly. 'You think it's wrong to pay for help? I thought you were for women's liberation.'

'Not if other women with worse lots in life have to pay the price.'

'What do you mean?' Anders asked.

'Exactly what I said.'

'Creating paying jobs isn't a good thing now?'

'Whatever,' Charlie said.

'What do you mean, whatever? Why do you always try to change the subject the second you run out of arguments? Charlie? What's wrong?'

Anders turned to her.

'I don't know,' Charlie said. She was clutching her chest, gasping for air, unable to take full breaths.

Anders turned down a smaller road and pulled over.

'I'm OK,' Charlie said after Anders jumped out and threw open the passenger-side door. 'It's getting better. It's just ... I think it was just a panic attack.'

'*Just* a panic attack?' Anders replied. 'That looked pretty serious to me.' He went back to the driver's side. 'Are you going to tell me what it's about?'

'I did tell you. It was a panic attack.'

'And why do people normally get those, would you say?'

'We don't have time for this,' Charlie said. 'Maybe you could drive while we talk.'

Anders turned back out onto the road. They drove in silence for so long, Charlie thought maybe he was going to drop the whole thing, but just as she did, he picked it back up.

'I can't work with you if you won't tell me what's going on. It feels unprofessional.'

'All right, so what are you going to do?' Charlie said. 'Turn around and demand a more psychologically stable co-worker?'

'I just want to know what's going on with you.'

'The last time I confided in you, you ratted me out to our boss.'

'You didn't confide in me,' Anders said. 'And you don't have to keep bringing that ratting-out business up. I did what I had to do to save the investigation and you.'

'You could have talked to me.'

'You're not the easiest to talk to when you're like that. I viewed it as an attempt to help you.'

'Thanks for the concern.'

'Charlie,' Anders said. 'We don't have time to fight right now. I just want to say that no matter how close we are as colleagues and friends, I'm not going to turn a blind eye to your downward spiral, and I'm not going to lie to save you in the moment. I know you'll hate me for it, but I just want to make it clear where I stand.'

'There was really no need,' Charlie replied, 'but thanks for the ... clarification.'

II

Karlstad town centre had changed since Charlie was last there. She'd been thirteen years old the time a classmate and her well-meaning mother had brought her along to go to the cinema. Karlstad had felt enormous then, but now, compared to Stockholm, it seemed to have shrunk.

'Did you come here a lot?' Anders asked when she mentioned it. 'I mean, it's not too far from Gullspång, is it?'

'I guess that depends on your point of view,' Charlie replied. 'We didn't really have a lot of money to go places.'

'I understand,' Anders said. 'Or, actually,' he corrected himself, 'I don't think I really do. It's like I keep forgetting where you're from.'

I should be so lucky, Charlie thought.

The high street was busy. Charlie thought she could detect worry in people's eyes. The news about the missing baby couldn't have escaped anyone.

'I need to go upstairs and change before we head over to the station,' Anders said after they had checked into their hotel. 'Meet back down here in ten minutes?'

'I need to run an errand,' Charlie said.

'An errand?'

'Yes, an errand.'

'You're not bringing your bag up first?'

'I'll just leave it at the front desk. Meet you outside in a bit.'

As soon as Anders had disappeared into one of the lifts, Charlie asked the receptionist for directions to the nearest pharmacy. It turned out there was one in the nearby mall, a block away.

Just inside the revolving doors of the small mall, coats and jackets hung in a long row along the wall. *The Wall of Kindness* proclaimed big letters above the hooks, and then: *Take a coat if you need one – Leave a coat if you can.*

A middle-aged couple were ahead of Charlie in the line at the pharmacy. They were talking about the missing girl.

'But who would do something like that,' the man said. 'Who would steal a baby?'

'A madman,' the woman replied. 'A psychopath. A normal person would never do something like that.'

Charlie had to agree. A normal person wouldn't take a child. Unless … unless he or she had very particular reasons to do so. But what could those reasons be?

Her mind began to wander, and she didn't notice when it was her turn. The man at the till cleared his throat and asked how he could help her. When she said she needed a morning-after pill, he fetched a box and asked with a pompous look on his face if she had ever taken one before.

'Why do you ask?' Charlie said.

'I just wanted to make sure you know how to use it.'

'It comes with instructions though, right?'

The man nodded and took her money. 'It's not to be used

as a substitute for contraception,' he said when he handed her the receipt.

'Thanks, good to know,' Charlie retorted.

As soon as she was back out on the street, she took the pill out of its packaging and washed it down with a few big gulps from her water bottle.

One less thing to worry about.

They drove over to the police station, which was located on the other side of the motorway from the town centre, in a red-brick building surrounded by something that looked like barracks. The press were already there, of course; about ten journalists were blocking the entrance.

'No comment,' Anders said before anyone even had a chance to ask a question. 'At the moment, you know as much as we do, and you need to let us do our job.'

The pack parted to let them through and they stepped into the lobby, where a tall woman in her fifties and an older man who was breathing heavily came to greet them.

'Stina Ryd, lead investigator,' the woman said. 'And this is Carl Antonsson,' she continued, with a nod to the man. 'He's in charge of the search team and the door-knocking operation.'

Is he mute? Charlie wondered briefly before the man said hello and told them he had to run.

'Why don't you come with me, and we'll do a quick brief,' Stina said.

They followed her past a reception desk with passport-photo machines and glass windows. Charlie liked that she skipped the small talk, kept a brisk pace, and didn't smile.

'There are just three of us here at the moment,' Stina explained. 'Everyone else is out knocking on doors. As you'll understand, we're focusing on the search operation right now, actively looking for clues in the immediate area around the house. We've put out a description of Beatrice, too, of course. The fleece overalls she was wearing, the teddy bear she was sleeping with, and the pram. It's a black Bugaboo,' she went on, 'an expensive but very common pram. What we need your help with is the investigative side of things: interviewing people, gathering any information that might help us understand what happened, who might have taken her.'

She showed them into a conference room, where two of her colleagues were seated at an oval table.

'This is Sebastian Sandström and Roy Elmer.'

Stina nodded towards the two officers who both looked like they were in their forties. Neither of them got up to shake hands.

'Coffee?' Stina asked.

Anders and Charlie both said yes and were soon holding chipped cups of black coffee. Charlie waited for Anders to ask for soy milk or some other lactose-free alternative, but he didn't.

Stina turned to the big whiteboard on the wall. On it were labelled photographs of the Palmgrens and, above them, a photo of the main character in the drama, Beatrice. She was wearing a pink, turban-like hat. Her hand was outstretched as though she was trying to grab the camera and she was smiling so wide that her two bottom teeth showed.

'All right,' Stina said. 'I assume you're familiar with the basic facts of the case, and I'm afraid that's more or less all we have.'

She sat down and began to go over the course of events in slightly more detail. Not even her warm local dialect could hide the gravity of her words.

Frida had been home alone when it happened. She had put Beatrice out on the veranda in her pram eight hours ago. Then she had gone back inside to tidy up a little in the kitchen, which was located at the back of the house. Beatrice usually slept for at least an hour and Frida hadn't checked on her until half past nine. That was when she discovered the pram was gone.

Charlie noted the pained look on Anders's face when Stina went on to update them on what they'd accomplished so far. They'd scoured the terrain around the house, talked to most of the neighbours, and got what they could out of the dismayed parents.

When Frida discovered that Beatrice and the pram were gone, she had called her husband, Gustav Palmgren, who had immediately contacted emergency services. Stina took a sip of coffee and then told them that the faint scent the dogs had picked up may not have come from the perpetrator.

'What possible scenarios have you mapped out?' Charlie asked. 'What motives? The parents, for instance, what's your sense there?'

'For now, nothing about them seems suspicious,' Stina said. 'Except ... that we know what the statistics say.'

'They're wealthy,' Roy put in. 'Gustav Palmgren's very successful.'

'We know,' Charlie said.

'Let me finish,' Roy snapped.

'I apologise,' Charlie said. 'Please, go on.' She was annoyed. Wasn't snapping at someone ruder than unwittingly interrupting?

'Most people in this town know who Gustav Palmgren is,' Stina said when Roy didn't go on. 'The local press has written about him, and the national press, too. He's well-known and, inevitably, there's quite a bit of talk about the family.'

'What kind of talk?' Charlie asked.

'Mostly gossip, I suppose. Gustav and his business partner sold their company for an inconceivable amount of money, so ... well, I guess people like to talk about that. Maybe you know more?' Stina said, turning to Roy. 'He's personally acquainted with them,' she explained.

'No, I'm not. I did move in the same circles as Frida for a while, but that was years ago.'

'And what is she like?' Anders asked.

'She was very popular,' Roy said. 'Smart and good-looking,' he continued tentatively, as though that was an equation he couldn't figure out. 'She had a rough time growing up, but you really couldn't tell from looking at her. But then again, I mostly saw her in bars, and I suppose everyone's happier than usual when they're out drinking.'

'In what way did she have a rough time?' Charlie asked.

'Her parents were alcoholics. Proper derelicts, both of them. So she's certainly living a different life now.'

'If this is about the fortune,' Anders began. 'If it's a kidnapping, shouldn't we hear about a ransom demand soon?'

'We should,' Stina said, 'and we have people there to help them if that happens.'

'And their families?' Charlie asked. 'Parents? Siblings?'

'Gustav's an only child,' Stina replied. 'His father's dead and his mother's in a home. She has dementia. Both of Frida's parents are dead, but she has a brother, who ...'

'Who what?'

'Who's in rehab. He's a junkie, with a criminal record.'

'What's on it?'

'The usual: burglaries, possession, drunk driving.'

'And what's his relationship with Frida like?'

'Not great, I'm assuming. The guy has a substance-abuse problem and that usually destroys most relationships. But right now, he's in rehab, like I said.'

'That doesn't necessarily mean he's locked up, though, right?' Charlie said.

'From what I've been told, he is,' Stina replied. 'We haven't looked into him yet. It didn't feel like a priority.'

'It can be hard to tell which leads to prioritise, when there aren't really any proper leads,' Charlie said.

'Would you like me to check to make sure he hasn't absconded?' Roy asked.

'Yes, please,' Charlie said and thought to herself that that should already have been done. 'Do you have a sample of Beatrice's DNA?'

Stina replied that they had sent two dummies and the bottle she'd drunk from that morning over to the NFC.

'And the parents?' Charlie asked. 'Have you swabbed them?'

Stina nodded.

'We need to talk to them as soon as possible,' Charlie said. 'Anders and I will head out there now. Meanwhile, keep knocking on doors. And we need to dig into the parents' background. And set up a tip line.'

'Already done,' Roy said.

'We need to give a press conference, as well,' Stina added. 'The journalists are hounding us.'

'Let them,' Charlie replied. 'We can't waste time on answering questions right now, and besides, we don't have any answers.'

Sara

We were all welcome to today's group therapy session, Marianne said after taking a seat next to Emelie in the circle of girls. Picco was strutting between our legs. Marianne said that for anyone who hadn't noticed, there was a new girl. Yes, maybe I could introduce myself?

I looked down at the notebook and pen in my lap and said my name was Sara and I was fifteen years old.

'Why are you here?' a skinny girl sitting across from me asked.

'I'll ask the questions,' Marianne said. Could I tell them something about myself? she wondered. Maybe something I was good at. This was something she asked every new girl because she felt it was important for us to focus on our strengths and not just our weaknesses.

I was silent for a long time because I'd never really thought about it. I pictured Jonas's grandmother's big cross-stitch embroidery, the one she hadn't had time to finish before she died and which I'd almost completed when I was taken away to Rödminnet. *Bright memories, bright days*. But my stitches were uneven and ugly, so I couldn't exactly say I was good at it.

'Maybe something that makes you stand out, then?' Marianne said when I didn't reply.

My mind was still a blank. The only thing I could think of was that I didn't seem to have a gag reflex. But that would probably be viewed as a bad thing, so I said I was good at riding.

'That's nice,' Marianne said. 'And you're not the only equestrian here.' She nodded to a girl I hadn't seen before.

'I don't know how to ride,' the girl said. 'That was just something I said.'

Marianne dropped the subject and said we should start as we usually did, by writing in our notepads whatever popped into our heads.

When all the pens around me in the circle began to rasp, I had a sudden school flashback, that horrible feeling of not knowing the answers, of just killing time, the loneliness of it. I picked up my pen and slowly wrote: *This page used to be empty. Now it isn't.* And then, when everyone else was still scribbling away, I wrote the same two sentences again, slower. *This page used to be empty. Now it isn't.*

I glanced over at Lo next to me. Her pen was flying across the pages as though it had taken on a life of its own. What was she writing? I tried to see, but she held her notebook at an angle that made it impossible.

When the writing part was over, Marianne started to talk about hope. It was important that we don't lose hope, she said. We should keep a positive outlook and not stand in our own way.

'Maybe it's not us standing in our way,' Lo said.

'Let me tell you about a girl,' Marianne went on, ignoring Lo's comment.

And then Marianne told us about a girl who used to live

at Rödminnet once upon a time. I only half-listened to the protracted story about all the things that had gone wrong for this girl and how everything had worked out for her in the end. Now, she had a job and was married to an accountant.

'What a nightmare.'

'Did you say something?' Marianne turned to Lo.

'A dream,' Lo said. 'It sounds like a dream.'

'She's a true sunshine story,' Marianne said after a long pause and then she looked at each of us in turn and said we could become one, too. We could become anything we wanted, if we just wanted it enough.

'What was her name?' Lo asked. 'What was the sunshine girl called?'

'Her name doesn't matter.'

'It does,' Lo said. 'A person's name matters a lot.'

That night, I lay awake, staring at the bottom of Lo's bunk, thinking about the series of events that had brought me to Rödminnet: Mum leaving, Dad drinking himself to death, Rita not wanting me. I thought about the parties at Vall's, the games that had left me scarred forever. When I closed my eyes, I saw the attic room, the stained old mattress and the moth-eaten blankets, the curtains fluttering in the wind. I thought about all the hands that had groped me, about the fact that I was fifteen and already so sick of everything.

12

The Palmgrens' big white house was built on a hill. The waters of Lake Vänern sparkled between the trees in the enormous garden. Two columns framed the main entrance on the other side of the veranda where the pram had been parked. When they got closer, Charlie noticed a baby swing hanging from the branch of an oak tree. A big SUV and a Tesla were parked in front of a two-door garage.

Charlie rang the doorbell. A woman in her mid-thirties opened the door. She introduced herself as Charlotte Jolander, a close friend of the family.

'The other officers are upstairs,' she said. 'We're just waiting for someone to call, for someone to tell us they have her and that she's alive and ... If this is about money, it can be worked out. It has to be.'

Charlie looked around as Charlotte led them through rooms with heavy drapes in neutral tones, blonde wood furniture, and dark paintings.

The other officers came downstairs and briefly introduced themselves. It was a man and a woman, both of them looked grave.

Frida Palmgren was sitting at the kitchen table, holding a

beige snuggle blanket with a rabbit's head. She looked nothing like the happy new mother in the pictures on her social media, but even though her make-up was running, and her hair was tangled, she was strikingly beautiful.

A man Charlie recognised as Gustav's business partner was standing by the kitchen counter. He came over, shook her hand, and introduced himself as David Jolander.

Charlotte went over to Frida and gently told her the detectives from Stockholm had arrived.

Without being asked, Frida launched into a description of how she had put Beatrice out on the veranda as usual in the morning and that she had then gone back inside to tidy up a little and the next time she checked ... She shook her head.

David put a glass of water in front of her. Charlie wondered where Gustav was and just as she did, he entered the room. He was tall and well dressed. His hand trembled when he held it out to her.

'I just put her outside for her nap,' Frida started again. 'She always sleeps on the veranda ... and then ... when I went back out there, the pram wasn't there, and she was gone. She's gone.'

Anders asked Charlotte and David to step out. They needed to talk to the parents alone.

The kitchen was impersonal, Charlie noted. No doctor's appointments on the fridge, no calendar, no pictures. The only signs that a child lived in the house were a handful of bibs on the counter and a highchair at one end of the table.

Frida compulsively started her narrative again. She hadn't heard anything, hadn't seen anything, Beatrice was there and then she wasn't.

She should be given a sedative, Charlie thought to herself.

Something to mute the tornado of terror, guilt, and panic before she falls apart.

'Frida,' Anders said. 'We know this must be horrible, that it's hard to think clearly now, and—'

'What do we do if she doesn't come back?' Frida cut in, as though the thought had only just occurred to her. She looked at Charlie and then Anders. 'What do we do if—'

'We're going to do everything we can to find your daughter,' Charlie said. The words felt lamer than ever.

Gustav put a hand on Frida's shoulder. His face was grim and his jaw clenched.

'I need to go out and look for her,' he said, turning to Charlie. 'I can't just sit here.'

'We have people out looking,' Charlie replied. 'The most helpful thing you can do is to answer our questions.'

Gustav nodded and sat down.

'Do you remember what time it was when you realised Beatrice was missing?' Charlie asked, turning to Frida.

'Half past nine,' Frida replied.

'And when did you leave her out there?'

'Half past eight.'

'And then?'

'What?'

'What did you do after that?' Charlie clarified.

'I cleaned up after breakfast and made coffee and—'

'And you didn't see anyone near the house at any point?'

'No.'

'Did you hear anything?'

Frida shook her head. 'Nothing. And then I read for a while, and when I checked the time, I saw it was half past nine and I thought I should make sure Beatrice wasn't awake, just to be safe, even though she usually sleeps for longer. So I went out to check on her and—'

'Would you normally notice if there was a car in the driveway?' Charlie cut in.

'You'd hear it,' Gustav said.

'You, too?' Charlie asked, looking at Frida.

'Yes.'

'And you didn't hear a car?'

'No, I heard nothing. She was just gone.'

That doesn't necessarily mean the perpetrator didn't have a car, Charlie thought. They could have parked down the road, walked up to the terrace, and pushed the pram back to the car.

'And you didn't see anything outside?'

'The only thing I saw was that the pram was gone.'

'And then what did you do?' Anders asked.

'I screamed,' Frida said. 'Or, actually, I don't remember, but I think I screamed.' She clutched her throat. 'And then I looked around, but I didn't see anything, and ... I shouldn't have left her outside. I shouldn't have ...' Frida trailed off and put her hands to her face. 'My cheeks are going numb,' she said. 'It feels like pins and needles.' She stood up.

'Where are you going?' Gustav asked.

'I don't know,' Frida answered. 'I don't know what to do. It's ... It hurts too much.'

'I think you should sit back down,' Gustav said. 'The police need our help.'

Frida did as she was told, and Gustav took over. He told them Frida had called him, screaming that Beatrice was missing and that he had called the emergency services straight away. Then he got stuck on details about what the operator had said and how many minutes it had taken him to get home.

'And you haven't been contacted by anyone today?' Charlie asked. 'I mean, before the other officers arrived?'

'No.'

'I just want to make sure you're not going to run off and do something without our involvement,' Charlie said, trying to read Gustav's facial expression. He was clearly a man who was used to taking charge and trusting his instincts. She prayed he wasn't planning to exercise those traits in this particular situation. 'Do you have any enemies?' Charlie went on. 'Have there been any conflicts recently?'

'Your colleagues have already asked us about all of this,' Gustav said. 'Don't you people talk to each other?'

'You're going to have to answer some questions more than once,' Charlie replied.

'We don't have any enemies. At least none that we know about.'

'My husband is successful,' Frida piped up, as though Gustav wasn't in the room. 'He ... has had disagreements with quite a few people—'

'I don't think this has anything to do with my work,' Gustav broke in.

'Is it true?' Charlie said. 'That you've had disagreements with a lot of people?'

'It's just business,' Gustav replied. 'Nothing serious.'

He clearly wanted to change the subject.

'Can you tell us a bit about your work?' Anders said.

'David and I run a company together. Our most recent project was developing a site for classifieds ads in Russia. We sold it six months ago. It was after that we moved back from Moscow.'

'How long were you in Moscow?'

71

'Just over a year,' Gustav said.

'And nothing happened there? I mean, no business deals that went south or anything else?'

'Business was good,' Gustav said. 'And what do you mean by anything else? Like what?'

'I don't know,' Anders replied. 'We just want as complete a picture as possible so we can help you better.' He was interrupted by Frida bursting into tears.

Charlie put a hand on Frida's shoulder and looked her in the eyes. 'Frida,' she said. 'We're going to do everything we can to find Beatrice. I know the pain and the fear are unbearable, but—'

'I shouldn't have let her sleep outside,' Frida wailed. 'I shouldn't.'

'A lot of people let their babies nap outside,' Charlie said, though she had no idea if that was the case.

'I ... I'm cold,' Frida said.

'Gustav,' Anders said. 'Would you mind fetching Frida a cardigan or a blanket?'

Gustav nodded and disappeared.

'She doesn't sleep,' Frida whispered as soon as Gustav was out of earshot. 'She doesn't sleep at night, and only takes short naps during the day unless I leave her outside in the pram. That's why I let her sleep out there. I've been so tired. I—'

Gustav returned with a cardigan that he draped over Frida's shoulders.

'I can't do this,' Frida said. 'I can't.'

'I know it feels that way,' Charlie said, 'but—'

'She's my only child,' Frida went on. 'She's the only family I have. I have nothing else to live for.'

Charlie wanted to say something comforting, but all the

phrases that came to mind sounded trite. No family, she thought. Was it her original family Frida was referring to, her dead parents and the brother who was walking down the same dark path they had? But she still had Gustav – or didn't she count her husband as family?

Charlie's phone rang. It was a number she didn't recognise. She apologised, said she had to take it, and left the room. When she answered, she realised it was a telemarketer, but instead of hanging up as she usually did, she listened to the information about some kind of highly advantageous loan offer. She walked past a wall with framed black-and-white wedding photos, a happily smiling Frida with a more solemn-looking Gustav by her side. And then, playful photos, silly faces, and something that was possibly meant to come off as spontaneous horseplay: Frida with her veil as a cape and Gustav standing diagonally behind her in some kind of peculiar pleading pose.

She continued further into the house and looked through an open door into a nursery. The colour palette matched the rest of the house: beige, white, and grey, with a few touches of pink. There was a tepee in one corner, a rocking horse in the other, and big stuffed animals and toys everywhere else. She studied the pictures on the walls: numbers and letters with funny animals, and then a framed text. Charlie moved closer and realised it was the Erik Lindorm poem from Frida's Instagram, but here in its entirety:

> Is it true that I'm holding a child in my arms
> and see myself in its eyes,
> that the sea is sparkling and the ground is warm
> and above us immaculate skies?

What is the time, what is the year,
who am I, what is my name?
My laughing bundle with sun-bleached hair,
what was life before you came?

I'm alive, I'm alive! Standing firm on the earth,
gone are the things I've been through.
I must have waited a million years
to spend this minute with you.

13

As they stepped out of the Palmgrens' house, Charlie spotted a shadow over by the garage.

'Stop!' she shouted when a woman set off at a run down the driveway.

But the woman didn't stop, she kept running towards the road, her long red skirt flapping around her legs. It didn't take Charlie long to catch up with her. When she did, she grabbed her arm hard.

'Why are you running from us?' Charlie asked.

'Sorry,' the woman said in a foreign accent. 'I don't like when people yell at me.'

'What are you doing here?' Charlie demanded.

'Please, let go of me,' the woman said.

Charlie relaxed her grip on the woman's arm. She knew she could catch her if she tried to run again.

'I clean there,' the woman said, pointing up at the house. 'I heard about what happened, so I ... I just wanted to come and help, but then I felt I didn't want to intrude and—'

'You shouldn't have run,' Charlie admonished.

'I know, I'm sorry.'

'What's your name?'

'Amina,' the woman replied. 'Amina Khalil.'

'Do you have ID?'

Amina shook her head.

'We need your contact information and your personal identification number,' Charlie said. 'And I want you to come back to the house with us so Frida and Gustav can confirm who you are.'

When Amina entered the kitchen and saw Frida, she began to mumble in Arabic, a sing-song chant that gradually grew faster and louder. Frida got to her feet and walked over to her.

'I'm so sorry,' Amina whispered. 'I'm so sorry.'

It was a touching sight, the conservatively dressed Frida and Amina in her washed-out clothes, holding each other and crying.

Amina had taken the bus out to Hammarö when she heard Beatrice was missing. Charlie offered to give her a ride back into town.

'I don't live in town,' Amina said. 'I live in Kronoparken. It's further out.'

'Then we'll drive you there,' Charlie said. 'We need to ask you some questions anyway.'

Kronoparken was a suburb about three miles from Karlstad town centre. They parked between two old rusty cars and walked past a playground with a large sandbox and a ramshackle climbing frame. A little boy was riding a squeaking tricycle round and round, and a girl of about ten was walking along a few steps behind him.

Amina and her husband lived on the second floor in a row of two-storey houses that looked like they were built in the sixties. The paint was peeling here and there.

A man met them in the hallway.

'This is Jamal,' Amina said. 'He doesn't speak a lot of Swedish, but he understands everything.'

Jamal nodded and shook their hands.

'You don't have to take your shoes off,' Amina said. 'The floors are dirty. I work so much, I don't have the energy to clean at home. I hope you understand.'

Charlie nodded. If there was one thing she understood it was people who didn't keep their homes clean. But Amina and Jamal's flat wasn't actually dirty at all, she realised as she followed Amina into the small kitchen; it was clean and tidy. On the wall above the kitchen table hung a framed photograph of three little girls, all wearing identical red dresses and ribbons in their hair. The oldest had her arms around the younger two. Were they Amina and Jamal's daughters? Charlie hadn't seen any other signs of children in the flat, no toys, no tiny jackets or shoes in the hallway.

'My girls,' Amina said when she noticed Charlie looking at the photograph.

Charlie wanted to ask where they were, but she could see the answer in Amina's eyes.

'They were one, three, and four when they died,' Amina said. 'Their father is also gone. We're from Syria.'

'I'm so sorry,' Charlie said.

'Me too,' Anders added.

Amina turned to the sink and filled the kettle with water from the tap. Charlie studied her chapped red hands as she set out cups for them and thought about her children, the family she'd once had. She pictured Amina with a husband and three little girls and pushed down the images of explosions, bombs, and children's bodies.

Jamal sat down at the table, and Charlie realised the thumb and forefinger on his left hand were missing. When he noticed her looking, he quickly put his hand in his lap under the table.

'How long have you been working for Frida and Gustav?' Charlie asked, after taking a sip of her tea.

Amina looked at her husband as though she needed help remembering. She looked nervous. Maybe she gets paid under the table, Charlie mused.

'Six months,' she replied after a long pause. 'It's a very good job. I work when I'm not in school.'

'What do you study?' Charlie asked.

'I'm training to be a healthcare assistant,' Amina said. 'And if I can do that, I'll try to become a nurse after.'

She looked at Jamal, who smiled back proudly.

'We've only been here three years,' Jamal said, holding up three fingers. 'But my wife is very good, very good.'

'I just like to learn,' Amina said.

'How often do you clean?'

'Frida and Gustav's house?' Amina asked.

'You clean other houses, too?'

'Yes, but mostly Frida and Gustav's.'

'Frida is very good to us,' Jamal added.

'You work for them, too?' Charlie said to Jamal.

'Yes, I've helped them with some carpentry and I—'

'And he painted,' Amina said. 'He painted the whole house and the garage, and now he's building a sandbox for ...' She broke off and swallowed hard. 'Frida and Gustav have been very kind to us,' she finished.

'So, how often do you clean their house?' Anders asked, turning to Amina.

'At least once a week. Usually more. Beatrice has had

stomach pains and hasn't been sleeping much, so I've been over more often to clean and ...'

'And what?' Charlie urged.

'Nothing.'

'Anything you can think of could be important right now,' Charlie said.

'I don't want to gossip about the people I work for,' Amina replied. 'It's not right.'

'But this is a missing child,' Charlie said. 'This is about Beatrice. You have to tell us everything you know.'

'I watched her sometimes,' Amina said. 'I took her for walks in the pram so Frida could sleep. But we didn't tell Gustav. Frida didn't think he would like it.'

'Why not?'

'I don't know.'

'He doesn't trust you?'

'He does, or at least I think he does. Frida just didn't want us to tell him, so I didn't.' Amina cupped her hands around her teacup. 'Where do you think she could be? I mean ... who would take a baby?'

'We're going to do everything we can to find her,' Charlie said.

'You have to find her,' Amina pleaded. 'She's ... she's so little and she doesn't like strangers. It's horrible to think ... how scared she must be ...'

'I understand,' Anders said. 'The best way for you to help right now is to answer our questions to the best of your ability.'

Amina nodded.

'How would you describe Gustav?' Anders asked.

'Gustav is ... We don't know him as well as Frida,' Amina said. 'He works a lot.'

'He gets angry sometimes,' Jamal offered.

'He's just very busy at work,' Amina said, shooting her husband a look.

'What does he get angry about?' Charlie asked.

'I don't know,' Amina replied.

'Have you ever seen Gustav get angry at Frida, have you seen him be violent towards her?'

They both said they hadn't. But that was neither here nor there, Charlie thought. Clever violent men didn't beat their wives where there were people to see it. And even if Amina or Jamal had seen something, they may not want to tell the police. They had their jobs to think about.

'Have you noticed anything unusual at Frida and Gustav's house recently?' Charlie asked.

'What do you mean?' Amina said.

'Anything that stood out to you. Maybe someone came to the house you hadn't seen there before, or has the mood been different? Just anything.'

Amina shook her head.

'When were you last there to clean?' Anders asked.

'It was … three days ago.'

'Can I ask where you were this morning?' Charlie said. 'Where were you when Beatrice disappeared?'

'I was cleaning another family's house,' Amina said and put her cup down so hard some tea spilled.

Charlie could tell that Amina understood why the question had been asked. But her fretfulness didn't necessarily mean she had something to hide. The police often made people nervous, even if they were perfectly innocent.

'What's the name of that family?' Anders asked.

'Jolander. Frida and Gustav's friends.'

'Charlotte and David Jolander?'

'Yes.'

'What are you doing?' Jamal said when Amina suddenly stood up. Her face had turned ashen.

'I'm just going to … fetch some more tea,' Amina said. She took two steps, stopped, and collapsed on the floor.

Charlie and Anders jumped up, but Jamal was quicker. He squatted down, lifted up his wife's head, and gently slapped her cheeks. After a few seconds, Amina came to. She sat up, mumbled something, and closed her eyes again.

'Stress,' Jamal said and looked up at them. 'She's very stressed.'

He pointed to the wall with the photograph of the lost children.

'She becomes … She … panics and now … Beatrice. She likes her very much.'

Amina stayed on the floor with her arms around her husband's neck. Her breathing was shallow.

'Amina,' Charlie said and put a hand on her back. 'Is there anything we can do for you?'

'She'll be OK,' Jamal said. 'She'll be OK soon.'

'Are you sure you're all right?' Anders asked when Jamal helped her back onto her feet.

Jamal nodded.

'Maybe you should contact your doctor, though, just to be safe.'

'No,' Amina said. 'No doctor. I'm fine now.'

Charlie thought to herself that she was clearly far from fine, that Amina was seriously struggling.

'Here, take our cards,' Anders said. 'They have all our contact info on them. Call us any time if you think of anything else.'

'Or if there's anything else we can do,' Charlie added. 'Anything.'

'Bloody hell,' Anders said once they were back in the car. 'I don't know how people who have lost everything carry on living. Losing all your children, how the hell do you get through that?'

'You get through it,' Charlie said, 'or at least most people seem to.' She thought about how proud Amina had been about her studies, how hopeful about her future. And then, how everything had turned in just a few seconds, how she'd lost control of herself. 'I feel like she was holding back about something, though,' she continued.

Anders turned to her. 'Are you suggesting she fainted on purpose?'

'All I'm saying is that there might be something that's so hard for her, she can't tell us. Or maybe she's afraid to.'

'About Beatrice?'

The question hung in the air. Charlie looked out the window. Dusk was falling. She googled how cold it was going to get at night. Only a couple of degrees above freezing. What if Beatrice had been left outside somewhere? How long could a nine-month-old baby survive that kind of temperature? How long could a nine-month-old baby survive without care?

She thought about Amina, about her dead children. About Frida, what her life would be like if they didn't find Beatrice alive. So helpless, she thought, we humans are so very helpless.

Sara

The room was pitch-black when I woke up. Something was wrong. It took a while before I realised it was the silence. No sound of breathing from the top bunk.

'Lo?' I whispered.

No answer.

I sat up. 'Lo?'

She wasn't there. I put on my slippers and went over to Nicki's room. Another empty bunk bed.

I heard the clicking of claws behind me. I turned around and saw Picco wagging her tail.

'Where is everybody?' I said. 'Where are the girls?'

Picco's misshapen tail wagged even harder and then she ran off towards the stairs. I followed. After leading me all the way down to the basement, Picco got up on her hind legs and scratched on a closed door.

'Is there someone in there?' I whispered.

Picco whined and scratched again.

I hesitated for a second before I pushed the handle down and opened the door.

They were sitting in a circle on the floor, in their nightgowns, slippers, and Thorazine hats. For a split second, I thought they were asylum patients who had lingered on the wrong side of life, unhappy souls who had failed to find peace after being subjected to treatments like rotation therapy, surprise baths, and lobotomies.

'Who's there?' a voice said. 'Step into the light, stranger.'

'It's me.'

'Come in, Sara,' Lo said. 'We were just about to have story time.'

I entered the room. Candles in bottles burned in the middle of the circle. Their flickering flames cast long shadows across the girls' pale faces under the wide brims of their straw hats.

'What happens if we get caught?' I asked.

'We're not going to get caught,' Lo replied and made room next to her. She accepted a bottle from Nicki.

Heart's-ease, Dad used to call spirits, *a bottle of heart's-ease*. And he was spot on, I thought to myself as the burning liquid trickled down my throat and the pressure in my chest eased.

'Go on, Nicki,' Lo said.

Nicki bowed her head and went on: 'Once upon a time, there was a girl ...' She looked up and asked us to close our eyes.

I closed my eyes and wished I was a girl who believed in fairy tales and sunshine stories. I wanted there to be hope for us somewhere, wanted us to leave the asylum strong, healthy people, capable of building normal lives for ourselves. Nothing fancy. Just regular lives.

I kept my eyes closed while Nicki told us about the girl in the sublet studio flat in the suburbs. I kept them closed while she talked about how there was never enough money, about how cold the flat was, about the hunger and the jobs her mother had to take. I kept them closed while she talked about her younger brother, whom she had to look after when their mother didn't come home at night.

'Why didn't she come home?' someone asked.

'Shh,' Lo hushed. 'Don't interrupt the story.'

We listened to the rest in silence. Furtive sips of wine turned into cigarettes and pills, and then heavier stuff. Because she wanted to feel calm. She just wanted to feel calm and happy sometimes.

'Go on,' Lo said when Nicki trailed off.

'I don't know if you want to hear it,' Nicki said. 'It's pretty unpleasant.'

'It'll feel better if you talk about it,' Lo said, sounding exactly like Marianne. 'Let us go back there with you. Take us to the place that hurts the most.'

'Fine,' Nicki sighed. 'Let's go then. Come with me to a flat in a suburb, to a bed with a filthy mattress. OK, so, close your eyes.'

I didn't want to go there with her. I'd had enough of filthy beds and stained mattresses.

They were football players, Nicki thought, or maybe hockey players – same difference. She'd forgotten how many but thought five or six. And they had tied her up. 'Why did you go with them in the first place?' someone asked.

'That's not part of the story,' Nicki said. 'But if you really want to know, I don't remember.'

'Go on,' Lo said.

'They tied me up like an X,' Nicki continued. 'They tied each of my feet and my hands to a bedpost. Then ... they touched me everywhere they could and—'

'Give me the bottle,' Lo suddenly said to me. 'Or were you planning to hog it all night?'

I handed her the bottle. Lo took three long pulls before passing it on.

'They touched me everywhere,' Nicki said. 'I felt like I was going to be torn in two. I thought I was probably going to die, and I was OK with it, it would be good to stop existing, to stop breathing.'

I wished Nicki would stop talking because I felt sick and didn't want to hear any more. I felt like it was me spread out on that mattress.

'Then something started to drip onto me,' Nicki went on. 'At first, I thought it was water, because I had my eyes shut. I figured maybe they were trying to clean me off, but then the smell ... I opened my eyes ... and realised they were pissing. They were pissing on me.'

No one said a word. I blinked to try to erase the images of Nicki spread-eagle on the bed, the swaying genitals above her, the piss running down her body.

'Afterwards, they said I was in on it,' Nicki whispered. 'They said I wanted them to piss on me.'

Charlie lay down on her hotel bed and turned the TV on. A smooth-skinned anchor informed her of the latest news, or, rather, the lack of news in the Beatrice Palmgren kidnapping case. Pictures of the house on Hammarö, a close-up of Stina solemnly urging the public to let the police know if they had any information. Then, a short street interview with a young mother who was holding a little boy's hand and staring straight into the camera, saying it was all just so terrible, that the town was in shock.

Just as Charlie was about to drift off, an image surfaced in her mind: a man in a leather jacket, the smell of it and the sound of laughing. She opened her eyes, stared out into the darkness, and tried to remember more – his face, hair colour, anything. When she was unsuccessful, she closed her eyes again to recreate the state she had just been in, but it didn't work. Her pulse was racing. What the hell had just happened?

She forced herself to think calmly and rationally. No need to fret. It wasn't the first time she'd dragged a man home with her, and the only thing that set this bloke apart was that she'd forgotten him. And, at the end of the day, she was alive, unharmed.

But her rationalisations did nothing to calm her.

She got out of bed, went over to the window, and pulled open the heavy blackout curtains. Two young, scantily dressed women were staggering down the street arm in arm, and after them, a group of men in suit trousers and coats. It was Saturday night and people were on their way out, or possibly home. It was twenty past midnight. She should really go back to bed, but instead she shuffled over to the minibar.

The tiny bottle of red wine was sitting there as though it were simply begging to be drunk. She downed it in three big gulps and waited for the feeling of temporary calm to come. She didn't care that the effect wore off so quickly, or that the consequences were so dire, it was still worth it.

She found herself thinking about her latest therapy session. *Tell me about a childhood memory*, Eva had said. *The first one that pops into your head. What do you remember?*

Mum.

Your mum?

Yes.

What is she doing?

She's ... dancing. She's dancing in our garden in Lyckebo.

And you? What are you doing?

I'm sitting at my bedroom window, watching her. I want her to come inside, because it's cold out and she's too lightly dressed, but it's as though she can't hear me. So I ... I go out into the garden to try to catch her, but she's too fast.

Let her stay in the garden and turn the music down. What would you say to her if she stopped and listened now?

I would tell her to come inside, that it's late ... that I'm scared of ...

What are you scared of?

Of her leaving me, of being alone.
Tell her.

And Charlie had closed her eyes and called up an image of the garden in Lyckebo where the music had gone silent, and Betty had frozen mid-twirl.

I don't want you to leave me, Mummy. I don't want to be alone.

Charlie went back to the bed, picked up her phone, checked the temperature, and noted that the forecast had been right. It was two degrees above freezing. She hoped Beatrice wasn't cold, that whoever had her was keeping her warm. Please, let us find her alive, she thought. And yet, the image of a frozen baby's body was the last thing she saw before she fell asleep. Blue lips, closed eyes.

Last night, I dreamt about a shooter in a mall. He was walking around with his gun loaded, shooting wildly in every direction. People were falling to the floor, bleeding out, dying. I hid with the baby behind some boxes. She squirmed and moaned, and I knew that if I couldn't keep her quiet, it would all be over. So I covered her mouth, too hard, for too long. I just wanted her to survive.

15

Charlie and Anders met in the lobby at eight the next morning. They had a quick breakfast in the deserted hotel breakfast room.

As they were walking towards the car, both holding paper cups of coffee, Charlie's phone rang. It was Stina.

'Are you on your way in?' she said.

'We're getting in the car as we speak,' Charlie replied. 'Has something happened?'

'Roy just checked with the facility where Frida's brother is in rehab, and … he's not there. He has been missing for three days.'

'But you said—'

'Yeah, that's on us,' Stina cut in. 'We—'

'No need to explain,' Charlie said. 'Just give me his home address, or have you already sent someone over?'

'You were my first call. He lives on Gruvlyckevägen 12.'

'His family wasn't contacted when he absconded?' Charlie asked.

'Apparently not. And another thing,' Stina said. 'Roy had another look at his criminal record. It seems the idiot who checked the first time missed something.'

'What?'

'Sexual activity with a child.'

Charlie felt her pulse quicken.

'When?'

'Ten years ago.'

'What's going on?' Anders said when Charlie put her phone down.

Charlie explained the situation while she typed Niklas Sandell's address into the GPS. Seven minutes later, they pulled up in front of a tired three-storey block of flats on Gruvlyckevägen.

'Talk about a brother and sister on divergent life paths,' Anders said. 'Proper extremes.'

'I honestly don't know which is worse,' Charlie said. 'I'm serious,' she added when Anders chuckled.

'You'd rather be a junkie than married to a billionaire?'

'I suppose it depends,' Charlie replied, 'on what kind of billionaire it is. Isn't it pretty much received wisdom, though, that people who climb all the way to the top have usually stepped on a lot of people along the way? I'm not sure living with the kind of person who'd do that is particularly wonderful.'

'And sacrificing everything else so you can get high all the time, that's wonderful?'

'The high probably is,' Charlie replied. 'It's all the other things that tend to suck.'

They parked and entered the building. The gravel on the floor crunched under their feet.

'What's with you?' Charlie asked when Anders pulled a face.

'You don't smell that?'

'It's just food.'

'More like rubbish.'

'You're exaggerating.'

Niklas Sandell's flat was on the second floor. They had to ring the doorbell three times before they heard the sound of footsteps inside.

'Are you Niklas Sandell?' Anders asked when a bleary-eyed man in pants and a tattered T-shirt opened the door.

'I am,' the man replied. 'Oh, now what?' he continued when Anders showed him his badge. 'What possible reason could you have for coming here and waking me up in the middle of the night?'

'It's almost nine,' Anders informed him.

'Morning or night?' Niklas asked earnestly.

'Morning,' Charlie said. 'We just need to have a word with you.'

The flat reeked of that familiar mix of ethanol, cat piss, and filth. Charlie could tell Anders wanted to turn around in the doorway.

'I can't go back there,' Niklas said after leading them into a kitchen with old yellow cabinet doors and piles of dirty washing-up in the sink. 'They should just give my spot to someone else. Someone who's not an idiot.'

'You're not an idiot,' said a voice from the next room.

'Shut up, Anton,' Niklas said.

'I'm just telling them you're not an idiot,' the bloke called Anton replied. 'Just because you like to have fun doesn't mean you're an idiot.'

Charlie recognised Betty's reasoning. *Who are the idiots anyway? Us, who know how to have fun, or the poor sods working in banks and at social services who are too uptight to ever let their hair down?*

LINA BENGTSDOTTER

'The police are here, Anton,' Niklas said.

They heard a loud thud, followed by a few hissed curses. Then Anton stepped out into the hallway with dishevelled hair and unbuttoned jeans.

'We didn't do anything,' he said. 'We just went on a good old three-day bender. Just booze, so you don't need to drive him back or anything.'

'That's not why we're here,' Charlie said. 'We've come to talk to you about something else. In private,' she added.

Anton held up his hands, turned around, and went back into the other room.

'What's this about?' Niklas asked.

He had taken a seat on a wooden chair. Charlie noted his bouncing knees. Nervousness? Withdrawal?

'It's about your niece,' Anders said. 'Beatrice.'

'Beatrice?' Niklas said, as though he'd never heard the name before. 'What about her?'

He reached for the ashtray on the table and picked up a half-smoked cigarette that he lit with trembling hands.

'She's missing,' Charlie replied.

'Missing?' Niklas stared at her blankly.

'Yes, you may have read in the papers or seen on TV that an infant recently disappeared from her home on Hammarö. The missing child is Frida's daughter. Beatrice.'

'I didn't know,' Niklas said. He stood up abruptly and walked over to the kitchen counter and the overflowing sink. When he turned on the tap, water sprayed onto the floor. 'What do you mean she's missing?'

Charlie briefly recounted the events of the past twenty-four hours. Niklas turned around and stared at her as though he couldn't quite wrap his head around what she was saying.

94

'But ... she has to be somewhere, right?'

'Yes,' Anders said. 'And that's what we're trying to find out, where she is.'

'But why ...?' Niklas said. 'Why didn't anyone tell me? Why didn't Frida call me?'

Because you're no longer part of her life, Charlie thought to herself.

'Maybe you should turn off the tap?' Anders suggested with a nod towards the sink, where the water was still running.

Niklas turned the tap off.

'So, what can I do?' he asked, turning back to them. 'Is there anything I can do?'

'You can answer our questions,' Charlie said. 'Have you met Beatrice?'

He didn't answer straight away, just stared out the window where a broken blind was hanging askew.

'I saw her once, in the town centre. Frida, I mean, she was pushing the pram. So I got to see her, Beatrice. She was ... she was so bloody lovely, like, the most beautiful baby I've ever seen. But I was high so she wouldn't let me hold her. I was barely allowed to touch her. Isn't that a bit much? I mean, it's not like it's contagious.' He looked at Anders.

'I don't think it's about that,' Anders said. 'Maybe your sister just doesn't want people under the influence around her child. That's understandable.'

'I just wanted to touch her,' Niklas said.

'How would you describe your relationship with Frida?' Charlie asked.

'It was good when we were little,' Niklas replied. 'We ... we looked after each other, or, well, mostly she looked after me, even though she's a year younger. She always felt like my big sister, maybe because I'm so fucking stupid.' He pointed to his forehead. 'But it was nice to have each other when Mum and Dad were drinking and raising the devil.'

'And later on?' Charlie said.

'Later on?'

'What happened with your relationship when you grew up? You said it was good when you were younger. What is it like now?'

'She changed,' Niklas said. 'She betrayed me.'

'What do you mean by that?'

'She refuses to help me out with money and she had me put in rehab against my will.'

'That doesn't sound like a betrayal,' Anders said.

'I think it does,' Niklas said. 'She won't even lend me money for rent, even though she's swimming in moolah since she got married. She says it's for my own good, but I don't believe her. I reckon it's because she thinks she's too bloody posh now. She has forgotten where she came from.'

'And where did she come from?' Charlie asked.

'What?'

'I just asked where she came from.'

'From Molkom,' Niklas said. 'She's the daughter of two alcoholics and the sister of a junkie.'

There was a long pause. Charlie thought about the brother and sister in the little town outside Karlstad, and it was as though she could hear the drunken rows, feel the anxiety caused by the unpredictability you had to live with when your parents had a substance-abuse problem.

'When did you last go to Frida's house?' she asked.

'I've never been to that house they bought after they got back from …'

'Moscow,' Anders finished for him.

'Whatever, I've never been there. Why? You don't think I would ... Bloody hell, if I ever get my hands on the prick who took her, I'd—'

'You should leave that to us,' Anders told him.

'How would you describe your sister?' Charlie asked.

'She's blonde, blue-eyed, and—'

'I was asking about her personality.'

'Sorry,' Niklas said. 'I should have figured, I guess. She's ... When she was little, she was pretty shy, but then she became more ... outgoing, and now ... it's like I don't even know her.'

'And what is your relationship with Gustav Palmgren like?'

'We don't have a relationship,' Niklas replied. 'That man wouldn't be caught dead fraternising with lowlifes ... at least not lowlifes like me.'

'Are you telling us he does fraternise with other kinds of lowlifes?' Charlie said.

'He's a bloody lowlife,' Niklas replied. 'Just the kind that comes in fancy packaging.'

'Could you expand on that?' Charlie said. His poetic turn of phrase surprised her.

'Well, both him and his mate ... what's his bloody name again?'

'David Jolander?' Charlie suggested.

'Right. They're not exactly above enjoying a bit of ...' he blocked one of his nostrils with a finger and mimicked snorting a line.

'How do you know?'

'Well, how do you think?'

'You sold them drugs?'

'I'm not answering that. I'm not quite that stupid. But, believe me, I know.'

'Is it serious ... an addiction, I mean?' Anders asked.

'People like Gustav and David don't get addicted to drugs. They're addicted to money and power. But they're recreational users, both of them. The third one's a different story, though.'

'The third one?' Charlie said.

'Yeah,' Niklas replied. 'That poor sod they dumped. He was bloody bitter about it.'

'Who are you talking about?' Anders asked.

'Half-White,' Niklas said. 'Not sure what his real name is. Anton!' he shouted. 'What's Half-White's real name?'

Anton returned to the kitchen. 'What are you shouting about?' he said.

'I'm just wondering if you know Half-White's real name.'

'Isn't it ... No, I have no idea. I thought Half-White was his real name.'

'It's obviously just a nickname,' Niklas said. 'How did you not know that?'

'I don't fucking know,' Anton bit back.

Niklas turned to Charlie and explained. 'It's like half his body's white, his skin, his hair, everything. It looks kind of funny.'

'Is he in trouble?' Anton asked. He had walked over to the fridge and was now staring at the largely empty shelves.

'No, it's about Frida's kid,' Niklas said. 'Someone took her.'

'Half-White?' Anton said. He closed the fridge door and turned to them.

'No,' Charlie replied.

'But, OK, then, we have to do something,' Anton said. 'How is Frida doing?'

'You know Frida?' Charlie asked. 'Are you ... friends?'

'We were in the same class all throughout school and, at first, she was pretty odd. Kept to herself mostly, read books during recess. But then something happened. I think it was the summer holiday after eighth grade ... when she suddenly ...' He cupped his hands in front of his chest to show them what had happened between eighth and ninth grade. 'She was just extremely bloody fit, simply put.'

'Shut up, Anton,' Niklas said. 'That's my sister you're talking about.'

'I'm just calling it like I see it,' Anton replied. 'I'm only telling them that every bloke with eyes and a brain wanted Frida. She was a good time, too,' he continued as though he'd only just remembered. 'She was fun to be around. But then when she got with that loser, it was like she withered. It was bloody sad to see.'

'Well, sure, she could have drunk her life away like you and me,' Niklas said, 'instead of marrying a billionaire.'

A phone went off somewhere in the flat and Anton disappeared.

Anders picked back up where they had left off when Anton joined them. 'What did you mean when you said they dumped him?' he asked. 'The third man, Half-White?'

'I'm not really sure,' Niklas replied. 'But he goes on about it sometimes when he's drunk, about Gustav and David fucking him up the arse. I mean, not literally, obviously, but—'

'We get it,' Charlie cut him off impatiently. 'But has he said anything else about it? Like ... has he described how they cheated him?'

Niklas shook his head. It's not like they were in the habit of having heart-to-hearts, and besides, he didn't have a lot of time for people who whinged about being hard done by. Didn't like their attitude.

'So you don't know if there's any truth to it?' Anders said.

'I imagine there probably is,' Niklas replied. 'Because if there's one thing I know about Gustav Palmgren, it's that he's not a nice bloke.'

'Have you ever had an argument?' Charlie asked.

Niklas frowned and said he couldn't remember, but that he had probably called and yelled at him once or twice when he was drunk.

'Why?'

'Haven't I already said?'

'You just told us he's not a nice bloke.'

'He's stingy, too,' Niklas added. 'Stingy and not nice.'

'Have you fought about money?'

'No, only with my sister.'

'Do you have any debts?' Charlie asked.

'What do you mean?'

'If you have links to the criminal underworld, that could obviously be relevant,' Anders said. 'If you needed money and—'

'I don't have links to people who kidnap children.'

'Speaking of children,' Charlie said. 'Can you tell me what happened ten years ago?'

'Did you have anything specific in mind?' Niklas asked, but the way his face had immediately gone stiff revealed that he knew full well what she was referring to.

'The child you raped,'

'Bloody hell!' Niklas took three quick steps towards Charlie. Before she could get up, Anders had placed himself between them.

'Sit down,' Anders said. There was a threat in his voice.

Niklas did as he was told.

Charlie didn't know if she felt demeaned or protected. She was perfectly able to tell him to sit down herself.

'Tell us,' Anders said. 'Tell us about that girl.'

'I didn't rape her,' Niklas said. 'She wanted to. I had no idea she was so young, and I've served my time. Can't you just read about it in your … case files or whatever.'

'Why don't you save us the time and tell us yourself. Your niece is missing. We're working against the clock here.'

'Well, I'm no fucking paedo, if that's what you're thinking.'

'Then tell us what makes you different from other people who have sex with minors,' Charlie said.

'It was ten years ago and—'

'And you've changed?' Anders said.

'Would you let me tell it then, since you're so bloody keen to know,' Niklas snapped.

He ran both hands through his hair and leaned towards Charlie.

'She was fourteen,' he said, sounding more composed now. 'She was fourteen and about to turn fifteen the next month. I was twenty-five. We met in a bar, so I had no reason to think she wasn't eighteen. Her dad reported me when he found out. She didn't want him to. I'm sure you can look all that up somewhere.'

Anders's phone rang. He checked the screen, apologised, and stepped into the hallway.

Niklas had found a packet of Marlboros on the windowsill and lit up a new cigarette.

'What were you doing yesterday?' Charlie asked.

'I was here,' Niklas said. 'We were drinking. Anton,' he called out. 'Come in here.'

Anton returned. Could they maybe make their minds up? Did they want him in there or not? He motioned for Niklas to pass him the cigarette.

'I just wanted to know what you got up to yesterday,' Charlie said. 'What did you do in the morning?'

'We partied ... or slept,' Anton said. 'I'm not sure about the timing. But I think we were here.'

'Think?'

'As far as I know.'

He looked at Niklas, who said that was right. They'd been in the flat all day and all night.

'Alone?'

There was a brief pause. Maybe they needed time to impose order on their jumbled recollections.

'Yes,' Niklas said. 'Alone.'

'So no one stopped by, or saw you, or—'

'You're not saying we bloody took the kid?' Anton said.

'Someone took her,' Charlie replied. 'That's all I know.'

'Well, she's not here,' Anton said. 'We didn't take her. Besides, I already have a kid.'

They were interrupted by Anders returning, his face ashen.

'I have to go,' he said. 'It's Sam.'

Sara

Lo was lying on her bed, laughing. It took me a while to realise what was so funny. She was reading my notebook.

'I'm sorry,' Lo said when I stepped onto my bed, heaved myself up, and ripped the notebook out of her hands. 'I'm sorry, I just couldn't help myself. Please, don't be mad at me.'

'Like you wouldn't be mad at me if I read yours,' I said.

'That could never happen,' Lo replied, 'because I keep mine locked up. In a place like this, you can't count on people leaving your stuff alone unless you lock it up. Look, there's always going to be some bastard snooping around.'

'You could have not taken it,' I said. 'Even though it wasn't locked up.'

'I said I was sorry,' Lo replied. 'I won't do it again. I didn't realise it was so secret.'

'I don't think that's the point,' I said. Because it wasn't. The only thing in my notebook was four pages of nonsense words and a botched portrait of Marianne, but I still felt horrible about Lo looking through it.

'You should use the time in group to write something serious,' Lo suggested. 'It feels good to get all the things you don't talk to other people about off your chest.'

'You must have a lot of things you want to get off your chest,' I retorted.

'I just like to write,' Lo said. 'It's one of the few things Marianne and I agree on, that it's healing.'

'You believe in sunshine stories, too?' I asked.

Lo shook her head and said she didn't, but she did believe there were exceptions and sometimes she felt like she might be one of them. Like she might be a person who could get through life without breaking. There was no harm in hoping anyway, right? Because maybe it was true what Marianne said, that nothing's more dangerous than people who have lost all hope.

'What's so dangerous about that?' I asked, suddenly worried.

'I guess it's dangerous not to care. There's no telling what a person who has given up might do.' Lo looked out the window. 'The sun's out,' she said. 'Want to go for a walk?'

'I thought we had to stay in the garden,' I said as I followed Lo out into the enormous field that spread out behind Rödminnet where the garden ended.

After what felt like an eternity, we reached the woods on the other side. We started walking up a steep, narrow path. Below us, there was water.

'It's Lake Vänern,' Lo said when I stopped to look. 'Sweden's biggest lake.'

'I know what Sweden's biggest lake is,' I retorted. 'I'm not stupid.' The path was climbing very steeply now, and I wished Lo would slow down.

'Here,' Lo said when the trees thinned out and the wind picked up. 'Welcome to the Cliff of Insanity. Come on, come closer, look down if you dare. This is where the lunatics would jump to their deaths,' she continued. 'When they'd had enough, they would come out here and just throw themselves over. I reckon it made them feel good, knowing this place existed.'

I walked up to Lo, who was standing dangerously close to the edge now, and it was as though I could see the white-clad hat people from the photographs on the walls at Rödminnet, could see them step off the edge, one by one, and fall.

'Were they sure they would die?' I asked.

'God, yes,' Lo said. 'It's at least a sixty-foot drop and there are rocks just below the surface, too. Look.'

I looked down at the water, which was washing over sharp rocks far below. The height made me dizzy. Lo took my hand and laced her fingers into mine. If either of us suddenly felt like jumping, the other would be dragged along.

'Can you feel the pull?' Lo asked.

I nodded. I didn't want to die, and yet, I felt it. The pull.

16

Please, don't tell me he's dead, Charlie thought. She pictured Anders's little boy, his tousled blond hair, the mischievous glint in his eyes, and his energy, courage, and utter inability to assess risk.

'Anders,' she said. 'Is Sam OK?' She had followed him into the stairwell.

'It's ... Where's my phone?'

Anders started to pat his trouser pockets even though he was holding his phone in his hand.

'He fell. It's serious.'

'But he's not ... I mean ...'

Charlie couldn't finish the sentence.

'Maria's in the hospital with him now. Can you just give me the car keys?'

The hand he held out to her was visibly shaking. Was it really a good idea for him to drive up to Stockholm by himself? That was all she had time to think before he snatched the keys from her and sprinted towards the car.

Charlie pulled out her phone and called Stina. She explained what had happened and that Anders had taken the car and was on his way back to Stockholm.

Stina said she could come pick her up. She would be there in a few minutes.

After they hung up, Charlie called Anders. Busy signal. She tried Challe instead. He sounded stressed, so she got straight to the point.

'You heard?'

'Yes, I just spoke to Anders.'

'Do you know anything?'

'He doesn't know much himself. I'll keep you posted. How are you getting on down there?'

Charlie summarised their progress so far, told him about Amina and the dead children, Niklas, and the potentially disgruntled former business partner.

'Does she have an alibi?' Challe asked. 'The cleaning lady?'

'Yes. But I have a feeling she knows more than she's telling us.'

'And the uncle?'

Charlie thought about the confused look on Niklas Sandell's face.

'Yes, but it's a bloke he parties with, so it's not exactly watertight.'

'But what would his motive be?'

'I don't know,' Charlie said. 'I'm just giving you the facts, that's what we have so far. Besides, he might not need much in the way of motive, other than being high, having an idea and ... well, stranger things have happened.'

'You'll have to keep an eye on him,' Challe said. 'I just talked to Greger, by the way. He's going to come down and take over from Anders.'

*

Stina pulled up in front of Charlie in an unmarked, dark blue car.

'Have you heard anything else about Anders's son?' she asked, after leaning across the passenger seat to open the door.

'Nothing,' Charlie replied.

'It's just awful,' Stina said. 'I hope it's not too serious.'

Charlie thought about the conversation she and Anders had had in the car. The one about how he wouldn't be able to live without Sam. She didn't think those were empty words.

'Another colleague of mine is on his way down,' Charlie said, while she pulled out her phone and texted Anders to ask him to let her know as soon as he had news.

'I know. Your boss just called. What did Niklas Sandell have to say?' Stina continued as she cut off an angrily honking car at an intersection.

'He has been on a three-day relapse bender with a mate of his, Anton Eriksson.'

'I know him,' Stina said. 'His record's similar to Niklas's.'

'Well, he gave Niklas an alibi, for what that's worth. And the whole sexual activity with a child thing,' Charlie went on. 'It was—'

'I know,' Stina said. 'I just looked it up.'

'Is it true she was fourteen and got into the bar by lying about her age?'

'Yes, she even had a fake ID.'

'And I found out some other things, too,' Charlie said. 'According to Niklas Sandell, both Gustav and David are recreational drug users.'

'I'm not surprised,' Stina replied.

'And he said there might be a third man, a business partner who feels cheated by Gustav and David, called ... well, they only knew him as Half-White. Apparently, he has no pigment in one half of his body.'

Stina turned to Charlie. 'Pascal Byle? It must be him. At least he's the only person I know who fits that description.'

'You know him?'

'No, but I know of him. Karlstad's not exactly a metropolis.' She indicated and turned left before adding, 'He's from a wealthy family, too.'

'Did he used to work with Gustav?'

'No idea,' Stina said, 'but I don't imagine it would be hard to find out.'

Charlie pulled out her phone and googled Pascal Byle. He was forty-six years old and registered at an address in Karlstad. She added Gustav Palmgren to the search bar but could find no connection between the two, business-related or otherwise.

'I'll try calling him,' Charlie said. She looked up his number and dialled it. It went straight to voicemail. Then she tried his wife's number because it said he shared his home with a Mathilda Byle. But there was no answer there either.

'We'll try again after the meeting,' Stina said. 'If they don't answer, we'll just have to go over there.'

Back at the station, Charlie went straight to the bathroom. She leaned on the sink, closed her eyes, and tried to impose order on the thoughts racing through her head. It was almost eleven. Beatrice had now been gone for over twenty-four hours. Where was she? With whom? Or was she alone? Was she alive?

Charlie pictured a giant hourglass, sand rushing to the bottom. Time was everything and they were absolutely nowhere. They had nothing.

17

Stina had called a team meeting in the conference room. She informed them Anders had had to go back to Stockholm for personal reasons and that a new colleague from the NOD was on his way. Then she went over the results of the search operation so far.

The door-knocking operation on Hammarö had yielded nothing. They were now casting the net wider, talking to the staff at the train station and local bus drivers, among others. Had they noticed any person or persons with a baby in a pram who had seemed stressed or had stood out to them some other way?

'What about the tip line?' Charlie asked.

'We've had nothing of immediate interest. There's a lot of empty chatter, as you know.'

Charlie nodded. Appeals to the public always attracted the lonely and the paranoid, self-appointed detectives and psychics. But among the dross, there was sometimes a nugget of gold that could turn an investigation around and lead to a crime being solved. The biggest challenge for the officers manning the phones was identifying those nuggets in the torrent of nonsense.

'This morning, Charlie and Anders went to see Frida's brother, Beatrice's uncle, Niklas Sandell.' Stina pointed to the picture of Niklas on the whiteboard. The picture must have been taken some years ago, because in it, he was less marked by his substance abuse. His dark-blond hair was glossy and his eyes clear.

'Niklas Sandell is a heavy drug user. He has been convicted of burglary, theft, and possession, as well as sexual activity with a child ten years ago. Hold on,' Stina added when a colleague opened his mouth to say something. Then she explained the circumstances, how they'd met in a bar, the fake ID, and that it had been the girl's father who reported it.

'It still says something about him,' Charlie said.

'Yes, it does. And his only alibi is his junkie friend, but as things stand, we don't have anything on him,' Stina replied.

'I'm sure we can turn up the pressure on him,' Roy said.

'Absolutely,' Stina agreed. 'You and I will go talk to him again. But the conversation with Sandell also brought up something else. Maybe you could tell us about that, Charlie.'

Charlie recounted what Niklas had said about Pascal Byle's bitterness against Gustav Palmgren. A quick preliminary search had revealed no business links between Palmgren and Byle, but that didn't mean none existed.

'Have you talked to Byle?' Roy asked.

'His phone is turned off and his wife isn't answering hers,' Charlie said. 'I'll be going over to his house after we're done here. One of you will have to ask Gustav Palmgren about it, get his side of the story. And one more thing,' she went on. 'Niklas Sandell told us that both Gustav and David Jolander are cocaine users. According to him, it's recreational, but I'm not sure we should trust his judgement on that. And apparently, Byle is a more serious case.'

'So you think the kidnapping might be linked to drugs?' Roy said.

'I didn't say that,' Charlie replied. 'If Niklas Sandell is to be believed, it's not that kind of drug use, and Gustav and David can both afford to finance a habit without risking too much, but ...'

'But what?' Roy pressed.

'I just think it would be good to know for sure,' Charlie said. 'So we have as complete a picture as possible of the people in Beatrice's life.'

Stina pointed out that they also needed to verify the alibi provided by Amina, the cleaning lady, who had lost all three of her own children and occasionally looked after Beatrice. They were also going to continue to look into the Palmgrens' background. Could there be a connection to Gustav Palmgren's work, after all? Perhaps Pascal Byle was just one of many people who felt cheated? Or was it a case of blackmail, had someone kidnapped Beatrice to extract money from Gustav Palmgren? It couldn't be ruled out just because there hadn't been a ransom demand yet.

'Does anyone have anything to add?' Stina asked after handing out assignments. 'Any questions?' She looked around the room. No one spoke.

Charlie drove through the Bergvik Retail Park thinking the GPS must have led her astray, but before long, superstore signs gave way to forests and beautiful lakeside properties.

Byle's house was a newly built black villa. There were diggers and machines parked in the garden. Apparently, they were installing a pool, Charlie concluded after studying the logos on the vehicles.

She crossed a muddy lawn criss-crossed by tyre tracks and walked up the front steps.

The house was dark. Charlie knew before she pushed the doorbell that no one would come to the door. On her way back to the car, she pulled out her phone and looked at the picture of the three boys in bathing suits at Adamsberg Boarding School again.

Gustav was in the middle as the winner of the swim meet. The other two, whom he had his arms around, were not named, merely described as his friends. When she zoomed in, she noticed that the young man on Gustav's right had dark hair on one side of his head and blond, almost white hair on the other. There could be no doubt it was Pascal Byle. And now she realised the boy on the other side of Gustav was David Jolander.

Sara

We were back in the basement. I was supposed to tell my story. It made no difference that I said it was uninteresting. I had to tell it anyway.

'I grew up in a small village,' I began and looked around the circle of girls in nightgowns and hats. 'At first it was … OK, I guess, but then my dad … he liked drinking a lot.'

'Who doesn't?' Nicki said and took a swig from the bottle that was being passed around.

'Shut up,' Lo said.

'And then, well, my mum left,' I continued, looking straight at Lo. 'She took off with a Spaniard and Dad started to drink even more.'

I thought about all the drunken parties at our house. The bottles, the cigarette butts, the guitar strumming, the men's laps. *Come sit with me and tell us if you have a boyfriend. Oh, go on, have a sip – a little sip never killed anyone.* I thought about the fact that I'd promised myself never to become like Dad, but what else was there?

'Tell us more,' Nicki said and handed me the bottle.

I took several long pulls and thought about the parties at Vall's, about the weed room and the fucking room and all

114

the things I'd let boys do to me out of … guilt? Gratitude? Because I didn't have anything better to do?

'Was your dad violent?' Nicki asked.

'No. He was … nice. He just couldn't catch a break.'

And then I thought about my thirteenth birthday, about the shampoo bottle, conditioner, and soap Dad had wrapped, how I'd thrown it in the bin when he said that was it, that there wasn't anything else, that, unfortunately, he'd …

I thought about Dad's bowed head, his thinning hair, the tears on his work shirt and I just wanted to die and rot in the ground like him.

'You were just thirteen,' Nicki said when I told them. 'You were just a little kid who wanted nice presents on your birthday.'

'But I was still an idiot,' I replied.

'You were a child,' Lo said.

'I was an idiot child.'

I didn't tell them about the time with Svante in the gazebo in the garden behind Vall's. Nothing about that dreamlike state in which my body had no longer belonged to me, the limpness of my arms and the numbness of my tongue. I didn't tell them about the faces in the window, about waking up the next day thinking it hadn't really happened. I said nothing about the horror and the shame when I realised it had, that it was all real.

18

Stina and Roy had gone to speak to Gustav again. Charlie texted Stina to let her know that no one was home at the Byle residence, and that she had decided to drive over to talk to David Jolander about the purported business relationship between him, Gustav, and Byle.

She had just parked outside Jolander's house when Challe called.

'Sam?' she said. 'Tell me he's OK.'

'He's OK,' Challe confirmed. 'I just talked to Anders. His wife called again and apparently it's just a concussion.'

'Thank goodness,' Charlie said, and couldn't help but think that maybe Maria should have known it wasn't too serious, that she had exaggerated. It wouldn't surprise her considering how Maria had behaved both before and after the divorce, what with her constant jealousy and attempts at manipulation.

'And Greger?' Charlie asked. 'Is he on his way?'

'Yes, I just spoke to him, too, he's about an hour away.'

After hanging up, she called Anders. No answer. She fired off a text instead, saying she'd heard things were under control and that he could call any time if he wanted to talk.

*

The Jolanders lived less than a mile from the Palmgrens. Their house was similar to Gustav and Frida's in both style and colour. Charlie looked out at the garden and noted a treehouse with a zipline, a trampoline, and a swing set of the type you'd normally find in a park.

A boy of about ten opened the door seconds after Charlie rang the bell. Behind him stood a girl who looked to be a couple of years younger.

'Is your dad home?' Charlie asked.

'What do you want?' the boy said.

'I want to talk to your dad.'

The boy gave her a suspicious look, then turned around and shouted, 'Daaaaaaad!'

Charlie heard quick, heavy footsteps coming down the stairs. David Jolander pulled up short in the hallway when he saw her.

'Is there news?' he asked.

'I just need to have a word with you,' Charlie said.

David nodded, then he told the children to go to their rooms and play video games.

'But we already used up all our screen time,' protested the girl, who had lingered after her brother had raced up the stairs, clearly curious.

'You can have another thirty minutes,' David said. 'Can I offer you something to drink?' he asked when they entered the kitchen. 'Tea? Coffee?'

'I'm good, thank you.'

But David must not have heard her declining the offer, because he took down two cups and started to make espresso in a light-pink machine sitting on the kitchen counter.

'I was hoping for good news,' he said as he put the cups down on the table.

'Unfortunately, I don't have any.' Charlie took a sip of the strong coffee. 'I've come to ask you a few more questions.'

'Go ahead,' David said.

'How long have you known each other, you and Gustav?'

'A very long time. Since primary school, I guess. And then we were in the same class at Adamsberg, and we started the company together, so ... well, I guess we've been mates pretty much our entire lives, really.'

'How would you describe working with him?'

'Well, I think our results speak for themselves,' David said. 'We sold our company for—'

'I know how much you sold your company for,' Charlie said.

'Then why did you ask?'

'Because maybe there's more to it than just the results.'

She looked at David, who seemed not to comprehend that there could be more to it.

'Your relationship,' she clarified.

'He's my best friend,' David said. 'We're both pretty competitive, so I suppose we've fallen out on occasion, but never seriously.'

'And what happened with Pascal Byle?'

David looked nonplussed. 'Aren't you kind of heading out into the periphery now?' he said.

'Is there a reason you don't want to answer the question?'

'What have you heard?'

'That he was cheated, that you and Gustav cheated him.'

'We disagree on that.'

'Then tell me your side of it. What happened?'

'Pascal was on board when we first started to plan to break

into the Russian market. He had some good ideas, did some work on the layout of the site, and invested some funds. But then we had different opinions on how to move forward, so Gustav and I bought his share of the company. He was happy with the sum we paid him, until we sold the company a year later. Then he suddenly got in touch, saying he wanted more. Several of his investments had failed and he was in desperate need of money. But we had a deal, and we didn't feel there was any need for charity.'

Charlie thought about the billions they had made from the sale of the site. 'Can I ask how much you paid him?'

'Two million.'

'And the company was sold for almost three billion.'

'Sure, but a deal's a deal.'

'Maybe it wouldn't be charity exactly, though,' she said, 'if you were to give him a bit more after the fact, considering how things turned out?'

'That's not how this business works.'

'And how have things been between you since?'

'He's upset,' David said and took a sip of his coffee. 'He has called both me and Gustav to yell at us.'

'Has he threatened you?' Charlie asked, wondering why Gustav hadn't mentioned this man when they asked him about potential enemies.

'I suppose you could say that, but we don't take him very seriously. He was always an angry drunk.'

'I understand Pascal Byle also attended Adamsberg,' Charlie said.

'That's right.'

'How were things back then?'

'Just normal, I guess,' David replied. 'We were in the same

class and on the swim team and rowing team together and ... I'm not sure what you're getting at ...'

'And then you partied together,' Charlie said.

'Sure, what of it?'

'I've been told it's not just alcohol,' Charlie replied. 'That there's cocaine involved ...'

'That was years ago. Maybe not for Pascal, but ... I'm a family man,' David said, as if that had anything to do with it.

'So is Pascal.'

'Well, regardless, I don't do that anymore. It was just a handful of times when we were out partying, but Pascal ... I suppose you could say he has some impulse-control issues.'

'When did you last hear from Pascal?'

'A few weeks ago, maybe. Why?'

'And what did he say?'

'It was the same old griping about us destroying his life, and he went on and on about deserving more money. Is this really something you should be prioritising right now? Pascal has nothing to do with Beatrice's disappearance, I promise.'

'You're just going to have to trust that we're doing our jobs.'

David gave her a look that plainly said he didn't. Then he leaned forward slightly and fixed Charlie intensely.

'You have to find her,' he said. 'Frida and Gustav will fall apart if you don't. I don't think you can imagine how important Beatrice is to all of us.'

The front door slammed shut and, seconds later, Charlotte Jolander came into the kitchen. She put her handbag down on the counter and greeted Charlie with a question in her eyes.

'She's just following up on a few things,' David said.

A shrill shriek from upstairs.

'Could you?' Charlotte said, turning to David.

David nodded and left.

'Do you have any suspects?' Charlotte asked. She had taken a seat across from Charlie.

'We're talking to everyone who's close to the family, to find out what might be behind this.'

'What could that be?'

'It's hard to say,' Charlie replied. 'Can you think of anything that has struck you as out of the ordinary recently?'

'I don't know,' Charlotte said after a long pause. 'I don't know.'

They were interrupted by the daughter, who came running into the kitchen. 'Love took my stickers!' she howled.

'Talk to Dad,' Charlotte said.

'But he went into his office and locked the door,' the girl replied. She had come all the way up to her mum now and was tugging on her jumper.

And that was when Charlie saw it, a long scar on Charlotte's forearm.

Charlotte quickly pulled her sleeve down and looked Charlie in the eye. 'Would you mind holding on for just a moment?' she said.

They left the room and soon Charlie could hear Charlotte yelling at her son to give back what he'd taken, no, not in a bit, right now.

Charlie thought about what she had just witnessed. She was pretty sure Charlotte had an identical scar on the other arm, suicide scars. That didn't fit in with her image of a woman on the sunny side of the street. But, she corrected herself, mental illness doesn't care about socioeconomic status. It doesn't discriminate.

'So, where were we?' Charlotte said when she returned.

'Are you close with Frida?' Charlie said, even though what she really wanted to ask was: What happened? Why did you slit your wrists? Why didn't you want to live? But how was a healed suicide scar relevant to the case?

'I suppose you might say that,' Charlotte replied.

'Suppose?'

'Well, Frida is ... She doesn't let people in, but I think you could say I'm her closest friend. When we lived in Moscow, we spent almost every day together. David and Gustav travelled a lot, so ... But since we've moved back to Sweden, I see her less. Frida has been very tired since Beatrice was born.'

'Can you tell me more about that?'

'There's nothing else to say,' Charlotte replied. 'Having a child is always an adjustment and Beatrice hasn't been sleeping well. It's no wonder she needs to rest and have some alone time while the baby naps. It was like that for me, too.'

'I understand,' Charlie said. 'Do you know anything about Frida's background?'

'She doesn't like to talk about it, but I think her parents were alcoholics, so it was hard, of course. Why are you asking me this? You don't think Frida ... Frida loves Beatrice more than her own life.' Charlotte seemed about to expand on the subject of motherly love, but Charlie managed to cut in.

'How well do you know Amina?'

'She cleans our house,' Charlotte said as though that answered the question.

'Do you see her socially?'

'No, but I like her very much.'

'Has she ever looked after your children?' Charlie asked.

'She has babysat on occasion. They adore her.'

'Amina claims she was here cleaning yesterday morning around the time Beatrice disappeared. Is that true?'

'If you're suspecting Amina, I can assure you you're on the wrong track. She is the kindest person in the world, she—'

'None of us want to offend any of the people who love Beatrice. We just want to find her, just like you. I hope you understand that.' Charlie gave Charlotte a grave look. 'Are you sure there's nothing else you want to tell me?'

'No,' Charlotte said. She shook her head. There was nothing else.

'Here's my number, in case you think of something later,' Charlie said and put her card down on the table in front of Charlotte. 'Don't hesitate to contact me.'

If you change your mind, Charlie wanted to add, because every part of her was screaming that this woman was hiding something.

19

Greger was sitting in the conference room with Stina when Charlie got back to the station. His hair was even more unkempt than usual, maybe because he'd left in a hurry.

'Have you been caught up?' Charlie asked after shaking his hand.

'Yep,' Greger replied. 'Unless I've misunderstood something, we have a very wealthy dad, a distraught mum, a cleaner who lost her own children, has looked after Beatrice, and knows the family's routines. And then there's the junkie uncle who absconded from rehab just before Beatrice went missing.'

'Spot on,' Charlie said. 'An uncle who's bitter about his sister not helping him out financially and has been convicted of sexual activities with a child, I might add.'

'Alibi?' Greger asked.

'Just a mate he parties with.'

'Got it,' Greger said. 'And then there's the third business associate. The one who was bought out and is feeling hard done by.'

'Yes,' Stina said, turning to Charlie. 'What did David Jolander have to say about Pascal Byle?'

Charlie briefly told them that David had confirmed that

Byle had been a participant and investor in the project in its early stages, had sold his share of the company to the other two, and had then been in touch after the sale of it to say he wanted more money. That Byle had called David and Gustav repeatedly, making threats, but that David was convinced he had nothing to do with Beatrice's disappearance.

'That matches what Gustav told us,' Stina said.

'And what about Frida?' Charlie asked.

'We didn't see her. She was upstairs with Charlotte Jolander, and we didn't want to disturb them.'

'Did you ask Gustav about the cocaine?'

'We did, but he said it was empty gossip, that the rumours about Byle's addiction had rubbed off on him.'

'Was that why Byle was bought out?' Greger asked. 'Because of his addiction?'

Stina shook her head. 'No, according to Gustav, it was because they had different ideas about the direction of the company.'

'That sounds like something he came up with after the fact,' Greger said. 'What does Pascal Byle himself have to say about it?'

'We haven't been able to reach him yet,' Stina replied. 'Neither he nor his wife is answering their phone. But we will keep on it, of course.'

'I would like to see Beatrice's parents straight away,' Greger said and got to his feet.

Charlie was about to object, to say that the Palmgrens had barely had time to close the door after the last police visit, but she could see why Greger wanted to form his own opinion of the victims.

*

Charlie drove out to the Palmgrens'. By now, the route to Hammarö was starting to feel familiar. She asked Greger to call Frida to let her know they were coming.

'Text her,' she said when neither Frida nor Gustav picked up.

Greger did as he was told.

'What are they like?' he asked. 'The parents?'

'It's hard to get a clear impression of them right now,' Charlie replied. 'I mean ... they're not exactly themselves.'

'True,' Greger said. 'That's understandable.'

'They come from very different backgrounds,' Charlie added. 'Gustav Palmgren is from a wealthy family, went to boarding school, and then made it big with this site in Russia.'

'I've heard about it.'

'Before this?'

'Yes, I read about it in the paper. What?'

'Nothing. I just didn't think you were the business-section type.'

'You don't like the business-section type?'

'I didn't think I did, but I guess I'll have to reconsider my position now.' She turned to him and smiled.

'I like people who have the ability to change their minds,' Greger said.

'Then I'm sure we can make this work.'

'Do you mind if I ask you a personal question?' Greger said.

I would prefer if you didn't, Charlie thought as she shook her head.

'Do you have something against Hugo Frilander?'

'No,' Charlie said. It was the truth. She had no feelings for Hugo. It was strange, she thought, that such fierce passion could turn into loathing, only to then fizzle out into utter indifference. Not even the feeling of humiliation had lingered. *I'm never going to be able to leave my wife, Charlie.* Hugo Frilander was simply a colleague she preferred not to work with, not because it was painful, but because she preferred working closely with people she could trust.

'Why would you think I did?'

'It's just ... I don't know,' Greger said. 'He's the natural choice for this assignment, and I accidentally overheard a conversation between him and Challe, and ...'

'And what?'

'Well, I guess it was clear Challe didn't think it was such a good idea for him to go and I was just wondering why.'

'God, I don't know,' Charlie said. 'Maybe Challe just wanted to give you an opportunity to prove yourself.' Don't let him down, she wanted to add. Let's find this baby already.

It was a while before the Palmgrens' door opened after they knocked. But, eventually, Gustav appeared.

'Nothing has happened,' Charlie said. 'We tried to call to let you know we were coming, but neither of you picked up.'

'Then what do you want,' Gustav said, 'if nothing has happened? Why aren't you out looking, trying to find her?'

'We are, I promise,' Charlie replied.

'My name is Greger Vincent, I'm from the NOD,' Greger said and stuck out his hand. 'Our colleague Anders had to return to Stockholm. I wanted to meet you personally to get a first-hand impression of the situation.'

Gustav pretended not to see the extended hand. 'It's just me,' he explained. 'Frida went out for a walk. She can't bear to be here.'

'I'm not so sure she should be alone right now,' Charlie said.

'I tried to tell her that,' Gustav said, 'but she left anyway.'

'Did she say where she was going?'

Gustav shook his head. 'But she usually walks out to the lighthouse.'

He explained how to get there to Charlie's retreating back.

Five minutes later, Charlie gingerly picked her way across slippery cliffs towards the lighthouse. Ahead, she could see a lonely-looking figure sitting by the water's edge.

Frida gave a start and whipped around when she heard someone approaching.

'What are you doing here?' she asked.

'Gustav said you might be here.'

'I need to be alone.'

'Is that Beatrice?' Charlie asked, looking at the phone in Frida's hand where a video had been paused.

Frida nodded and pressed play. And there she was: Beatrice. Sitting in her highchair, wearing pyjamas with a floral pattern, bright-eyed and with food all over her face. Listening raptly to Frida's happy voice.

How big is Bea now? How big?

A toothless smile.

Hooooow big is Bea?

Beatrice laughed and raised her stubby arms into the air.

Thiiiiiiis big!

Charlie's eyes began to sting as the video started over from the beginning.

How big is Bea now? How big? The smile, the laughter, the arms in the air.

Frida stopped the video, turned to Charlie, and asked what she wanted.

'Honestly, I was worried when I found out you had walked off by yourself,' said Charlie. 'But, originally, I came out here because I wanted to talk to you some more.'

'About what?' Frida's eyes were glazed, possibly from sedatives.

'I'm trying to get a picture of what life was like before Beatrice disappeared.'

'I don't know what else to tell you,' Frida said. She slowly pulled out a cigarette.

'Can I bum one?' Charlie asked.

Frida held out the packet and a lighter and pulled her coat tighter around her. A cold wind was blowing in from the lake.

Charlie took a deep drag.

'I quit two years ago,' Frida said, as though Charlie had asked. 'But now I've gone through almost an entire pack. I don't know what else to do with my hands. Or myself.'

'It helps in the moment,' Charlie said, 'like focusing on your breathing.'

'Nothing helps until she's back,' Frida said.

Charlie nodded. It was true. Not even time could heal the wounds left by a missing child. The pain wouldn't be acute forever, but it would never completely fade either.

'My grandad used to take me here when I was a little girl,' Frida explained. 'His grandad had been the lighthouse keeper. Grandad had this idea that his spirit lived on and had become one with the lighthouse and could give him guidance in life. Lead him through the darkness.'

'And did it?'

'It's not the kind of lighthouse that leads you right,' Frida said. 'It only shows you when you're going the wrong way. It warns ships about the rocks out there.' She pointed out at the lake.

'Isn't that just another way of leading you right?' Charlie said. 'Alerting you to hazards?'

Frida nodded.

They said nothing else for a while. The wind had picked up and the waves were growing bigger. It looked more like the sea than a lake now.

'I need to ask you some … uncomfortable questions,' Charlie said.

'Fine, ask,' Frida replied.

'When young children disappear, it can be due to … accidents … Something may have happened, a mistake, I mean, that you … can't bear to tell anyone about …'

'That wasn't a question,' Frida said. Her eyes looked more alert now, guarded. 'But I can see what you're getting at, and the answer is no, I would never harm my daughter. I love her. I love her so much I …' She trailed off.

'I've talked to your brother,' Charlie said. 'Niklas. He told me what it was like for you, growing up, I mean.'

'OK?'

'Would you mind expanding on that?'

'Mum and Dad were alcoholics.' Frida shrugged as though that fact bored her. 'It's hard to explain to someone who hasn't been in that situation …. what it's like to be the child of parents who can't be trusted, who alternate between being idiots and being children themselves.'

'I've been in that situation,' Charlie said.

Frida turned to her. Charlie didn't care that she had crossed a professional boundary.

'I know what it's like to be the child of someone who

alternates between being an idiot and being a child,' she added.

'Then you know,' Frida said. 'Then you know how guilty you can feel about ... things you were powerless to control.'

'Yes,' Charlie said and thought to herself that the guilt was actually the worst part, the guilt of not having been able to save Betty from destroying herself. It didn't matter that she knew she hadn't stood a chance, the feeling was still there.

'I want to be a different kind of parent to Bea,' Frida went on. 'The kind who loves unconditionally, who makes her feel safe, who is ... there for her. And that's why I'm so scared I don't have it in me – that I'm going to break my child because that's what I am, broken.'

Charlie nodded. She recognised that kind of reasoning. The fear of harming other people just by being who you were, who you had become.

'When did you and Gustav meet?'

'My first year at uni. I was studying literature, but Gustav wanted me to help him with his company, so I ... well, I dropped out. I don't know what I was thinking, but I suppose I was sick of ...'

'What were you sick of?' Charlie asked, because Frida seemed to have lost her train of thought.

'The loneliness,' Frida said. 'I couldn't take it anymore.' She stared at the glowing tip of her cigarette. 'Imagine if I'd known then that some relationships only make you lonelier.'

'Is that how you feel about Gustav?'

Frida nodded.

'How come?'

'Because there's no getting close to him. I've come to realise that he chose me the same way he chooses cars and gadgets. I suppose he thought I was the ... prettiest. But is that love?'

'I'm not an expert in that field,' Charlie said.

'But then, I had Bea ...' Frida threw her cigarette away and raised Beatrice's snuggle blanket to her cheek. 'It hurts too much. It hurts so fucking bad. I thought I knew everything there is to know about pain, but I had no idea. Where I am now ... this place is ... it's dark.'

Charlie moved a little closer and put her arm around her. For a long while they just sat there, Frida with her face in her daughter's blanket and Charlie with her eyes on the foaming waters of Lake Vänern.

Sara

'I'm not sure exactly what time Mum will get here,' Lo said. She was lying on her bed with her feet up on the wall next to the photograph of the woman who, according to her, was the most wonderful person in the world. 'It's a visiting day, you know,' she went on, as though there was any way I could have forgotten. Lo had been going on about it for a week. 'She can't come until after work. I told you, right? That Mum got a new job?'

I told her she had.

'At a hairdresser,' Lo said. 'Right in the centre of town. Soon, they're going to let her start cutting customers' hair and do perms and stuff.'

'Isn't that what people do at a hairdresser's?'

'She's not a hairdresser, though, not yet.'

'I'm sorry,' I said. 'I just thought ... So what does she do there, if she's not cutting hair?'

'I guess she sweeps and whatever,' Lo said. 'I don't fucking know what she does.'

I thought about Rita. She had only called once since dropping me off at Rödminnet, and I sincerely hoped she had forgotten all about the visiting days.

'Check this out,' Lo said and lowered her styling head so I could see. Its hair was in a plait that wrapped all the way around its head.

'Nice,' I said. 'I bet your mum's going to love it.'

'Do you have anyone coming?' Lo asked.

'I doubt it.'

'You can hang out with my mum and me,' Lo said. I should, come to think of it, because it was important for the two of us to meet properly since we were going to work and maybe even live together.

It was the second time Lo had brought up living together. It made me happy. I'd started fantasising about a small house in the country. We would drive to our salon in the nearest village and maybe take in some foster kids. *Look at us*, we would say to them, *we were delinquents in care once, too, but look at us now . . . look at what can happen if you hold on to hope.*

20

Charlie had given Frida a ride home and picked Greger up. After a conversation with Stina, they had decided to go by Pascal Byle's house. Neither Pascal nor his wife had answered their phones yet, and given how imperative it was to reach Byle, they figured they might as well give it a try.

'You really think he might have taken Beatrice?' Greger said.

'I don't know,' Charlie replied. 'That's why we need to find him.'

'We will. What did Frida say?'

'She's not doing well. Really not doing well.'

'That's understandable,' Greger said.

'She wasn't doing well before this happened either.'

'How come?'

'Well, you know, her childhood, her marriage … she's lonely.' Charlie thought about Frida, about her growing up with a couple of drunks for parents, the university studies she had dropped out of, her loneliness, and her hope of curing it forever. Maybe she could have used Betty's warnings.

Never trust a man. Never think a man can make you happy.

*

A woman of about thirty-five with a little boy in a nappy next to her opened the door when they rang the bell at the Byle residence.

'Has something happened?' she asked.

'We would like to speak to Pascal,' Charlie said and flashed her badge. 'We've been trying to call, but—'

'He's not home,' the woman said.

The boy whined and tugged on the woman's trousers. She picked him up, put him on her hip, and shushed him.

'Are you Mathilda Byle?' Greger asked.

The woman nodded.

'Do you know where your husband is?'

'I'm afraid not. We're ...' Mathilda glanced down at her son before finishing, 'separated.'

'Could we come in?' Charlie said.

Mathilda Byle led the way into a kitchen with dark-grey cabinets and clean, open surfaces.

'As you may have heard, a child has gone missing on Hammarö,' Charlie said once they were seated around the kitchen table.

'Yes, I know.' She hugged the happily squirming boy in her lap tighter.

'Then you may also know it's Gustav and Frida Palmgren's daughter,' Greger said. 'That the missing child is Beatrice Palmgren.'

Mathilda nodded. Yes, she knew. But why did they want to talk to Pascal about that?

'We've been told Pascal and Gustav aren't on friendly terms,' Greger said. 'And now someone has kidnapped Gustav's daughter and your husband is nowhere to be found ...'

'I don't understand ... What are you saying?'

'We would very much like to know where he is,' Charlie said. 'If only to cross him off our list. How long has he been gone?'

'It has been ... five days since he left,' Mathilda said.

'And you haven't heard from him since?'

Mathilda shook her head. The little boy began to cry.

'Do you want me to take him?' A girl entered the kitchen. She was about thirteen and had pink highlights in her curly blonde hair. The little boy held his arms out to her when she walked up to them.

'Thank you, Antonie,' Mathilda said and handed her the little boy.

The girl called Antonie said a brief hello to Charlie and Greger without asking who they were. Then she turned to the boy. 'Do you want to read stories? Want to read the one about the big tractor and the little mouse?'

'Pascal's daughter,' Mathilda said after they'd left. 'Right now, I don't know what I'd do without her.'

'And she hasn't heard from Pascal either?' Greger asked.

Mathilda shook her head. No one had heard from Pascal, as far as she was aware. Not his ex-wife, not their closest friends. Not even his parents had been in touch with him. They lived in Paris and since her mother-in-law was in ill health, Mathilda hadn't wanted to worry them unnecessarily, but reading between the lines, she'd concluded they hadn't heard from him either. And he wasn't in their summer house in Torekov, she had checked with the neighbours. Maybe she should have reported him missing, but he was a grown man who had asked to be left alone and told her he was going away for a while. A few days ago, she had called him anyway, but his phone had been turned off.

Charlie asked if she could give them the contact details of any friends he might have gone to see or called.

Mathilda said she would do that right away. She got up and fetched a pen and a notepad, started to write, and then consulted her mobile for phone numbers. Charlie experienced the feeling of fellowship she always had whenever she saw someone write with their left hand. She pulled out her phone and texted Stina: *Byle has been missing for five days.*

When Mathilda was done, there were about ten names on the list.

'I don't have everyone's number,' she said as she handed the piece of paper to Charlie. 'But I assume you can find them online. They all have unusual surnames, so you should have no problem.'

'Do you think he may have left the country?' Greger asked.

'No,' Mathilda replied. 'Or at least, he left his passport here.'

'And his car?'

'He took that.'

'May I ask ... why are you separated?' Greger said.

'Isn't that kind of personal?' Mathilda said. 'But if you really want to know, Pascal has been on a downward spiral ever since he was cheated by Gustav and David. He started to drink and turned into ... well, into someone else.'

'In what way?' Charlie asked.

'He became ...' She lowered her voice. 'He became withdrawn, stopped talking, and couldn't sleep at night. It was like living with a ghost. It affected the whole family. It's frightening to watch a person change like that.'

'I understand,' Greger said.

'And then he started to drink and stay out all night.'

'Was he aggressive, violent?' Charlie asked.

'He never hit anyone, if that's what you mean, but it's still unpleasant when someone flies off the handle.' She pointed towards a door at the other end of the kitchen, which had a big hole in it.

'And all of this happened because he felt cheated by Gustav and David?' Greger said.

'He *was* cheated,' Mathilda replied. 'It wasn't just a feeling. Gustav and David had him do the things they couldn't do themselves and once they had what they wanted, they dropped him like a hot potato.'

'From what I'm told, they bought him out,' Charlie said.

'Yes, that's what they say. But that's not how it was. They forced him to sign the papers. They would never have been able to sell the company for all those billions if it weren't for Pascal.'

'Then why did he agree to sell his share of the company?' Charlie said.

'When I asked him exactly that, he just said he had needed the money at the time, that he had wanted to invest in other things. I found out afterwards that he had big debts. From failed investments, gambling ... I'm not really sure what he got up to. My lawyer is going to try to sort it all out in conjunction with the divorce.'

'It seems your husband keeps secrets from you,' Greger said.

'Yes, that's beyond clear,' Mathilda replied. 'But that doesn't mean he would kidnap a baby.'

It was, perhaps, not surprising she would think her husband incapable of something like that, Charlie mused. But she had just told them herself how wronged and angry he felt, how much he had changed. Plus, there was the inescapable fact that Pascal Byle seemed as impossible to find as Beatrice.

'We need to locate him as soon as possible,' Greger said.

'I want to find him, too,' Mathilda said. 'I want to find him and put an end to all of this.'

'Can you tell us a bit more about Pascal's and Gustav's relationship?' Charlie asked. 'Have they known each other a long time?'

'They were classmates,' Mathilda said. 'Pascal, David, and Gustav attended Adamsberg Boarding School together and they've kept in touch. But we've all lived abroad on and off, so ... well, we haven't spent much time with their families. Mostly because of me. I didn't want to.'

'How come?'

'Because they're ... unpleasant, David especially.'

A scream from the little boy reached them and Mathilda broke off to listen, only to conclude it had been a shriek of joy.

'What do you base those feelings on?' Greger asked.

'It's just my impression,' Mathilda said. 'I ran into David in a bar once and he ... came onto me, and when I rejected him, he turned pretty nasty.'

'In what way?' Charlie asked.

'He asked me if I knew who he was and bragged about his business success, and—'

'When was this?' Charlie said.

'A few years ago,' Mathilda replied. 'I don't remember exactly, but it was before I met Pascal. Gustav was with him. They were celebrating some kind of deal they'd made and were very pleased with themselves.'

'So nothing else ...?' Greger asked.

'No,' Mathilda replied. 'Other than that they've ruined my husband's life and destroyed our family.' She excused herself, saying she needed a drink of water.

'Do you think Pascal could have taken Beatrice to get back at them?' Charlie asked when Mathilda sat back down.

'No,' Mathilda replied. She shook her head. 'Pascal loves children. Gustav and David are the ones he's mad at. It was all he talked about before he took off, that he was going to ...'

'Going to what?' Greger asked.

'Give them what they deserved,' Mathilda replied. 'I realise what that sounds like now, but ...'

'Tell us more,' Charlie said. 'Tell us what words he used when he talked about giving them what they deserved.'

'I don't remember exactly, but it was something about hoping their lives would be hell, and ...'

'And what?' Greger urged.

'That they deserved a punishment worse than death. But they're just words,' Mathilda continued when Charlie stood up. 'He didn't mean it.'

21

When they got back to the car, Charlie called Stina to update her on Pascal Byle. But Stina cut her off.

'A call just came in,' she said. 'A woman found a pram in a ditch. It looks like it might be Beatrice's; same make, same colour.'

'Where?'

'A few miles from the Palmgrens' house. We're on our way there now.'

'What's the address?'

'It's a gravel road in the woods.'

Charlie typed the nearest address into the GPS.

Stina asked where they were, and Charlie looked around for some kind of landmark.

'We're fourteen minutes away,' Greger put in.

'We can be there in ten,' Charlie said.

'Then you'll probably beat us there,' Stina replied.

Eight minutes later, Charlie turned onto the gravel road. Another car did the same behind them. Charlie was relieved to discover it was Stina and Roy. She knew it was only a matter of time before news of the pram reached the press. They were probably already on their way.

'We need to cordon off the area,' Charlie said after introducing herself to the distraught woman who had spotted the pram. 'Cordon it off and get forensics and the dog handlers out here.'

Stina told her they were on their way.

The pram was lying on its side in the ditch. Water seeped into Charlie's shoes the moment she stepped down into it for a more thorough examination. Inside the hood was a tangle of feathers. She moved closer and realised it was a dreamcatcher. She photographed the pram from several angles and sent the pictures to Gustav. Within minutes, what they already knew was confirmed. It was Beatrice's pram. But aside from the dreamcatcher, it was empty, no pink teddy bear, no black footmuff, no baby.

'Now what do we do?' Greger said. Stina and Roy had already left to start knocking on doors in the immediate vicinity. Uniformed officers had been called in to cover the rest of the area. 'Should we head back to the station?' he continued. 'I guess we have to—'

'Could I just have a moment?' Charlie said. 'I'll meet you at the car in five minutes.'

Greger nodded and turned back. Charlie continued down the narrow gravel road and then cut in among the trees. She took a few deep breaths, looked up at the swaying evergreens, and thought about the fantasies she'd had as a child. When she had lain under the thousand-year-old oak tree in Gullspång, thinking about all the things it could have told her if it'd had a voice. A thousand years of human history. Now, she would have settled for an account of the past twenty-four hours. But the forest was silent.

*

'I think it's a good sign, at least,' Greger said when they were back at the station. 'Whoever did this wanted to keep Beatrice warm and took her stuffed animal along.'

'Or it could just be a coincidence, and they just ripped out whatever was in the pram,' Roy countered.

'Yes, I suppose there's no way of knowing,' Charlie said.

'And what about the location,' Greger continued. 'Why was the pram found there?'

'It's only a couple of miles from the Palmgrens' house,' Stina replied. 'Maybe they had a car waiting there?'

'But no one we talked to in the area saw anything,' Roy said.

'Well, no one saw Beatrice disappear from her home either,' Charlie said. 'But that definitely happened.'

Sara

Lo was sitting on one of the wooden benches by the headless angel. How long had she been sitting there? An hour? Two? She was wearing a thin dress and her blonde hair had been brushed until it looked like a halo of candyfloss around her head. She was sitting dead still, with her hands in her lap and her eyes locked on the front gate. The clock struck four and then half past, but Lo didn't move.

I went down to the kitchen.

'I don't think she's coming,' I told Marianne, who was making coffee.

'Who?' Marianne asked.

'Lo's mum.'

'Not a lot of people come on visiting days,' Marianne said. 'A man called, by the way, asking for you.'

'Who?'

'I think he said his name was Jonas.'

'Why didn't you tell me?'

'I am telling you. It just happened.'

'Then why couldn't I talk to him?'

'I thought you were outside. I said you would call back.' She picked up the phone from the counter and held it out to me.

'Never mind,' I said.

'Is it someone you don't want to talk to?'

'I don't know.'

I thought about Jonas. He'd been kinder to me than most, had let me eat and stay at his house and had carried me home from Vall's when I was too drunk to walk. But to talk to him now ... all those things seemed so far away. What would we even say to each other?'

I said I might call back later, that I wanted to go outside and talk to Lo.

Marianne told me I should probably leave Lo alone.

On my way back up to our room, I stopped by the big window with the view of the forecourt. I stood there for a while, praying Lo's mum would show up soon, before Lo froze to death.

'She's not coming,' Emelie suddenly said behind me.

I turned around.

'Her mum, I mean,' Emelie continued. 'She has never been here. She hasn't visited once.'

'You're lying,' I said.

'Why would I lie about that? You don't have to get angry just because I'm telling you the truth.'

'I'm not angry,' I replied, even though I did feel angry, as though the whole thing were Emelie's fault.

'Do you get visits?' Emelie asked.

'Sure,' I said. 'They all come. Mum, Dad, and all my brothers and sisters.'

'As if,' Emelie retorted. 'I read in your file that you're an only child.'

'I have a file?'

'Everyone here does.'

'What does it say?' I asked, feeling distinctly uneasy about Emelie knowing things about me I hadn't told her.

'I'm afraid that's confidential.'

'Then why are you telling me at all?'

'Because I don't like being lied to.'

I wanted to tell her I didn't like bullies who poked fun at girls who lived in care homes and didn't have any visitors, but there was no point.

Emelie left and I stayed by the window, looking down at Lo. If I squinted, it almost looked like one of the old black-and-white photographs on the wall. *Girl on bench, waiting for her mother.*

22

It was ten o'clock when Charlie and Greger returned to the hotel. Because it was Sunday, the kitchen was already closed, but they agreed to make an exception and serve them a light meal.

'Drinks?' the waiter asked.

'Water,' Charlie replied.

'I'll have a glass of red,' Greger said. 'One glass is OK, right?' he asked, looking at Charlie.

She nodded and wished more than ever that she was a person who was capable of having just *one* glass.

While they waited for their food, Charlie went over the latest developments in her mind. The pram had been sent to the NFC for DNA analysis and technicians had combed a large area around where it had been discovered without finding anything else. She hoped Greger was right in his thinking about the teddy bear and the footmuff, that the fact that they had been taken was a sign that the kidnapper cared about the baby's well-being. The image of Beatrice being rocked in someone's arms calmed her a little before a torrent of other possible scenarios uploaded into her brain: a tiny bundle bobbing in a lake, a pale, frozen baby face in the woods, a mangled baby body in ...

The images made her think of Betty's sister, the unborn baby who had died from a punch to her mother's stomach. And then, the son of the man who had done the punching, the little boy who had been lured away and murdered in the woods, strangled by the same hands that had plaited Charlie's hair. It had been an accident, Charlie had told herself when she found out. Betty had just wanted to scare him. She would never kill a child. Or would she? Maybe it had been planned, an eye for an eye, a child for a child? Had that been her reasoning? Like divine justice?

There is no justice. There is no God. Haven't you realised that by now, Charline?

'Are you OK?' Greger asked.

Charlie nodded.

'You look a little pale.'

'We need to find her,' Charlie said, ignoring his comment about her pallor. 'Time's running out.'

'Do you think Pascal Byle took her?' Greger asked.

'I don't know. But if he wanted to punish Gustav with something worse than death ...'

'Still a drastic thing to do,' Greger said, 'kidnapping a child over a business dispute.'

Charlie agreed, but they couldn't ignore the fact that he had vanished four days before Beatrice. And even though his wife had assured them he wasn't the type to take a child, she had also told them he'd been a different person recently.

So far, the search for Pascal Byle had yielded no result. They had put out an APB on his car as well, but there had been no word on that yet either. His phone had last been pinged by a mast in central Karlstad. Now, it was dead, and it hadn't been used since he left home. There had been nothing of interest in his call list or messages. Was that because he was staying away voluntarily? He hadn't used his credit card since he disappeared, but according to Mathilda Byle, he usually carried a lot of cash. He was either dead or very good at lying low.

'So, what's your thinking?' Charlie said when their food arrived. It was some kind of weird goop that made her want to head out to the nearest fast-food restaurant. 'What's your take on all of this?'

'It bothers me that we can't seem to get anything else out of Gustav,' Greger replied. 'I felt like I had to drag the words out of him when surely he should be ... I mean, his child's missing. How can he be so sure her disappearance has nothing to do with his work? Why doesn't he want to turn over every stone?'

'Maybe he's busy turning over stones we know nothing about. He does seem genuinely upset.'

'So he thinks he can do a better job than us?'

'Maybe. Don't forget that he's used to being the best at whatever he does.'

Charlie put a forkful of food in her mouth and swallowed it without chewing; it tasted even worse than it looked.

'OK, let's come at it from a different angle,' she went on, well aware that focusing too much on one lead risked leaving you blind to other possibilities. 'Say this isn't Pascal Byle exacting revenge. Then what happened?'

'Well, statistically, the parents ... And let's not forget that Frida was alone with Beatrice when it happened, and—'

'Mothers rarely kill their children,' Charlie said. 'Unless there's post-partum psychosis involved, but we've had no indication Frida suffered from that. And doesn't that actually just increase the risk of suicide, come to think of it?'

'There are exceptions,' Greger countered. 'I went on a call-out many years ago. It was in a posh suburb; a woman who had never had any mental-health issues or run-ins with the law had slit her daughter's throat with a kitchen knife. We got there before the ambulance, and ... going into that house and seeing it ...'

Greger trailed off and took a big gulp of wine.

'She was a lawyer,' he continued, 'and her husband ... I don't recall what he did for a living, but they were both successful. The whole family was described as nice and polite by friends and neighbours. No one understood how it could have happened.'

'The human psyche is as unfathomable as outer space,' Charlie said. 'And the deeper you dig, the more complex it becomes.'

'I didn't know you liked to dig into the human psyche,' Greger said.

'I don't know if you can say I ever have, but I did study psychology.'

'Where?'

'Stockholm University,' Charlie replied. She thought about how triumphant the knowledge she had gained during her years in the psychology department had made her feel. It had been like being given the keys to her own brain.

'When did you have time to do that?'

'Before the Academy. I couldn't apply straight out of school, I was too young. The cut-off was twenty back then and I was only seventeen when I graduated upper secondary.'

'Why did you graduate early?' Greger asked.

'Because I skipped a year.'

Her phone dinged. It was a text from Anders. A picture of him and Sam and the words *Everything under control.*

Great news, she texted back.

'That was Anders,' she said.

'I'm glad everything turned out all right.'

'Anders wouldn't be able to go on,' Charlie said. 'If something happened to his son, I mean.'

'In my experience, people can survive more than they think,' Greger said and raised his glass to his lips again.

'Sure, but everyone has their limits,' Charlie replied and thought about Betty.

There's a limit, and once it's reached, there's no way back.

What was it Frida had said about Beatrice? *She's the only family I have. I have nothing else to live for.*

A different waiter came over and asked in a heavy local accent if everything was to their liking, if they wanted any more drinks.

'I'll have another glass of wine, please,' Greger said.

'A beer for me,' Charlie replied without thinking. 'A pint of whatever you have on tap.'

What's the point of having the keys to your own brain, she thought, when you can't seem to use them?

The waiter returned quickly with another glass of wine and an ice-cold, frothy pint.

'When did you get that?' Greger asked, nodding towards the tattoo on Charlie's left wrist as she raised her glass to drink.

'A year and a half ago,' Charlie said.

'What does it mean?' Greger said. 'I've never understood what it's used for, the semicolon, I mean.'

'It's a half-pause,' Charlie replied. 'A half-pause, but not an ending.'

She thought that, for her, having it done had felt like an

ending. A sequence of flashing images: Gudhammar, the smelter, and then, no matter how hard she tried to push it down, Johan's shattered skull. *He's in a critical condition.*

Charlie would never forget the call from the hospital. She'd had a childish belief in their ability to save Johan.

But there had been haemorrhaging, complications, and extensive internal injuries. Again and again, she had asked them: He's still alive, right? He's not dead, is he?

But he was. Johan Ro had passed away on 28 October at twenty-two minutes past ten.

Who cares about the exact time, Charlie had thought, and yet, the digits had been dancing around her head ever since. Johan's heart had stopped beating at 22:22. At 22:21, he had still existed; at 22:22, he had gone.

The first week after he died, she had lain in bed, telling herself she was going to go back to work before further sick leave required a fit note. But that hadn't happened because you can't work with a brain that's stuck in a loop of catastrophic thinking. Suddenly, she'd felt a compulsive need to make sure the hob was turned off, that there were no candles burning. It had made no difference that she hadn't cooked or lit any candles, she had to check several times anyway. She hadn't been able to trust her senses. It was the front-door lock, the security chain, the hob, and then the lock again until she was exhausted. When she was little, she'd suffered bouts of obsessive-compulsive behaviour from time to time. She had poked at the rows of goods in the supermarket aisles, stomped her foot twice every time she crossed a threshold, and counted things out loud.

Cut it out, Betty had said. *Stop it. I said stop it!*

But Charlie couldn't stop because if she failed to obey her compulsions, Betty would die.

You should know that's not how it works, Betty had told her when she tried to explain. *You're smarter than that, Charline. You do get that you can't affect life and death by prodding some milk cartons, right?*

But the compulsions weren't about being smart or dumb, Charlie knew that now. Nor were they about knowledge or awareness. She had established that by trying to cure herself and rediscovering just how difficult it was.

'So, why the half-pause?' Greger asked.

'It's Project Semicolon,' she said.

'Is that something I should have heard about?'

'Not necessarily. I think it's mostly a young-people thing. It's supposed to represent a sentence you could have chosen to end but instead you took a half-pause and continued. The sentence is life, and the author is you. It sounds simple,' she continued, realising she wasn't making much sense. 'But deciding to keep going isn't easy. A person's willpower is a severely limited resource, especially if that person is in the throes of a depression. Whether or not you get through it has more to do with luck than anything else.'

Greger asked her to explain what she meant, so she talked about the danger of putting too much on the shoulders of someone who was sick, like the kinds of things you often hear others tell people who suffer from depression or have cancer, advice about not giving up and staying strong. That was putting too much on the individual, because illness isn't about lack of willpower or personality.

'So you believe in luck over agency?' Greger said.

Charlie opened her mouth to say something smart, but her brain was tired and her thoughts fuzzy. It had been a long day.

'It's not like they're mutually exclusive,' she replied. 'And I guess it depends on what you mean by luck, how you define that concept.'

'How would you define it?' Greger asked.

'I think you can be lucky enough to be born into a context in which you're free to realise yourself fully. You can be lucky enough to have genes that make it easier for you to be good at things, lucky enough not to be afflicted with serious disease or other things of that nature.'

'So, what you're saying is that it's all luck?'

'Yes,' Charlie said, realising that was what she meant.

'So you're saying human beings don't have agency?'

'That's not quite how I see it.'

'But if you take your argument to its logical conclusion, that is, in fact, what you're saying.'

'What do you think?' Charlie countered. She enjoyed that he argued with her, that she had to put effort into finding the right words.

'I'd like to think people can take charge of their own lives, that we have the power to create the life we want to live.'

'Even if we're unlucky enough to be born with a brain that's not so good at making smart decisions?' Charlie said. 'Then how do you explain all the things you see in the world?' she continued. 'Do you think people want to beg on the streets, be addicted to drugs, sell their bodies, be hungry, lonely, are you saying they ... chose that?'

'I didn't say I *think*,' Greger replied. 'I said I'd *like* to think. There's a difference.'

'But I didn't ask what you'd *like* to think. I asked what you think.'

'True,' Greger said. He smiled resignedly. 'I don't know what I think, except that it's all bloody complicated.'

'Then we're in agreement,' Charlie said. 'About it being complicated, I mean.' She took a long pull on her beer. It tasted wonderful.

Greger's phone rang. He excused himself and left the table.

Charlie had another sip, closed her eyes for a moment, and suddenly he was there again, the stranger with the leather jacket. She'd fallen down, he'd helped her up. Who had been laughing? His face … There was no face. He was faceless.

'Charlie?' Greger said. 'Is everything OK?'

'Yes.'

'Are you sure? You don't look OK.'

'I'm fine,' Charlie said, and when she could tell he wasn't convinced: 'Don't tell me you're the kind of person who thinks he can read people after just a few minutes' acquaintance?'

'You sound upset,' Greger said. 'Do people usually read you wrong?'

'I'm not upset, but sure, I've been read wrong.'

'I wasn't trying to read you, I just thought you looked … sad. But let me try again.'

Charlie said she believed him, that he didn't have anything to prove, but Greger insisted, and in the end, Charlie acquiesced. But she let him know that if it turned out he had been listening to people at work gossiping about her, she would know immediately.

'Why would people at work be gossiping about you?' Greger asked.

'People gossip about other people at work,' Charlie replied. 'It's not just me.'

'Well, some of it seems to be true, at least,' Greger said with a smile.

'Like what?'

'I've heard you're sharp.'

'Oh, come off it.'

'I'm serious,' Greger said. 'But come on, let me try to analyse you.'

'Fine,' Charlie replied. She felt it was a silly thing to do, especially under the present circumstances, but she also knew you had to switch your brain off sometimes so you could then switch it back on again.

'You're not big on food,' Greger said.

'Wrong, I like to both eat and drink.'

'You can't tell from looking at you.'

'High metabolism,' Charlie replied. 'Keep going.'

'You have a … pretty hot temper.'

'Hearsay,' Charlie said.

'True, sorry. You have a profound sense of justice,' Greger continued. 'What?' he said when Charlie sighed. 'Am I wrong?'

'No, but that's too generic,' Charlie said. 'What are you going to say next – that I hate war?'

Greger laughed.

'You're hard work but attempting to puzzle you out is intriguing. I like being surprised.'

Me too, Charlie thought, but it almost never happens.

'Keep going,' she said. 'Give your best shot. Who am I?'

What am I doing? she thought. Why am I acting like a self-absorbed teenager?

'You're unafraid, unmarried, and … unreachable.'

'And you like alliteration,' Charlie countered.

'And it turns out that thing about you being sharp wasn't just hearsay,' Greger said and smiled.

'Or maybe it's just that everyone else is dumb. What makes you think I'm unmarried?'

'No ring,' Greger said, pointing to her left hand.

'I could have taken it off. Some married people do that.'

'I don't think you're that kind of person.'

'No, I'm just not the marrying kind.'

I stare at the pillow I've fluffed up to keep her from falling. How easy it would be to put it over her face, just put it over her mouth and nose, press down, hold it still, and end it all.

I pick up the pillow, lean in closer, and tell myself I'm going to do it. I'll do it, and then ... then I'll off myself. But then she whimpers in her sleep and waves her arms above her head.

And I can't do it.

23

Charlie woke up half an hour before her alarm. She picked up her phone from the nightstand and scrolled through her newsfeed. Beatrice's disappearance was the lead story in all the big papers. *Who took Beatrice? The lack of leads confounds the police. No word yet on a ransom.*

She went into the bathroom and felt relieved that she had stopped after one pint the night before. She couldn't remember the last time that had happened.

She washed her face with cold water and rubbed some lotion on it from one of the hotel's miniature bottles. Then she grabbed her phone again, sat down on the bed, and went to Flashback. There was a lot of crap on Sweden's biggest discussion website, but among all the idiocy, you could occasionally find something of substance. She hadn't seen anyone talking about Beatrice's disappearance the day before, but she was pretty sure she was going to today. And, lo and behold, there it was, a thread: *Beatrice nine months missing.*

The first post was a brief background note, followed by a question by the original poster of what everyone thought might have happened.

When a child as young as that goes missing, it's almost always the parents, a user called Justitia had written, adding a link to a page with child murder statistics.

Gargamel2 had chimed in: *Wouldn't surprise me if it were the mother. We went to the same school growing up and she was bloody weird.*

User 666 had asked in what way she was weird and Gargamel2 explained that she'd always worn clothes that were several sizes too small and hadn't exactly loved to bathe. *Hehehe.*

What are you on about Gargamel2? the next user, who used the logo of the local hockey team as his profile picture, had asked. *Frida Sandell, as she was known back then, was the fittest girl in school.*

Gargamel2 had replied almost instantly. *Sure, in secondary school, but when she was younger, she was just odd.*

Charlie thought about what Anton, Niklas Sandell's friend, had said about Frida, that she had been odd through eighth grade but had then transformed into the girl all the boys wanted.

She quickly skimmed a long series of observations about the Sandell family from so-called schoolmates. It was everything from little anecdotes about Frida's dad, who apparently used to drive around town drunk, knocking over letterboxes with his car, to stories about her mum, who had sung along far too loudly at end-of-year ceremonies and used to wear so much make-up she looked like a clown. And several posts mentioned *the junkie*, her brother.

And then, a new perspective, from user Ladylove: *I assume Gustav Palmgren fucked some psycho on the side.*

Charlie paused for a second before reading Justitia's comment: *What proof do you have of him having done that?*

The reply from Ladylove had been posted just a few minutes later: *Reliable sources tell me Mr Palmgren will shag anything with a pulse, and sooner or later, he was bound to stick his cock in some crazy bitch who wants revenge.*

You've watched too much TV, wrote Anonymous.

I've seen too much of that man-whore, was the reply.

Then Gargamel2 had re-entered the conversation and once again steered it towards Frida: *Wouldn't surprise me if Frida killed the kid herself to get back at him.*

Far-fetched, Justitia had protested.

Charlie had her own Flashback account, username Missblue, and now she wrote: *How do we know Gustav Palmgren fucks people on the side? Do we have names? And what about Frida? Does anyone actually know her? Do we have anything on her aside from the way she used to dress?*

Charlie checked the time. They had to be at the station in twenty minutes. She pulled on the same clothes she'd worn the day before and went downstairs to have breakfast.

'Good morning,' Greger said behind her as she was pouring coffee into a paper cup. 'I see I'm not the only one who prioritises a few extra minutes of sleep over eating.'

'I picked up some things to go,' Charlie said. 'Shall we?'

'Do you have a statement for us?' a voice called out from the constantly growing gaggle of journalists waiting for them outside the police station. The man was wearing a jacket with the logo of the local TV channel on it.

'I'll refer you to the upcoming press conference,' Charlie said.

'Do you have any leads?' the man asked. 'Any suspects? Any theory about what might have happened?'

'You heard her,' Greger said when the gaggle pressed in closer. 'You'll have to wait for the press conference.'

They didn't have a press conference scheduled yet. And if they did decide to hold one, it wouldn't be to keep the journalists informed, though they seemed to think so. It would be to advance the investigation. So far, they had simply issued an appeal to the public to report any observations to the police and leave it to them to decide what was relevant and what wasn't.

Now, they were forced to listen to the usual griping from the assembled press corps, about the public's right to know. That argument always rang false to Charlie, as though the journalists were trying to give the impression that they were motivated by societal duty, rather than a desire to dig up the most salacious content possible in order to drive up their own professional stock.

And what about me? she thought. What's my motivation? I want to do a good job, feel successful. But there was something else, too. She had experienced it in the search for both Annabelle and Francesca. And now, it was back, the feeling that she would go to pieces if the case wasn't solved.

Stina wasn't in the conference room. Charlie asked Roy where she was.

'In her office,' Roy replied.

'Would you mind getting her.'

'I'm a detective,' Roy said, 'same as you.'

'I know that,' Charlie said.

'Then why are you treating me like your assistant?'

'I was just asking you to do me a favour.'

'You're making sure I know you're my superior,' Roy said. 'Don't you think I can tell?'

Charlie sighed.

'I'll get Stina,' Greger said.

Charlie turned back to Roy.

'I don't know you,' she said, 'but let me give you some friendly advice. The Police Authority is a hierarchical organis-ation. It's not always pleasant, especially when you're sitting on a low rung. But if you want to climb higher, you're simply going to have to do as you're told sometimes. If you don't like it, learn to keep that to yourself or change careers.'

'Sorry,' Roy said. 'It's just that Stina—'

'Shh,' Charlie said and put a finger to her lips. 'Keep it to yourself.'

Roy nodded. He wasn't just easily offended, Charlie thought to herself. He was stupid, too.

'I'm sorry I'm late,' Stina said as she and Greger entered the room. 'I was on the phone with Antonsson. They've talked to the staff at the larger public transport hubs, the local bus drivers, and anyone else who might have seen something, but they've come up empty. Antonsson is on his way to Vålberg right now to chase down a tip that just came in. He wasn't particularly hopeful, apparently it was just someone who had been spotted walking along a road with a child in a carrier, looking stressed. But we have to follow it up.'

Stina went on to tell them that there were no matches for the fingerprints the technicians had lifted from the pram and that the DNA material they'd found was being sent to the NFC as soon as possible.

'And Byle?' Charlie asked. 'Any news on him?'

'No, he seems to have vanished without a trace.'

Charlie looked at the whiteboard, which now had a picture of Pascal Byle on it, and underneath his name the list of the people Mathilda Byle had given them. Contacting them had turned out to be more involved than expected because many of them owned several properties. They had all denied having talked to Pascal about staying in any of them, but each location still had to be checked out. Stina had spoken to Pascal Byle's parents in Paris, who had been very alarmed and were now on their way back to Sweden.

'We're going to focus on finding Byle,' Stina said.

Charlie nodded. He was without question their most promising lead. She excused herself and went to the bathroom. Checking Flashback, she saw that her question about Gustav's philandering had been answered.

A new user called ThePhilosopher had written: *The last person I know he boned was Madelene Svedin.*

How do you know that? Justitia had asked.

Believe me, I know, ThePhilosopher had replied.

Charlie closed Flashback, opened Instagram, and found the Madelene Svedin ThePhilosopher had referred to. *Karlstad girl, living on a prayer*, the caption under her profile picture read. The account was public, and her feed consisted primarily of party pics, selfies and then, a picture of a man by a lake, standing with his back to the camera. The picture was taken from so far away, the man was little more than a silhouette. Charlie checked the date: 15 November 2017 – five months ago. Could it be Gustav? She read the comments under the picture. It was heart emojis, two high-fives, and a *looovely*. And then, a different tone:

There's a special place in hell for women who steal other women's men.

Madelene had replied to it: *No one can steal a man who doesn't want to be stolen.*

The anonymous poster had replied instantly: *I hope you get what you deserve. I hope you get what you deserve for all the marriages you've destroyed.*

Charlie clicked on the anonymous account. It was private.

She went back to the conference room, showed the others the Flashback thread and told them what she'd found. Her phone was passed around so the handful of officers who were still there could see the picture of the man by the lake in Madelene's Instagram feed.

'I know her,' Roy said.

'You're friends?' Charlie asked.

'Not friends, exactly,' Roy replied. 'But Karlstad's not very big. She goes out quite a bit. She's …'

'She's what?' Charlie said.

'Loose,' Roy said. Then he corrected himself: 'She's rumoured to be loose.'

'I'll look into this,' Charlie said.

'Is that really something we should be prioritising right now?' Stina asked. 'We need to talk more about the tip line, keep looking for Byle, and—'

'But we haven't had any promising tips,' Charlie said. 'We're putting out an APB on Byle and half the team is already looking for him. Surely we have to be able to pursue more than one lead at a time?'

'Fine,' Stina replied. 'You look into Madelene Svedin.'

Fifteen minutes later, Charlie had unsuccessfully tried to call Madelene, but had found out from her sister that she was at work. Madelene Svedin worked as a tour guide at Selma Lagerlöf's Mårbacka.

Sara

There was a racket down in the main lobby.

'Let go of me!' Lo screamed. 'I just want to go for a ride with my mum.'

Emelie said she wasn't allowed to because it was too late, and Donna had been drinking.

'But I'm not driving,' the woman called Donna slurred. 'My friend's driving and he hasn't had a drop. Tell them!' she shouted. 'Tell them you haven't had a drop, Stefan.'

But Donna still wasn't allowed to take Lo anywhere. She had to come back during visiting hours if she wanted to see her daughter.

More raised voices. Donna roared about not giving a toss about visiting hours, and Lo said she was going with her mother, that no one could stop her.

But they could. Frans and the support staff blocked her way. Lo flailed and kicked to get by them, but they wrestled her down onto the floor and held her there.

Emelie told Donna she could either leave voluntarily, or they could call the police. Yes, she was serious.

*

'Why are you still up?' Emelie said after she had locked the door behind the fuming Donna and spotted all of us at the top of the stairs. 'Go to bed.'

'Where's Lo?' Nicki asked.

'Lo's going to stay down here for a while and calm down,' Emelie replied.

'You can't lock her up,' Nicki said. 'Or restrain her. Promise you won't restrain her.'

'You're going to bed,' Emelie said. 'Right now.'

I couldn't sleep. I'd grown used to hearing the sound of Lo breathing in the top bunk. Why wasn't she coming back? Had they given her sedatives? I thought about what Nicki had told me about places that made Rödminnet seem like heaven, homes where they strapped you down and drugged you. Where they kept you isolated until you lost your mind and started seeing things that weren't there.

I had just got out of bed to go and make sure Lo was still in the building when she returned. Her hair was dishevelled and her face almost as white as her nightgown.

'Leave me alone,' she said, even though I hadn't said anything. Then she walked past me and climbed up into her bed. I wanted to climb after, hold her, whisper that everything was going to be all right, but what did I know about that? Things could just as easily go the other way and get even worse.

24

The road to Östra Ämtervik was narrow and winding. Charlie had wanted to visit Mårbacka ever since she read *The Emperor of Portugallia*. It was less than two hours from Gullspång, but Betty had neither car nor driving licence, so they never ended up going. The landscape Charlie drove through alternated between fields, forests, and meadows. From time to time, she caught a glimpse of Lake Fryken on her right. She drove as fast as the road allowed, which was considerably slower than she would have liked due to the many sharp, unpredictable turns.

Mårbacka. It was even more beautiful than the pictures she had seen of it. Scilla dotted the lawn in front of the big, yellow manor, and when she looked up at it, she could almost see the gentlemen from *Gösta Berling's Saga* leaning against the columns on the veranda.

There wasn't a soul in sight. Charlie walked up the stone front steps and turned the handle. Unlocked. The heavy wooden door creaked and then she was in the hallway. Straight ahead hung a large painting of a wintry evergreen forest, and in front of that stood a stuffed goose.

'I'm sorry, the museum is closed.'

Charlie looked up to see a young woman in plaits, with a shawl around her head and dressed in clothing that looked like it was from the earliest days of the previous century.

'The guided tours don't start until May,' the woman added.

'That's not what I'm here for,' Charlie said and held up her badge. 'I'm looking for Madelene Svedin.'

'That's me.'

Charlie was surprised. She would never have guessed that this young woman, whose solemn face bore no trace of make-up, was the same one she'd seen making duck lips on Instagram.

'Has something happened?' Madelene asked.

'I would like to have a word with you about the missing baby. I'm sure you've heard that a little girl has gone missing.'

Madelene looked nonplussed, but she nodded. 'I heard,' she said. 'It's just terrible. But I don't understand what I can—'

'Maybe we could sit down somewhere?'

'I just have to tell the others,' Madelene said and nodded towards the back of the house. 'I'm training new guides, but it's fine; they can have a coffee break.'

Charlie followed Madelene through a large drawing room and then a dining room. The walls were hung with portraits of grave-looking men in priests' frock coats and large pencil sketches of houses and farms.

In the kitchen, they found four women, all dressed in historical garb. Madelene told them they could take a quick break and if she wasn't back in ten minutes, they should start to practise giving the tour to each other. Then she turned to Charlie and said they could go upstairs. Charlie followed Madelene up a narrow staircase behind the kitchen.

Madelene showed Charlie into a small room, where they sat down at a round table next to a window with delicate white lace curtains.

'This is lovely,' Charlie said.

Madelene nodded and said that they were sitting in the housekeeper's parlour. She had run the household and been deeply loved by the owner of the house.

'How long have you worked here?' Charlie asked.

'Since I was twenty-one,' Madelene replied. 'So that makes it nine years. I've loved Selma ever since I was a child, so this is a dream job for me. I play her sister, Gerda,' she continued and looked down at her dress. 'It brings the story to life for the visitors when I tell them about our childhood, about what it was like to grow up here with Selma.'

'And the rest of the time?' Charlie said. 'I mean, what do you do when this place is closed for the season?'

'I've taken some university courses. But this is practically a full-time job now since the museum is open around various holidays and on Christmas as well. And I've been given more responsibility, so ... I guess I'm supposed to have more high-flying life plans, but I like it here.'

'I can see why,' Charlie replied. She took a deep breath and got to the point. 'Can I ask you what you were doing Saturday morning between eight and ten?'

'What do you mean?' Madelene's voice had hardened. 'Am I being interviewed under caution or something? I think you're supposed to tell me if I am.'

'It's just a question,' Charlie said. 'One I'm sure you don't mind answering.'

'I was at home,' Madelene replied. 'Probably still in bed. I'd been out the night before, so ...'

'Can anyone confirm that?'

'No ... I was alone. Look ... I don't feel good about this. Am I under suspicion?'

'I assume you know that this is about Gustav Palmgren's daughter,' Charlie said. 'We've been told you're having an affair with him.'

'Who told you that?'

'I'm afraid I can't answer that,' Charlie said. 'Is it true?'

'No,' Madelene replied. 'I'm not having an affair with him.'

Charlie waited for her to go on, but she didn't.

'Madelene,' she said after a long pause. 'I'm sure you realise the gravity of the situation. A baby is missing.'

'Of course I do,' Madelene said. 'But what am I supposed to do about it?'

'You can tell me about your relationship with Gustav.'

'It wasn't a relationship,' Madelene replied. 'Not the way you mean it. And whatever it was, it's over. He told me he was getting a divorce,' she continued, 'and I believed him. I never meant to ...' She looked down at the table.

'I make no judgements about your relationship with Gustav,' Charlie said. 'I just want to find Beatrice.'

'But I have no idea what happened to her!'

'Why did it end between you and Gustav?' Charlie asked.

'I guess it was because ... well, like I said, I don't think he ever planned to get divorced. He's full of lies. You can't believe a word he says.'

I suppose that's the problem with a man who cheats on his wife, Charlie mused, you can't trust him.

'What did he lie about?' she asked.

'Everything,' Madelene replied. 'He said I was the love of

his life, but it turned out I wasn't even the only one he had on the side.'

'And you found out?'

'Yes, I even saw it with my own eyes.'

'Do you know the other woman?'

Madelene shook her head and said she didn't, but she assumed there was more than one, that she was just one of many. At least that's what she had been told when she asked around.

Charlie thought about what she had read about Gustav Palmgren on Flashback, that he was a man-whore who shagged everything with a pulse. Might a woman scorned be their best lead? Could the perpetrator be sitting in front of her right now, disguised as a farm girl?

'Do you know the names of anyone else he has been seeing?' she asked.

Madelene said she didn't. And she didn't want to dwell on it, just wanted to move on.

Charlie could relate. She knew how easy it was to let yourself be deceived by someone when you were in love, even though your brain was screaming itself hoarse about all the red flags. Before her relationship with Hugo, she would never have fallen for that kind of nonsense. But infatuation, or passion, or whatever it was, could knock out a person's good sense, at least temporarily.

'I don't really like to talk about it,' Madelene added. 'Like I said, I just want to put it behind me.'

'And how is that going?' Charlie asked.

Madelene smiled and said it was going OK, that time was the best healer.

'Have you ever met Frida Palmgren?' Charlie went on.

'Depends on what you mean by met,' Madelene replied. 'I've seen her around. I know who she is. Karlstad's not exactly big.'

'But you've never ... spoken to her?'

'No, not that I recall, anyway.'

'And Beatrice?'

'Just once. It was out in town. Gustav wanted to meet for coffee while she slept in her pram, but she never went to sleep, so ... it was just for a little bit...' Madelene looked out the window. 'Do you think ... I mean, do you think she's alive?'

'We don't know,' Charlie said. 'But we're doing everything we can to find her as quickly as possible.'

'I suppose that would be the worst,' Madelene said. 'Never finding out. I imagine even bad news is better than living your whole life not knowing.'

'Are you speaking from personal experience?' Charlie asked.

'No, but if my child went missing, I think it would tear me apart.'

'Do you have children?'

A brief pause.

'No,' Madelene said. 'No children.'

Charlie circled back to the reason she was there. 'Did Gustav ever talk to you about being on bad terms with anyone or feeling threatened?' she asked.

'No, I think the only person he fought with was his wife.'

'What did they fight about?'

'Anything and everything. He used to tell me all the time that he was sick of her, that she was clingy and couldn't stand on her own two feet and that he felt more like her carer than her husband.'

'Her carer?'

'Yes, Frida struggled with mental-health problems on and off.'

'Gustav told you that?' Charlie said, thinking to herself what a betrayal it was for him to discuss his wife's mental health with his mistress. Was it even true, or was it just something he'd said, like another version of the my-wife-doesn't-understand-me card?

'Yes, he did,' Madelene replied. 'It's why he wanted a divorce.'

'Did he ever tell you how serious Frida's mental-health problems were?'

'He said she was disturbed, that she would fly into sudden fits of rage. One time, she threw herself down a flight of stairs. Just threw herself straight down. I mean, what normal person does that?'

Normal people don't, Charlie thought, not unless they have a really good reason.

'Gustav said he thought it was a way to get attention,' Madelene went on. 'I guess it's no wonder he wanted a divorce.'

'But in the end, he didn't?' Charlie said. She wondered whether Madelene perhaps hadn't put the relationship as far behind her as she claimed.

'No, and maybe he never did.' Madelene shrugged.

'How would you describe Gustav?' Charlie said.

'I don't know. He's slippery.'

'In what way?'

'He's different from one moment to the next. One second, he can be caring, thoughtful, charming, and the next, he's completely cold. He can do mean things and not care.'

'Can you give me an example?'

'Sure. I remember one time he was supposed to fire someone

he'd hired to work for his company. The way I understood it, this person hadn't done anything wrong, he just didn't make the cut. And when Gustav told me about it, it seemed like he'd enjoyed firing him, like he got a kick out of seeing this guy's reaction. It was … unpleasant.'

A voice reached them from the stairs, someone saying they were now approaching Selma's favourite room in the whole house.

'Felicia,' Madelene said when the aspiring guides passed by the room they were in, 'you can't talk while you're climbing the stairs. No one will hear what you're saying.' She turned back to Charlie. 'Let's go back downstairs, otherwise I'll just be listening to them the whole time.'

Charlie said they were pretty much done anyway and followed Madelene back down to the ground floor. When they reached the front door, she realised she'd forgotten to ask if Frida knew about her affair with Gustav.

'No idea,' Madelene replied. 'But given as how I'm not the only one he's been with, I don't see how he could have kept his infidelity from her entirely.'

When Charlie climbed back into the car, she saw one of the guides cross the forecourt, dressed exactly like Madelene. The scene could easily have been from a hundred years ago. She felt like a time traveller, a time traveller fighting the clock. Beatrice had been missing for over fifty hours now and they were still treading water.

25

'I didn't want to bring it up,' Gustav said. He was sitting on the big living-room sofa, sweating in the same suit he'd worn the day before. From time to time, he glanced nervously towards the kitchen, where Greger was talking to Frida. Gustav had just confirmed his relationship with Madelene.

'Because I'm absolutely certain she has nothing to do with this,' he said when Charlie asked why he hadn't told them right away. 'And this is hard enough on Frida as it is.'

'You don't get to decide what's important in this investigation,' Charlie said. 'So if you have any other secrets, this is the time to tell us.'

Gustav shook his head. There was nothing else.

'You said that before, though,' Charlie noted, 'and then we found out about your conflict with Pascal Byle.'

'It's not a conflict,' Gustav said. 'He's just unhappy about the amount he was paid for his share of the company. He has gone off his rocker. How many times do I have to tell you that?'

'He seems more than just unhappy,' Charlie countered. 'And now both he and Beatrice are missing. You would have thought that would be enough to make you at least mention it.'

'There's nothing to say,' Gustav retorted. 'And I don't know where he is.'

Charlie changed tack.

'Tell me about you and Madelene,' she said. 'Tell me about your relationship.'

'It wasn't really a relationship,' Gustav said.

'Then what was it?'

'We met right after I moved back from Russia; I was out with some business associates. Frida and I had been going through a rough patch, and … well, I met Madelene, and she came onto me, and … I don't know.'

So predictable, Charlie thought, and so cowardly to blame his bad decisions on his wife and the seductive mistress.

'And then?' she said, because she couldn't bear to listen to how he'd become an innocent victim to circumstance. If there was one thing she hated, it was people with no self-awareness. Moral lapses and mistakes she had no problem with, as long as you didn't blame others for them. She had to remind herself Gustav Palmgren was also a father, a father whose daughter was missing, who didn't know if he was going to ever see her again, dead or alive.

'Then?' Gustav repeated, as though he didn't understand the question.

'Yes, after that first night. I assume you saw her more than once.'

'I did.'

'For how long?'

'A few months, maybe three.'

'And how often did you see her during this time?'

'What does that matter?'

'Just answer the question, please.'

'A few times a week. But it ended a couple of months ago.'

'Why?'

'Because I didn't want to do it anymore. I wanted to be with my wife, my family. For me, it was never meant to be anything serious.'

'And how did Madelene take it?'

'She went crazy. Said she was going to tell Frida everything and ruin my life.'

'And what happened? Did she tell Frida?'

'No, but she has threatened to many times. It's bloody unpleasant, let me tell you.'

Charlie thought about Madelene, about how serious she came off in her role as a tour guide, but also about the other side of her she'd seen online. The Madelene on social media was very different from the woman who told stories about a bygone era at Mårbacka. And now, a new facet, the scorned, furious mistress.

Madelene hadn't said anything about threatening to ruin Gustav's life, but then, that was hardly something you told other people about, and certainly not the police. And even though Madelene had seemed composed, more violent emotions might have been lurking beneath the serene surface. Rejection had a way of bringing out the very worst in people.

'Have there been other women?' Charlie asked.

'I'm not going to sit here and discuss things like that right now,' Gustav replied.

'Let me remind you that this is a police investigation,' Charlie said. 'It's not up to you what you discuss or don't discuss.'

'Let me remind you that my daughter is still missing,' Gustav said. 'You're wasting time on dead ends.'

'I understand that you're frustrated,' Charlie said, 'but this is my job. I will ask the questions that need asking.'

Gustav sighed, leaned forward, and glanced towards the kitchen.

'I suppose you might say my moral compass has been ... slightly wobbly.'

'Could you be more specific?'

'Yes, there have been other women.'

'Have any of them threatened you or your family?'

'No, no,' Gustav replied. 'Never. And Madelene's behaviour ... look, she may have been livid, but ... I just found her pathetic. She's not the type to kidnap a child.'

'Do you know anyone who is the type to kidnap a child?' Charlie asked. And when Gustav made no reply: 'Exactly, a lot of people have trouble imagining that type of person. But they do exist.'

Gustav nodded.

'I want you to make a list of everyone you've had a relationship with,' Charlie said.

'All of them?'

'At least since you got married.'

'I don't understand why that's necessary.'

'Because we will need to talk to them.'

'OK, but it's going to be a waste of time. And anyway, what counts as a relationship? Some of them I just ... I just met them once, I don't even remember their names.'

'Just do the best you can,' Charlie said.

'Fine,' Gustav replied. 'I will. Listen, I'm sorry if I'm ... I don't know.'

'Just try not to obstruct the investigation,' Charlie said,

'that's all I'm asking. We both want the same thing here. We want to find your daughter.'

Gustav nodded. 'I just feel like I'm running out.'

'Running out of what?'

'Hope. Look, I know what the passing of time means,' he continued. 'I know how quickly the chances of finding her alive decrease. And I'm just sitting here ... completely powerless.'

That might be a new feeling for him, Charlie thought, not having any power, not being able to control events.

'Has Frida ever had mental-health problems?' she asked.

'I wouldn't call it mental-health problems,' Gustav replied, 'but she has been tired. Why?'

'We've been told it's more serious than that.'

'Who told you that?' Gustav asked. And when Charlie didn't answer. 'It's her, right? It's Madelene. She'll say anything to hurt us. She's just angry about me breaking it off with her. If anyone's mentally ill, it's her.'

'I didn't say it was Madelene.'

'No, but I know it was. I know the games she's playing to try to hurt me. As if that would make me want her back.'

'But why didn't you tell us about this? I mean, a woman you yourself call mentally ill, who has threatened your family ...'

'Like I said, I never thought she was *that* crazy, and I was just trying to save the situation. Frida would be done with me if she found out. But I guess ...' He looked over at the kitchen again, 'it's already too late.'

'Yes,' Charlie replied. 'It is.'

'I'm not a bad person,' Gustav said.

'I'm not the one you should be trying to convince,' Charlie said. 'And this is more important than your ... wobbly moral compass and your marriage.'

'Don't you think I know that? This is a fucking nightmare, and if there was anything I could give to have Beatrice back – *anything* – I would. This house, the stuff, my companies. I would trade it all in a second to have her back. Are we clear?'

Charlie nodded and thought that it was a shame there was no one to bargain with.

Charlie left Gustav and went to the kitchen, where Greger was sitting at the table with Frida. Frida was smoking a cigarette. It looked out of place in the spotless environment.

'I'd like to talk to you,' Charlie said, 'if you're up to it.'

Frida nodded.

Greger stood up and said he'd go stretch his legs in the garden. He needed to make a few calls.

'Did you know?' Charlie said. 'Did you know Gustav was having an affair?'

'He has had many affairs,' Frida replied flatly and tapped ash into a small flowerpot in front of her.

'How many?'

'I don't know. I caught him cheating on me several years ago. He swore it was just a rough patch and that it would never happen again, but it has.'

'Did you know about Madelene Svedin?'

'No, but I do now.'

Frida didn't seem upset, probably because she had no space left for such feelings. Or maybe she had known after all? Charlie thought to herself, as possible motives for Frida to do something to the child swirled through her head: revenge, loneliness, vulnerability, sleep deprivation, mental illness. She thought about the wives of all the cheating husbands who had come out to Lyckebo to confront Betty. Their shrill voices.

Stay away from my husband. Stay fucking miles away from my husband, Betty Lager.

'If we find Beatrice, I'm going to pull my head out of the sand and divorce him,' Frida said. 'I should have left him a long time ago, but … I've been so tired. I've had neither the energy nor the money to leave.'

Charlie nodded. She had never been in that situation herself. She had never counted on someone else to support her and protect her from the world. That was one good thing about growing up with Betty Lager: you learnt not to trust anyone but yourself.

Sara

The real stories were told in the basement. Underground, we talked about the things we never so much as mentioned in group therapy. Down there in the dark, there were no sunshine stories, no accountants to marry, no happy endings.

Then, one night, we found the letters. Lo was the one who broke open the rusty lock on a trunk we found in a small room behind the one we used to gather in.

'Just a bunch of crap,' Nicki sighed.

'Hardly,' Lo replied. She had picked up a letter in an envelope and started to read it aloud.

'I've told Flora I'm going crazy, that I can no longer tell dreaming from waking, fantasy from reality. I tell her all I can think about is my girls and that they don't just visit me in my dreams. I see them on the footpaths, see them under the wings of the victory goddess. I hear my little girl babbling, my big girl laughing. I hear and see it, even though they've both been taken from me – one by life, the other by death.'

I don't know why, but the hairs on my arms stood up when Lo read that. It was as though we were suddenly in direct contact with the shadows in the empty hallways, the vacant eyes in the photographs.

'That's bloody creepy,' Nicki said. 'Who wrote that?'

'It seems like a part of something longer,' Lo said. 'There's no beginning or end.'

She turned the page over and continued.

Yesterday, a mouse family in human clothing came strolling across the floor. It was Father Mouse in a suit and hat, Mother Mouse in a blouse and skirt, and the children in shorts and dresses.'

We burst out laughing. We could just picture the little mouse family.

'Edenstam watches our every move,' Lo read on. *'Most of the time, he's standing on the roof, keeping watch. Yesterday, he flew past the dormitory on a swan. The whole thing is hard on my nerves, let me tell you, being always under his gaze.'*

'Who was Edenstam?' I asked.

'The head doctor. The guy in the suit with the ridiculous moustache in the picture outside the dining hall. He was the last head doctor here before they closed the mental hospital. At least that's what Frans told me.' Lo picked up a stack of documents from the trunk. 'These look like old patient files,' she said and read to us from a yellowed sheet.

'Pat 154, restless, says she sees beetles and snakes in her bed. Says she wants to die.'

'Pat 96, unkempt, oscillates between retardation and mania, must be kept away from the male ward as she is sexually provocative. Medicated with 300 milligrams thorazine.'

'At least they gave them plenty of drugs,' Nicki said. 'They could get high as kites without having to sneak around.'

Lo picked up another letter. 'That's really sad,' she said.

'Read it aloud, then,' Nicki urged.

I miss my girls
I miss my girls

I miss my girls
I miss my girls'.

'That's horrible,' I said. 'Who wrote that?'

'The handwriting's the same as the other one,' Lo said. 'She signed it *Mummy.*'

'Do you think they're dead?' Nicki asked. 'Her girls?'

'One of them seems to be alive, at least,' Lo replied and carried on reading.

'The dreams are back. Last night, it was the three of us, you, me, and the little one, the way it should have been. We were walking down the path to the lake, autumn leaves and sunshine, past the house on the hill.

He wasn't there.

In all the world, it was just us, me and my daughters, and it was so real I never wanted to wake up.'

'That doesn't mean she's alive,' Nicki remarked.

'But she's writing to her daughter,' I said. 'Surely that means she's alive, or was at the time, anyway.'

'Not necessarily,' Nicki said. 'She might not even have had daughters. She was in a mental hospital, don't forget.'

'I know that, but it would still be weird for her to write letters to a daughter who's dead.'

'No weirder than seeing doctors riding swans,' Nicki countered.

26

Charlie and Greger were sitting at window table in the hotel restaurant.

Charlie had learnt from yesterday's mistake and eaten a big burger on the way back from the station and now ordered only a Coke and a coffee. Greger seemed to experience the food differently, because he happily scarfed down the slop that looked every bit as unappetising as whatever it was they'd been served the night before.

'Where the fuck is Pascal Byle?' Charlie said. 'Why haven't we found him?'

'We will,' Greger replied. 'No one can hide from the police for long, especially a person with no experience. And if he has a child with him, that'll make it even harder.'

'You think it's too late?'

'I'm trying to tell myself it isn't,' Greger said. 'The alternative is too horrible. But the statistics aren't on our side.'

Gustav had given them a list of women he'd had extramarital affairs with. There were four of them. One who had just become a mother and had barely left her home in Gothenburg since the birth, another who lived in New York, and two that lived locally. Both had watertight alibis.

'But he may not have told us about all of them,' Greger said.

'Why would he hold back now?' Charlie asked.

'Potential consequences, perhaps,' Greger replied. 'He might have stepped out with the wives of his friends or business partners.'

'Still, it feels a bit far-fetched for a scorned lover or her husband to kidnap a baby because of an affair,' Charlie said.

Greger agreed. It did feel far-fetched.

'But, then again, maybe there is no clear motive,' Charlie put in. 'Something could have happened, an accident ... involving Frida.'

'How is she doing?' Greger asked. 'Do you think Madelene Svedin was telling the truth when she said she has mental-health problems?'

'I don't know,' Charlie replied. 'When I asked Gustav about it, he claimed Frida was just tired, that Madelene was in fact the unstable one.'

'So, what do we do now?' Greger asked. 'Where do we go from here?'

'We have to talk to Frida's brother again,' Charlie said. 'Him and other friends.'

'I guess the problem is that Frida doesn't have a lot of contact with her brother. And she doesn't seem to have a lot of close friends. I mean, not even Charlotte seems to really know her. What are you thinking about?' he asked when he noticed Charlie staring vacantly into space.

'About her, about Frida ... I don't know. She's so dependent on Gustav. She has no job, no income, no family, barely any friends. All she has is a junkie brother.'

'And a daughter,' Greger said. 'A daughter we can still find.'

Charlie nodded.

'I need a pint,' Greger said. 'Would you like one?'

'Yes,' Charlie answered. 'I'll have one, too.'

I'm a normal person who can have a pint, she thought. I did it yesterday, and today, I'm going to do the same thing. I'm not a broken person who drinks, takes drugs, and lets strangers into my home. I have a pint after a hard day's work. Can't it just be that simple?

'Tell me more about Madelene Svedin,' Greger said when their pints had been brought over.

Charlie told him about Madelene, about how different she seemed in person from the image she projected on her social media.

'But did she seem ... normal?' Greger asked.

'I don't know. She's hard to read. And she has no alibi. According to Gustav, she has been acting angry and threatening, but who doesn't get angry when they're dumped and feel betrayed?'

'I don't think everyone acts threatening, though,' Greger retorted.

'No, but even if she did, that's still a far cry from kidnapping a baby. She doesn't have a real motive.'

A group of four men sat down two tables away from them. They started talking loudly about some successful business venture and ordered in two bottles of champagne. Charlie envied their good mood. They seemed completely unaffected by the drama consuming the rest of the town.

They put the case aside for a while. Greger wanted to know more about her background. It didn't make any difference that Charlie assured him it wasn't very interesting. He wanted to know anyway.

'I grew up just fifty miles from here,' Charlie said, 'in Gullspång.'

'Do your parents still live there?' he asked after Charlie described the place.

'It was just my mum and me.'

'OK, then does she still live there?'

'No. She's dead, sadly.' Charlie was surprised at how easy it was to say the words. 'She died when I was fourteen.'

'Was she sick?'

An image of Betty on the sofa in the living room in Lyckebo: *It's the light, it's all the light that hurts.*

'Yes, she was sick.'

'That's terrible,' Greger said. 'And your dad? You don't have any contact with him at all?'

'He wasn't in the picture. He was just ...'

Charlie trailed off. She wasn't going to cling to Betty's lie about her dad having been a stranger just travelling through, a good man who had no idea she existed.

'My dad was an idiot.'

'So what happened to you? When your mum died, I mean.'

'Foster care.'

Greger looked at her as though he were expecting more. But there wasn't much more to say. It was just a regular family, the kind she wished she'd had with Betty.

'And you?' she said. 'It's your turn.'

'I grew up in Oskarshamn.'

'Oskarshamn,' Charlie said. 'I'm picturing a nuclear power plant.'

'You're not the only one,' Greger said with a smile. 'My dad worked there. He monitored a bunch of screens. Did it his whole life. Can you imagine a worse job, just sitting there, staring at a bunch of screens, waiting for something horrible to happen?'

'Yes.'

'Pardon?'

'I can imagine it, a worse job, I mean.'

'Well, anyway, for my dad, it was hell.'

'How come?'

'He made some kind of mistake and turned one of the reactors off. It wasn't for very long, but the costs were enormous. It didn't matter that everyone told him he shouldn't blame himself. He couldn't let it go, and so ...' Greger took a sip of his beer before continuing. 'He knew what it had cost to have the reactor offline, and it was more than all the money they'd paid him since he started working there at eighteen. It would have been cheaper for the company if he had never existed, if he had never gone to work a day of his life. And when you think about it that way, it's no wonder he became depressed.'

Charlie nodded.

'He never recovered,' Greger said. 'He just dwelt on his mistake and, in the end, my mum said she'd leave him if he didn't pull himself together.'

'And did he?' Charlie said. 'Did he pull himself together?'

'No, he didn't. It just got worse after that.'

'So they got divorced?'

Greger shook his head. 'He ... well, he just couldn't live with it in the end. One day, I came home and ...'

'I understand,' Charlie said. 'You don't have to say it.'

She felt a sudden impulse to tell him about the night she found Betty, about the flies in the room, the smell of blood and death. She wanted to tell him about the panic, her pointless resuscitation attempts. She wanted to tell him she knew how he felt. But the moment had passed.

'How old were you when it happened?' she asked.

'Sixteen,' Greger replied. 'I had turned sixteen two days before.'

'Can I ask what you did to move on?'

'I just kept breathing. That's all it was.'

'It's not as easy as it sounds.'

'I didn't say it was easy,' Greger said. 'I'm just saying it's what I did. And you? How did you get through it?'

'Same thing,' Charlie said and downed the last of her beer. 'Exactly the same thing.'

27

She's walking barefoot along the path from the water, roots and pine needles under her feet. Betty calls out that it's time to eat. But when she gets home, there's no one there. The kitchen is empty, the living room, too. A smell of iron. She goes upstairs and realises the entire first floor is a chicken coop the fox has been in; there are feathers and blood and half-eaten chickens everywhere.

What did I tell you, sweetheart? Didn't I say you can't take the wild out of them? Didn't I tell you it would all go to hell?

She runs, runs back out into the garden. A man without a face is standing at the edge of the woods, and next to him another, and then another. She turns away, looks down at the grass and there they are, the children. The boy has sunk into the soil, but the girl is still visible, vines twining around her cold body. She rips and tears at them. And then Betty, again: *You have to pull them up by the root, sweetheart, otherwise they just come back. All that work is futile if you don't pull them up by the roots.*

Charlie woke up winded. It was four in the morning.

It had been a while since she'd had one of her recurring

nightmares, but they always came back in times of stress. They were invariably set in Gullspång, in Lyckebo, and featured Betty Lager, sometimes alive, sometimes dead. It was usually summer, early morning or night, mist swirling across the fields, the grass glistening with dew, and always the same feeling of panic, impending disaster, and death. The part with the faceless men was new. It doesn't matter, she thought, how good I am at repressing things during the day since it all just strikes back twice as hard at night anyway.

It's like everything's coming back.

There was no going back to sleep, her head was throbbing. She could feel every beat of her heart as a jolt of pain in her temples. In the end, she got out of bed and dug an oxazepam and two ibuprofen out of her handbag. She wouldn't be able to function unless she could get a few more hours of sleep.

When she woke up three hours later, both the headache and the exhaustion had evaporated and the oxazepam had swaddled her feelings of panic and dread in a pleasant cocoon of temporary calm.

We're solving this case today, she told herself, and just as she did, her phone buzzed. It was Stina.

'A tip just came in,' she said. 'I think we've found Byle.'

A man in lumberjack clothes with an excited bird dog by his side was waiting for Charlie and two crime-scene technicians, Christoffer and Filip, when they arrived at his farm in Väse, just outside Karlstad. He tersely introduced himself as Åke Eriksson and then told his dog to sit and be quiet. He explained that his dog had run away from the farm that morning and come back with a bloody nose. Figuring she'd killed some animal, he'd followed her back into the woods. That was when he found the body.

'Is it far?' Christoffer asked.

Both he and Filip were decidedly taciturn. They hadn't said two words together during the twenty-minute drive from the police station.

Maybe that's what happens when you spend your days doing this kind of work, Charlie reflected.

'Less than a mile,' Åke replied and pointed towards the woods. 'It's not a pretty sight,' he added when they reached the edge of the trees. 'I've handled cadavers and dead animals all my life, and I'm definitely not delicate, but apparently it's different when it's a human.'

He ducked under a low pine branch. His dog took off into the undergrowth.

'You're going to have to put a lead on her,' Christoffer said.

'Sure,' Åke replied. 'Spana!' he called. 'Come!'

The dog was back in seconds and obediently let him put the lead on.

Charlie could feel her pulse quicken as they ventured deeper into the woods. She looked around at the mossy rocks and evergreen trees. Wisps of morning mist billowed across the forest floor.

It's the elves, sweetheart. It's the elves dancing.

Suddenly, the dog stopped. She pricked up her ears and started growling deep in her chest.

'Is there an animal or something?' Charlie asked.

'She always growls in this spot,' Åke said. 'No idea why.'

They kept moving. The trees thinned out and now they could see a hunting hide in the distance.

'He's over there,' Åke said, pointing.

*

The man lying on his back at the foot of the hide was dressed all in black. Next to him lay a rifle. The shot had gone straight through his chest. Animals had helped themselves to his remains, and the smell of corpse filled the air.

The technicians pulled on their white protective clothing before approaching. Charlie watched them work from afar. She could see the line splitting the man's face into a dark and a light half. There could be no doubt they'd found Pascal Byle.

'Is that a note?' Charlie asked and resisted the urge to walk up to the body and pull out the piece of paper sticking out of his pocket.

'It's Byle, isn't it?' Åke said behind her. He had stopped at a very safe distance with a firm grip on his barking dog.

'Do you know him?' Charlie said.

'We're on the same hunting team,' Åke replied, 'but we don't socialise outside of that. But why would he ... why would he feel he had no other bloody choice than to ...' He shook his head.

Stina had called a meeting of the whole team in the conference room. Charlie confirmed that the dead man was Byle, that it appeared to be suicide, that he had shot himself with a rifle.

'Could he have been dead by the time Beatrice disappeared?' Greger asked.

'It's probably too soon to tell,' Stina replied. 'We're going to have to wait for the autopsy.'

'But given the state of the body, I think it's safe to say it's likely,' Charlie said. She felt dizzy and there was something else, too, a prickling sensation in her fingers, a pressure in her skull. She sat down, took three big gulps of water, and tried to focus.

'If it's confirmed that Byle has been dead for more than three days, we can write him off,' Stina said. 'Which would mean that we're back to square one. I know that may sound like a setback, but let's hope for it anyway, because if it was Byle who took Beatrice, it's not very likely she's still alive. Charlie, why don't you go over what we're going to focus on while we wait for the autopsy report.'

'Sure.'

Charlie stood up.

'Are you OK?' Stina asked.

'Yep,' Charlie said. Then she collapsed.

28

Charlie was relieved to find that the hotel shower was properly hot. She leaned her forehead against the wall, closed her eyes and felt the water burn against her skin.

She had passed out a few times before, probably due to low blood pressure, but this was the first time it had happened at work.

She was mortified. It didn't matter that she couldn't help it, involuntarily checking out like that still filled her with shame. The feeling brought her thoughts back to the night she couldn't remember.

The man with no face. Who was he? What had he done to her? How was she supposed to cope with the fact that she might never know? She closed her eyes and tried to summon up his image. She had the leather jacket, the contours of his body and ... nothing else.

She thought about what Anders had told her once, that she should look up the men she dragged home in the police databases, that it was only a matter of time before she crossed paths with a real lunatic. She had laughed it off and told him she was a pretty good judge of character, but what good did that do you if you were unconscious?

The others had insisted that she should rest for a while, that there was no rush to come back. But how was she supposed to lie down and rest with things the way they were? When there was a child out there who could still be saved.

She turned the shower off, wrapped one towel around her hair and another around her body. When she stepped out of the bathroom, the neatly made bed and the clean surfaces made her think of the kitchen at Charlotte and David Jolander's house. She pictured the kitchen counter. It had ... not been clean. And then the smell, or rather, the lack of smell. Because it hadn't been there, the smell of cleaning products. How could she have missed it? How could she have missed the fact that their house hadn't been cleaned?

She called Greger.

'Aren't you supposed to be resting?' he said.

'Their house hadn't been cleaned,' Charlie said. 'The Jolanders' house. Amina can't have been there that morning, which means Charlotte gave her a false alibi.'

'The cleaning lady?' Greger said.

'I'm going over there right now. Tell Stina for me, OK?'

Before Greger could object, she'd hung up.

Charlotte and David Jolander's daughter opened the door. She was wearing a green leotard and black tights.

'You've been here before,' she said before Charlie could say anything at all.

'That's right,' Charlie replied. 'Is your mum or dad home?'

The girl shook her head. Her dad was in his office, and she had promised not to disturb him.

'And your mum?'

'She went to the shops.'

'Do you think she'll be back soon?' Charlie asked.

'I think so. What's your name?'

'Charlie,' Charlie replied and held out her hand.

'Mika,' the girl said and shook it. 'It's a boy's name, too.'

'No,' Charlie said, 'it's a name anyone can be called, just like Charlie.'

'What are you going to talk to Mum about?'

'This and that.'

'Like what?'

'It's secret,' Charlie said.

Mika seemed to ponder that for a moment. 'I'm great at keeping secrets,' she said.

'That's good,' Charlie replied.

'I never say anything if I promised I wouldn't. Last year, Love got a bike for his birthday. I knew about it for weeks, and he tickled me and everything, but I didn't tell him.'

'Good for you.'

They were interrupted by David coming down the stairs.

He asked Mika to go up to her room. Once she was out of earshot, he turned to Charlie and said he hoped she hadn't said anything to her about Beatrice.

'Of course not,' Charlie replied.

'So, what do you want? Has anything happened?'

'No. I would like to talk to you or your wife. May I come in?'

They had just sat down when David's phone rang. He apologised and said it was important, that he had to take it. He left the room and Mika appeared again.

'Is everything OK?' Charlie asked.

'I want to show you my room,' Mika said. 'I have a new desk, and—'

'Sure,' Charlie said.

'It's this way,' Mika instructed.

Charlie followed the girl upstairs. They stepped into a big, bright room with white sofas and a large, curved flat-screen TV on the wall.

'That's Love's room,' Mika said, pointing towards an open door. Charlie saw a tall black leather chair in front of a desk with a big screen on it.

The room next to his was Mika's. They stepped into a fluffy pink world full of stuffed animals, dolls, and princess dresses.

'Your room's lovely,' Charlie said. 'You like pink a lot.'

Mika nodded.

'This is nice,' Charlie went on and walked over to the desk. Above it was a large noticeboard with postcards, pictures of kittens, and a black-and-white photograph of a girl with a thick plait full of tiny flowers. The photograph was taken diagonally from behind.

'Is that you?' Charlie asked.

'Yes.'

'That's a lovely plait.'

'It's not a regular one,' Mika informed her. 'It's a fishtail plait.'

'It's very pretty.'

'Thank you.'

Charlie spotted another photograph in a frame on the windowsill. It was of a widely grinning Mika. She was sitting up very straight, holding a baby in her arms.

'That's me and Beatrice,' Mika said. 'My baby friend. Isn't she cute?'

'Super cute,' Charlie said.

'She's bigger now. She can talk and everything. Love says

she can't, that I'm just making it up, but I've heard her say lots of words.'

'What does she say?' Charlie asked.

'Mum, Dad, look, and lamp, and bye. She does this,' Mika said and waved her left hand at herself, 'byyyyeee.'

Charlie heard the front door open. She went downstairs to talk to Charlotte Jolander.

'Your daughter let me in,' she said. 'I have some more questions.'

They sat down in the kitchen. This time, it was clean. The counter gleamed in the sunlight pouring in through the windows.

'Has Amina been here?' Charlie asked.

'Yes, she was here a few hours ago.'

'But she wasn't here on Saturday, was she?'

'Yes, she was,' Charlotte said and met Charlie's eyes without blinking.

'Are you sure you don't have your days mixed up?'

'What difference does it make?' Charlotte said. 'Amina would never—'

'It's not a question of whether or not she would,' Charlie cut in. 'I just want to know if she was here on Saturday. Charlotte?' she said when there was no answer. 'I'm sure you know what the consequences are of providing someone with a false alibi.'

Charlotte nodded. 'She was here, but not the whole time,' she answered. 'She came around eight and did the upstairs, then she left.'

'What time was that?' Charlie asked.

'Around nine,' Charlotte said. 'Maybe a bit before nine.'

Charlie considered the distance between the two houses. It couldn't be more than half a mile.

'Does Amina own a car?' Charlie asked.

'No,' Charlotte replied. 'She always takes the bus here.'

'Did she tell you why she had to leave?'

'She was going to see a friend who ... needed her.'

'A friend?'

'Yes, a classmate. I think it's a man.'

'And why didn't you tell us this before?'

'Because ... Amina asked me not to.'

'So Amina asked you to tell anyone who asked that she had been here the whole time, cleaning?'

'Yes, but I would never have said it if I didn't trust her one hundred per cent.'

It was odd to think, Charlie mused, that there were people who had been alive for more than a decade and still trusted others one hundred per cent.

'Amina isn't capable of hurting anyone,' Charlotte added.

'You can't possibly know that,' Charlie said. 'Did she tell you the name of this classmate?'

'I'm sorry, she didn't. You're wasting your time if you think it's Amina,' Charlotte called after her as she got up and walked towards the front door.

As soon as she was back in the car, Charlie called Amina. She picked up after four rings, sounding winded.

'This is Charlie Lager, from the police,' Charlie said. 'We met the other day. I need to talk to you. Are you home?'

'No, I'm cleaning.'

'Where?'

Amina gave her the address.

'What's the name on the door?' Charlie asked.

'M Svedin,' Amina replied.

'You're at Madelene's? Madelene Svedin?'

'Yes.'

29

Amina opened the door to the flat but shook her head when Charlie asked if she could come in. That was against the rules.

'The rules don't apply in this situation,' Charlie said. 'But lying about your alibi is against the law. So either we go inside and talk about that here, or you're going to have to come with me.'

'OK, come in,' Amina said. 'I need to explain.'

They walked through a narrow hallway to a small kitchen. On the wall hung a picture of a young Selma Lagerlöf and next to it, a framed quote: *How much more common isn't being stung by a rose than being burned by a nettle?*

'You seem to work for a lot of people in Gustav's circle,' Charlie said.

'Yes, that's usually how it works out,' Amina replied. 'Word of mouth.'

They sat down at the small table. Amina's eyes darted back and forth. She was clearly nervous.

'So, what did you get up to during the time you claimed you were cleaning at the Jolanders'?'

'I went to see Kasim, a friend.'

'And why didn't you tell us that before?'

'You don't understand,' Amina said. 'A married woman can't be friends with a man like here in Sweden. We go to school together. Kasim lost his wife and son in the war. We help each other when it's extra hard. Last Saturday, when I was at Charlotte's house, he texted me and ... I was afraid he might hurt himself. I had to go see him.'

'You should have told us,' Charlie said. 'You should have told us the truth right away.'

'Yes,' Amina conceded. 'I'm very sorry.'

'What's Kasim's surname?' Charlie asked.

'Fardosa, Kasim Fardosa.'

'Do you have his number?'

'Yes, but he went to see his relatives in Denmark. I can't reach him either. I'm worried, he's not doing so well.'

'I need his number,' Charlie said.

'Of course.'

Amina took out her phone and read out his number.

'And can you show me the message he sent you?' Charlie asked.

'I deleted it,' Amina said. 'I didn't want Jamal to—'

'Does he get jealous?'

'No, it just wouldn't look good. But I called Kasim when I was on my way over. It's probably still in my call list.'

A moment later, she held up her phone, showing Charlie a call that fit with the time frame.

'I'm sorry,' Amina said again. 'So, what happens now? To me, I mean?'

'We're going to follow up on this to make sure what you're saying is true,' Charlie explained.

'Was there anything else?' Amina asked. She looked around the room. 'I need to finish here.'

On the way out, Charlie peeked through a half-open door into a bedroom. She stopped dead and felt her heart skip a beat. There, by the foot of the bed, stood a white cradle.

Sara

Marianne had gone to see her sick mother and taken Picco with her. Her mother was on her deathbed but apparently refused to die until Marianne came to see her. Emelie and Frans were filling in for her.

With Marianne away, we could go to the basement every night. We didn't talk about ourselves as much anymore, we mostly read the letters from the mental patients.

There was Orvar, who wrote about being watched, saying there was surveillance equipment everywhere and poisonous smoke in the vents. There was Vivianne, who, in a trembling hand and with no spaces between her words, appealed to various family members to come get her: *pleasetakemehome*.

And then there was her, the mother writing to her daughter. She was the most prolific writer and even though it was sometimes about things like mice in human clothing and doctors riding swans, there was something real underneath her words, grief and a longing for her daughters.

'Listen to this,' Lo said and read aloud:

'We were sitting on the bench by the pavilion, and I said to Flora: here she comes. Here comes my daughter. And then ... I saw the child in your arms. You were carrying your sister. Your sister had come back.

'*And I didn't want to scare you. I didn't want to take the baby from you. I just wanted to hold her awhile. I had dreamt about it for so long.*'

'She's hallucinating,' Nicki said. 'Come on, it can't be true, she wrote that the baby died.'

'Would you stop fucking interrupting,' Lo snapped. 'Let me finish.'

'Fine,' Nicki said. 'I just thought it was odd. Go on.'

'*I told Flora I probably needed help because now I could see you so clearly and I just wanted to run over and touch you. But Flora could see you, too. She could see you as clearly as I could.*

I didn't mean to frighten you. I was just so happy both my girls had come. What I had dreamt about since ... forever. I didn't want to take the baby from you, I just wanted to hold her awhile ... but then Edenstam came, and an army of white coats grabbed me and took me away from you.'

'Bloody hell,' Lo said. 'How the fuck can anyone do that?'

'You're leaving?' I asked when she got to her feet.

Lo said she just needed a break, that I could keep reading if I wanted.

I took the letter and did.

'*Edenstam says it's going to be a long time before you come back. He says your visit was a setback in my recovery. And the picture I have of you ... I'm not allowed to keep it because it makes me cry. That's why I'm sending it back. I didn't know what else to do with it.*'

'It's so sad,' said Lo, who had paced around the room and come to stand behind me.

'Can I see?' she asked when I took out the photograph.

I handed it to her without looking.

'Mother and daughter, it says,' Lo said. 'Maybe it wasn't her baby, but her ... grandchild? That would explain—'

'Let the rest of us see, too,' Nicki said. The photograph was passed around the circle. When it reached me, I saw that it had been taken in an overgrown garden. It was of a young woman with a baby in her arms.

'How can she be a mother?' Nicki asked, leaning in towards me. 'She looks like a child herself.'

'No, she doesn't,' Lo countered. 'She looks like a mother. You can tell from her eyes.'

'You can't tell things like that from someone's eyes, though, can you?' Nicki said.

Lo didn't bother to answer.

I asked if she was OK, and she said it was impossible to be OK when you had been torn away from your family, that none of us were OK.

I nodded, because I assumed that was true.

'I'm going to go to her soon,' Lo said. 'I'm going to steal a car and go see my mum. Who's coming with me?' She looked around the circle.

'I'll come,' I said. 'I guess I have to get to know her, right?'

'Thanks,' Lo replied. 'I knew I could trust you.' She looked back at the pile of letters. 'Why didn't those pricks post her letters?' she asked. 'How fucking hard is it to post letters from people who are completely cut off from the world?'

'Maybe there was a reason?' I shrugged.

'What fucking reason?' Lo said. 'What's so dangerous about these letters? Her daughter needed to read this. Do you have a cigarette, Nicki?'

Nicki nodded and handed her a packet of Marlboros.

Lo lit one and took three deep drags.

'A mother shouldn't be separated from her child,' she added. 'It's against nature. It's against everything.'

I thought about my own mother, who didn't seem to have had any problem defying nature.

But still, they couldn't entirely separate them, Lo went on. Because somehow, they were forever linked, the mother and her child. Even though they were separated in space and time, nothing could change the fact that they were one.

30

Madelene Svedin was sitting in an interview room at the police station and Charlie noted that she looked a lot more like her social media persona now. Gone was the solemn young woman with plaits and a dress. Today, she was wearing tight jeans and quite a bit of make-up.

She didn't want tea or coffee, just to know why she had been asked to come.

'I went to your flat earlier,' Charlie said. 'To talk to Amina, and I happened to see the cradle in your bedroom.'

'And is that against the law now?' Madelene said. 'Owning a cradle?'

'No, but considering that Beatrice is missing and that you, as far as we know, have no children, I hope you understand why we need to ask.'

Madelene looked out the window and took a deep breath before meeting Charlie's eye. 'I was pregnant,' she said.

Charlie waited for her to go on.

'Mum brought the cradle over when I told her,' Madelene continued. 'She had just sold her house and didn't have room for it, so ..,'

'What happened?' Charlie said. 'I mean ...?'

'Miscarriage,' Madelene replied. 'I had a miscarriage two weeks ago.'

'My condolences.'

'It's not a big deal,' Madelene said.

But Charlie could tell from her face that it was.

'How far along? I mean, how many weeks?'

'Fourteen.'

'And how did Gustav react to the news of your pregnancy?'

'How do you know he was the father?' Madelene retorted in a hard voice.

'I don't,' Charlie said. 'I just assumed.'

'He reacted badly because he was completely certain the baby wasn't his,' Madelene said.

'It wasn't?'

'No, I was with another man a few times, too.'

'Then how do you know who the father was?'

'I didn't at first,' Madelene said. 'But then Gustav told me he couldn't have children, that he was infertile.'

After Madelene left, Charlie went to find Greger to tell him what she had just been told, and that they needed to drive out to see the Palmgrens again.

'I thought you were supposed to be resting,' Greger said.

'I did rest.'

'It was pretty scary when you just collapsed.'

'I have low blood pressure,' Charlie said. 'It wasn't the first time.'

Greger looked at her as though he were expecting her to say more. Charlie looked away. Losing control in front of others was unpleasant and this thoughtfulness she hadn't asked for was even worse.

'If it makes you feel better, I'll let you drive,' she said and jingled the car keys as she started walking towards the exit.

David Jolander opened the door at the Palmgrens' house. He looked tired.

'Come in,' he said. 'I was just leaving.'

Frida and Gustav were sitting at opposite ends of the big sofa in the living room.

Frida's hair was dishevelled, and her eyes staring and bloodshot. She was still clutching the bunny blanket in one hand.

Charlie saw both hope and fear in their eyes when they entered.

'David let us in,' she said. 'We have no news about Beatrice, but we need to ask you some more questions.'

'Is it him?' Gustav asked. 'Is it Pascal they found?'

'I'm afraid we can't discuss that.'

'Then why are you here?'

'Let me get straight to the point,' Charlie said, fixing Gustav with a level gaze. 'Are you Beatrice's biological father?'

'What do you mean?' Gustav said.

'Who told you that?' Frida asked. 'We haven't discussed that with anyone.'

'So it's true?' Greger said.

Frida looked at her husband.

'Yes,' Gustav replied. 'It's true.'

'Who have you been talking to?' Frida asked. 'Who told you?'

'I'm afraid I can't tell you that,' Charlie said.

'But ...'

Frida turned to Gustav.

'How ... Who have *you* been talking to?'

'The source isn't important right now,' Charlie said. 'What we need to know is who Beatrice's biological father is.'

'We don't know his name,' Frida said. 'I was inseminated in a clinic in Russia. The donor was anonymous.'

Charlie exchanged a look with Greger. Maybe he was thinking the same thing she was, that it was extremely strange that they had kept this to themselves.

Gustav stepped in and told them about how they had tried to conceive for years, and how, when they finally decided to try IVF, it had turned out he was infertile.

'Do you understand what that feels like?' he said, looking from Greger to Charlie. 'Do you understand what it feels like not to be able to have what everyone else takes for granted?'

Charlie wanted to tell him that wasn't true, that lots of people didn't take it for granted, but Gustav seemed so upset about the unfairness of it all that he was unlikely to be receptive to that kind of statement.

Entitled, Charlie thought to herself. This is a man who feels entitled to absolutely everything.

31

It was past six when they got back into the car. The sun was still up, bathing the fields and forests in a warm spring light. In just a few weeks, the cherry trees would be in full bloom in Lyckebo. Charlie pictured the trees, Betty in her dress, the music from the open kitchen window. Betty laughing at her because she couldn't keep time or her distance. *You'll never be a dancer, Charline.*

She had let Greger drive again because her headache was back and the oxazepam had long since worn off.

'How are you feeling?' Greger asked.

'I'm OK.' Charlie looked out the window at the wind anemones blooming at the edge of the forest. She pictured a little girl with chubby hands, saw her bend down and pick a bouquet of flower heads with no stalks and smilingly hand it to her mother. 'All these things that are coming out,' she continued. 'It feels like they should add up to something.'

'I agree,' Greger said. 'But it's like they said: an anonymous donor can hardly have been involved in Beatrice's disappearance.'

'But what if they're lying?' Charlie said. 'What if it's not an anonymous donor, or a donor at all.'

'But they showed us the documentation,' Greger countered.

'It could be fake,' Charlie said. 'Frida could have slept with someone else.'

'Don't you think Frida would have told us? I mean, what's infidelity compared to a missing child? And she would have nothing to lose by it because if Gustav is infertile, he must have known, and why make fake documents anyway? It feels a bit … over the top.'

'True,' Charlie said. She leaned her head against the window and thought about all the loose ends they were failing to tie up: inadequate alibis, murky pasts, and secrets, a tangle of missing children, mistresses, and miscarriages.

'So, Beatrice was conceived through insemination,' Stina said once they were all gathered in the conference room for the last team meeting of the day. 'Why didn't they tell us?'

'Maybe because they figured it had nothing to do with this,' Charlie said.

'Still, they shouldn't have kept it from us,' Roy commented.

'I'm not saying they were right to withhold it, I'm just explaining why I think they did. An anonymous sperm donor from Russia who doesn't even know Beatrice exists. It's a bit far-fetched.'

'Still, it's weird,' Roy said, 'not to tell us.'

Stina reported that they were working their way through the calls to the tip line, but that Antonsson had let them know they shouldn't be holding their breath, that he didn't think any of it was particularly interesting.

'Have we had the DNA results?' Charlie asked. 'And the rest of the tests from the pram?'

'I haven't heard from the NFC,' Roy replied.

'Go call them right now, Roy,' Stina instructed. 'Make sure they know it's urgent.'

'Why would they be confused about that?' Roy asked.

'I'm sure they're not, but it doesn't hurt to keep on it.'

Roy nodded, picked up his phone, and left the room.

'And what about Madelene Svedin?' Charlie said. 'I mean, a miscarriage and a cradle is all we have on her.'

'She was dumped by Gustav Palmgren and has no alibi,' Greger put in.

'That's not enough,' Stina said. 'I've been calling the number you gave me, by the way. Trying to reach this Kasim. No answer.'

'According to Amina, he has gone to visit relatives in Denmark. He has mental-health problems,' Charlie explained.

'I know, I talked to one of the teachers at his school.'

'What if they did something together?' Greger said. 'I mean, what if this Kasim has the baby?' He looked at Charlie and then at Stina.

Charlie nodded.

'We're going to have to contact the Danish police, they'll have to find him.'

'What about Byle?' Greger asked. 'Have we had the reports from the technicians and the coroner?'

'Christoffer and Filip are on their way over,' Stina replied.

Ten minutes later, Christoffer and Filip were standing at the whiteboard in the conference room. The coroner had informed them that it was most likely suicide. And no, he couldn't give an exact time of death, but his best guess was that he'd been dead at least five days. Taken together with the time his phone was last used, everything pointed to Byle having been dead when Beatrice went missing.

'And what about the piece of paper in his trouser pocket?' Charlie asked.

'Yes, we were just getting to that. It was a letter. We scanned it so you can read for yourselves,' Christoffer said and turned on the projector.

The letter was one page long and perfectly legible despite some rather extensive damp damage.

To Gustav and David, it began.

Then followed a confused rant about how the two of them had used Pascal for his technical know-how and then forced him out of the company through blackmail, which concluded by saying they should consider this letter a middle finger from the other side.

He was never going to forgive them.

She just cries and cries. Sometimes, she dozes off, but then she wakes up, flails and squirms and it starts all over again. I rock, shush, feed, sing. Lullaby after lullaby.

But she keeps howling and whining.

She's warm, full, and dry, and yet ... She won't be soothed.

Rock-a-bye baby, in the treetop.

But it doesn't work. I can't protect her, not from them, not from me. And I'm starting to understand what you've probably known from the start, that this story isn't going to have a happy ending.

32

It was past eleven by the time they got back to the hotel. Earlier in the evening, Charlie had called Challe to update him on their progress. His thoughts and questions usually helped her to sort things out in her mind, but this time she'd felt nothing but frustration when they hung up.

'Nightcap?' Greger said when they stepped into the lobby.

Charlie nodded. They went to the bar, but it was closed.

'Want to come up to my room?' Greger asked. 'We could grab something from the minibar.'

Charlie argued briefly with herself. What she should do versus what she wanted to do.

'I just need to make a phone call,' she said. 'I'll be right behind you.'

'OK,' Greger said.

He gave her his room number and disappeared into the lift.

I'm just going to go up to my room and go straight to bed, Charlie thought as she walked towards the stairs. But when she reached her floor, her feet kept moving.

Greger opened a screw-cap bottle of red wine from the mini-bar, filled two glasses and handed her one.

Charlie didn't know where to sit, the bed felt too ... intimate, and the sofa was tiny. Greger solved the problem by taking a seat on the carpet and leaning back against the wall. She followed his lead.

'Bloody hell,' Greger said, 'everything's just spinning.'

'Agreed,' Charlie said.

'Tell me we're going to solve this.'

'We're going to solve this,' Charlie said.

'You don't sound very convincing.'

'No surprise there.'

'So, what are you thinking?'

'I wouldn't call it thinking, more like my mind's racing, bouncing around.'

'I feel the same way.'

'Summarise for me,' Charlie said. 'Take it from the top.' She took a big gulp of wine and closed her eyes to listen. But when Greger started with his thoughts about Gustav, she interrupted and asked him to start with Beatrice instead.

So Greger told her about Beatrice's disappearance, about the leads that never actually led anywhere. Then, he went on to describe Gustav, his infidelity, the rumours about his ruthless business practices and treatment of Pascal Byle, but also his concern for his child. He talked about Frida, her alcoholic parents, her junkie brother, her mental health, which seemed to be the subject of debate. And then: the inescapable fact that she had been home alone when Beatrice disappeared.

Greger paused for a second before outlining the parents' joint lie, or perhaps omission was a better term: Gustav wasn't Beatrice's biological father.

Why hadn't they told them? Was it because they thought it was irrelevant, or for some other reason? It seemed particularly strange given as how it would come out anyway when they got the results of their swabs. Granted, they didn't have those results yet, but it was only a matter of time before it was confirmed that Gustav wasn't the father. That being said, the parents were both in shock, of course, and that didn't make for rational behaviour.

Greger moved on to the people around Frida and Gustav: Amina, who had lost her own children and lied about her alibi. She knew the family's routines and had also looked after Beatrice on occasion. And Madelene, the dumped mistress, her miscarriage, and Gustav's claims that she had threatened the family, something she herself denied.

Half an hour later, when they had drunk everything in Greger's minibar and he asked if she wanted to move onto hers, Charlie thought she might have met her soulmate as far as colleagues went. She didn't know if that made her feel safe or frightened.

'We're not taking the lift?' Greger asked when Charlie set her course for the stairs.

'It's just two floors,' Charlie said.

'Are you claustrophobic?' Greger asked. He smiled at her.

'Perhaps,' Charlie replied.

'Well, you need to confront that, then,' Greger said. 'Come on, let's go.'

He held out his hand to her. Charlie sighed but took it. As soon as they stepped into the lift, she regretted it. It was as though her windpipe closed along with the lift doors.

'You're OK, right?' Greger asked.

Charlie shook her head because she felt like she was about to pass out.

'Don't worry,' Greger said, 'we're almost there. Everything's OK.'

Charlie made no reply. Every part of her had seized up: her thoughts, her lips, her body. She didn't regain control until the doors slid open a few seconds later.

'I'm sorry,' she said. 'I don't know what happened.'

'I'm the one who should apologise,' Greger protested. 'I had no idea it was that bad.'

'It's fine.' Charlie took out her key card and hoped the mini-bar had been restocked. It had been. She didn't bother with glasses, just opened the bottle, took a long pull, and handed it to Greger.

'It's odd,' Greger said. 'You come off as really tough, so I wasn't prepared for you being that scared of lifts.'

'I guess I'm contradictory. Look,' she said and held out her hand. 'I'm still shaking.'

Greger took her hand and held it firmly in his. Then he looked deep into her eyes.

'No,' Charlie whispered when he pulled her to him. 'We shouldn't.'

But when Greger backed away, she followed and put her arms around his neck. They kissed, gingerly at first, tentatively, as though they were about to stop any second, but then increasingly fiercely.

Sara

'Look what I have,' Lo said.

She was holding a set of car keys in one hand and her phone in the other. She slowly swiped between three pictures. They were taken in the big common room on the ground floor and showed Frans and Emelie naked on the sofa. Frans with his head tilted back, his eyes closed, and his mouth half-open, Emelie straddling him. Then another one almost exactly like it and then the last one: their flushed, horrified faces when they realised they'd been caught.

'Oh my god,' I said. 'Oh my fucking god.'

'Nicki caught them red-handed,' Lo said. 'So now Marianne's little assistant's tattling days are over.'

I couldn't tear my eyes away from the picture of Frans and Emelie.

'What do you say, want to go for a drive in Frans' car?' Lo asked, jangling the keys.

'Are we going to go see your mum?'

'I would have loved to,' Lo replied. 'It's just that I can't get hold of her. She moves a lot. And besides, it's pretty far, to Stockholm, I mean. Maybe we could just drive around because ... because it's fun. Do you want to? We can go right now.'

'Don't you want to get dressed first?'

'What? You don't think I look pretty?'

Lo twirled.

'I thought that was a nightgown.'

'It's both,' Lo said. 'And the best thing about it is that I have another one that's almost identical.'

'Aren't we going to freeze to death?' I said after slipping on Lo's spare nightgown.

'I guess we'll wear our coats over them,' Lo replied. 'Come on.'

We went outside. Fog had settled over the footpaths.

'Do you want to or should I?' Lo asked when we reached Frans' Volkswagen.

'I'll do it,' I replied.

'Wow,' Lo said, 'I didn't know you could drive.'

'I learnt a long time ago.'

It was still impressive, Lo said as I turned out from the treelined drive, that I could drive so well when I was only fifteen. Who had taught me?

'A guy from back home,' I said and thought about the driving lessons Jonas had given me in the football field behind the fire station. After Dad died, I'd driven our old Volvo around in broad daylight.

'What about you?' I asked, assuming Lo hadn't taken proper lessons either.

'A friend at another care home. She taught me to hotwire cars, too, but it's a lot easier with keys.' Lo leaned forward and started fiddling with the stereo.

'What are you doing?' I asked.

'Connecting to the Bluetooth,' Lo replied. 'Listen to this.' She turned the music up and began to sing along.

Night is warm, the city roars,
Traffic, bars, and open liquor stores,
Woken by the stellar sky
And a streak of faintly grey street light
What you don't have
You cannot lose

I glanced over at her. She looked happy.

'Where are you taking me?' she asked when I turned left at the next intersection.

'Home,' I said. 'We're going to my hometown.'

'Town?' Lo said as we drove through Gullspång town centre. It was dark, only a few street lights were on.

'I know,' I replied, 'it barely qualifies.'

'It looks abandoned. Are you sure you're not lost?'

'I've lived here my whole life,' I said. 'I can't get lost.'

'But it's completely dead,' Lo remarked. She had her face pressed against the window, looking out. 'It looks like ... like they just closed everything down and left.' Lo pointed to a few boarded-up windows that had once belonged to a gift shop. 'I wanted to party.'

'We're going to party,' I said. 'There's a pub down this street.'

'That's pretty hard to believe,' Lo said. 'What the hell is that?' she asked when we passed the smelter.

I slowed down and looked up at the rusty building. The street light outside was on and cast eerie shadows across the factory walls.

'GEA,' I replied. 'It's an old smelter.'

'What's a smelter?'

I told her about the iron, the ovens, and the freight trains that had once run all the way into the factory. We'd started hanging out there sometimes in middle school. We'd fallen from pipes, torn our clothes on old rusty things, and found rubbish that we burnt in the ovens to stay warm.

'Here it is,' I said when we reached the pub. The lights were on in the windows and cigarettes were glowing on the front steps.

'They're not going to let us in, though, are they?' Lo said.

I told her they would, that it wasn't a regular pub.

'But the age limit's the same everywhere in Sweden, right?'

'Sure, but people don't really care out here. It's a small place, everyone knows everyone else, and—'

'I grew up in the wrong place,' Lo said. 'I would have been much happier here.'

Don't be so sure, I thought to myself.

I greeted the gang huddled on the front steps. It was a few of the blokes who worked in the factory. I noticed them looking at our bare legs.

I paused for a while inside the doors and breathed in the familiar smell of beer and party. I showed Lo where we could hang up our coats. We heard laughter from the ladies' room.

'I'm absolutely certain,' Lo said as we walked into the bar section, 'that I'm going to like this place.'

Janis was up on stage, singing Dad's favourite song, a local folk song.

'What kind of funeral dirge is this?' Lo said.

'Calm down,' I said. 'There will be normal music later. But she sings this song once every night.'

'Why?'

'Because it's the Värmland anthem.'

'Are we still in Värmland?'

'No.'

'Then where the hell are we?'

'In Västergötland.'

'I'm confused,' Lo said. 'But whatever. I want a drink.'

We started towards the bar but were stopped after just a few feet by Lasse Smed, one of Dad's old drinking mates.

'There you are, Sara,' he said. 'Noddy and I were just wondering when you'd be back.' He pointed towards Noddy, who smiled his toothless smile at me. He didn't seem to have been wondering anything.

'I'm just visiting,' I said.

'You look skinny,' Lasse went on, pinching my bare upper arm. 'They're nice to you in that place, aren't they? Or do you want me to bring Sten-Henrik and Noddy over there and talk some sense into them?'

'I'll let you know if I do.'

'We'll be there in a heartbeat. Just give us a shout and we'll come rescue you. You know that, Sara. Anything for Svenka's girl.'

'Thanks,' I said. 'That's good to know.'

Lasse grinned at me. He didn't seem to realise he couldn't save anyone, not even himself.

'Do you know everyone here?' Lo asked when we sat down at the bar, and I nodded to the lady who ran the kiosk in the square.

'I know who they are, at least,' I replied. 'It's a small place.' I broke off when I saw Jonas come out of the kitchen. He stopped dead when he spotted me.

'Are you back?' he asked.

'I'm just visiting.'

'I've been trying to call you, but—'

'I know,' I said, 'I've had a lot on.'

'Aren't you going to introduce us?' Lo asked.

'Jonas,' I said. 'This is Lo.'

'Hi, Lo,' Jonas said.

'Hiya,' Lo replied.

'So, what can I get you ladies?' Jonas said and wiped his hands on a kitchen towel he had tucked into the waistband of his trousers.

'The usual,' I replied.

Lo wondered what the usual was, and Jonas told her it was liquorice shots.

'Oh come on,' Lo sighed, 'I want something that lasts longer than five seconds.'

'You won't finish these in five seconds,' I said and nodded towards Jonas, who had already filled half a water glass for me.

'Are you coming to Vall's later?' Jonas said. 'My shift ends at eleven and I'm heading over there when I'm done.'

'What's Vall's?' Lo asked.

'The place to be,' Jonas replied.

We picked up our glasses of liquorice shots and went over to the only free window table. I looked around the room. It had been seven months since I'd last been there, but it felt like much longer. Everything was the same, yet different. Dad was missing. He wasn't standing at the bar, buying rounds with money he didn't have, and he wasn't going to stagger in through the front door in the early hours of the morning covered in vomit and piss.

Those days were over.

33

Charlie woke up alone in her hotel bed. It took her a few seconds to remember the night before, the wine, Greger. She waited for the wave of anxiety and panic, but it didn't come.

It was half past seven. They were supposed to meet at the station in half an hour. She got out of bed and concluded that she was OK, that the hangover would strike later or not at all.

Greger was sitting in the breakfast room when she stopped by to pick up a cup of coffee and a piece of fruit on her way out.

'You OK?' he asked.

'Absolutely.'

She couldn't quite meet his eyes. All the things that had felt so right last night now felt ... so ... well, what, actually? Embarrassing? Scary? Or maybe it could just be what she had decided to see it as: a nice time. It didn't have to be a problem if they were both happy to leave it at that.

Greger brought it up on the way to the station.

'The thing that happened,' he said, his eyes firmly on the road. 'I mean last night. It was—'

'It was what it was,' Charlie cut in before he could finish the sentence.

She had a feeling that whatever he'd been about to say, it would have been bad. If he'd hinted at wanting to explore things further, she would have panicked, and if he'd said the opposite, she would have been offended. And they had more important things to think about right now than what had happened between them and why. It had simply happened.

Charlie studied the names and pictures on the whiteboard. Their investigation seemed to keep growing sideways, but not in depth.

Byle's name had been crossed off the list of suspects. Stina had checked with Antonsson; nothing else of interest had come in to the tip line. Most of the calls were from people who wanted to make sure they knew Gustav Palmgren was a nasty character. It had become increasingly clear that he wasn't well thought of. Someone had said that Frida didn't seem like a very loving mother since she'd left her baby to cry in her pram at a café. A psychic had been in touch, too, talking about dark water and open fields.

'So, nothing?' Charlie said.

'I still think it's worth noting that Frida let her baby cry instead of picking her up,' Roy put in. 'Isn't that contrary to the whole maternal-instinct thing?'

He turned to Stina as though he expected praise for his penetrating analysis, but Stina just shook her head and said most parents let their babies cry for a while before picking them up, that it was just human.

They were going to focus on finding Amina's friend Kasim Fardosa in Denmark, both to verify her alibi and to make sure he didn't have Beatrice. They were also going to try to find out if there was any truth to Madelene Svedin's stories about

Frida's mental-health issues. The main problem there was that Frida was increasingly clamming up in their conversations with her and they weren't getting much out of the people closest to her either: Gustav and the Jolanders.

'We could put the screws on Amina,' Charlie suggested. 'She does clean their house, spends several hours a week there and has watched Beatrice. She must know more than she's saying.'

'Lovely day,' Greger said as they drove out towards Kronoparken.

'Sure,' Charlie replied.

She'd barely noticed the weather, but looking out the car window now and seeing the sun beaming down on the pale-green leaves of the birch trees, she had to agree. She thought about Beatrice. Was she going to get to experience her first spring? Was she going to get to dip her feet in the lake, play in the sand, take wobbly steps in the new grass?

'Do you think we can make Amina talk?' Greger asked.

'I don't know. She's very loyal to her employers.'

'You don't sound very hopeful.'

'I'm not,' Charlie said.

But it was more than just hopelessness; the feeling of resolve and optimism she'd woken up with the previous day had been replaced by helplessness, frustration, and a growing fear that this case would remain unsolved. She knew it was the worst thing that could happen to a parent, to be left with a glimmer of hope and live forever in uncertainty. And then, that thought buzzing at the back of her mind: Unless they already know.

She showed Greger where to turn in and park. Amina opened the door before they could ring the bell.

'Come in,' she said.

They went into the kitchen and sat down. This time, Amina

didn't offer them tea. Jamal came in to say hi and then left them alone.

'We need to ask you some more questions about Gustav and Frida.'

'OK?'

'And it's important that you answer truthfully, do you understand?'

'Yes.'

'How has Frida been feeling lately?' Charlie asked. 'I mean before Beatrice disappeared. Have you noticed a change, seen her and Gustav argue, anything?'

Amina shook her head and said she'd already answered that.

'Amina,' Charlie said. 'We're trying to find a missing baby, we're trying to find Beatrice. Are you sure you can't think of anything?'

Amina looked away and then down at her chapped hands. They looked worse now, Charlie noted. She must have been scratching at them since they last talked.

'Frida hasn't been doing so well,' Amina said. 'But I don't think—'

'In what way?' Greger asked. 'How do you know she hasn't been doing so well?'

'I don't know.'

Amina's phone rang. She picked it up and looked queryingly at Charlie, who nodded.

Amina answered and started speaking quickly in her native language. She sounded upset, but maybe it was just the prosody.

Charlie couldn't keep her eyes from the photograph of Amina's dead daughters. It was difficult to comprehend that none of them were alive.

Amina ended the call.

'How can you tell she hasn't been doing so well?' Greger said again.

'She has been crying a lot, and also … she takes pills to sleep and sometimes she takes them during the day, and … well, I guess it's that mainly …'

'How do you know she takes pills?' Charlie asked.

'I clean her house,' Amina said. 'You get to know the people you work for, and Frida has been home a lot recently, too, so … well, I've seen it, she takes pills and becomes tired afterwards. She sleeps a lot and doesn't always hear Beatrice crying. She probably doesn't mean to …'

She trailed off.

'I feel horrible for telling you this.'

'It's good that you are,' Charlie said.

'She cries all the time,' Amina added. 'I think it's because she can't sleep. Beatrice is awake at night a lot. And once,' Amina continued with her eyes on the picture of her own daughters, 'she shook her … Frida shook Beatrice a little bit too hard. I don't think she meant to, but … I saw it.'

Charlie and Greger exchanged a look.

'Do you have to tell Frida?' Amina asked. 'She's going to know it was me.' Tears were running down her cheeks now. 'I'm sorry, but all of this … It brings back …' She looked up at the photograph of her children again. 'It makes me very sad.'

When they'd left Amina's flat and were walking across the car park, something squeaked loudly behind them. Charlie recognised the little boy on the tricycle from her last visit. The older girl who looked like she must be his sister was trudging along behind him. She was carrying a toddler on her hip this time and said something in Polish to the boy on the tricycle. Probably told him to stop. He didn't.

The girl met Charlie's eyes.

'He's not allowed to ride his bike here,' she said in perfect Swedish. 'But he won't listen.'

She shifted the toddler over to her other hip with a practised motion.

'It's because of the cars,' she went on. 'They don't see him when they back out. He's so little.'

'Is he your brother?' Charlie asked.

The girl nodded.

'What's his name?'

'Dobry.'

'Dobry,' Charlie said to the boy, who stopped pedalling and turned around in surprise. 'You're not allowed to ride your bike here. You could get hit by a car.'

The boy's bottom lip began to tremble. He quickly turned his tricycle around and pushed himself along with his feet until he almost ran into his sister's legs, then he burst into tears.

The girl tried to get her brother, his tricycle, and the wriggling toddler out of the car park.

'Would you like some help?' Greger said.

'Really?' the girl replied. 'Maybe you could take the tricycle?'

The children lived two doors down from Amina and Jamal. The girl thanked them for their help and Charlie and Greger were just about to leave when a woman came out and shouted something at the girl.

'We were just helping her with the little ones,' Charlie said. 'They were upset.'

'Who are you?' the woman demanded.

'We're from the police,' Charlie said. 'The boy was riding

his tricycle in the car park and your daughter had her hands full, so we just helped her get everyone home.'

'Who called the police? Was it her?' the woman said before Charlie could answer. She pointed towards Amina's door. 'Don't believe her. Don't believe what she says. Ask her what she did to my little girl instead.'

'What did she do to your little girl?' Charlie asked.

'She took her,' the woman replied. 'She snatched my baby out of her pram.' She looked down at the toddler her older daughter had handed back to her and who was now content in her mother's arms.

'What do you mean by snatched?' Charlie asked.

'I mean exactly that. My daughter was sleeping in her pram out here and Amina came and took her.'

Amina looked surprised to see them back.

'Is something wrong?' she asked.

'We were just talking to your neighbour,' Greger said. 'She says you took her daughter when she was sleeping in her pram.'

'No,' Amina's eyes went wide. 'No, no, no!'

Jamal appeared behind her. 'What's the matter?' he said. 'What now?'

'The little girl was crying,' Amina said. 'She was crying and had kicked off her blanket and she was cold. I knocked on the door and when no one opened, I picked her up and brought her inside. It was in the middle of winter. I didn't want her to be cold. I just didn't want her to be cold.'

'And how long was she with you?'

'I don't know … fifteen minutes, maybe twenty. Then I heard screaming outside and realised my neighbour had noticed her child was missing, so I went straight out there and tried to explain.'

'And where had the mother been?' Charlie asked. 'Why was the child unattended?'

'She wouldn't say,' Amina replied. 'She just screamed at me that she was going to call the police.'

'But she didn't?' Charlie said.

'No, because I said I would call them too, if she did, and tell them she had left her baby outside in the cold all alone. Then she said it was all a misunderstanding, that it wasn't going to happen again, and that I shouldn't poke my nose into her affairs. And then ...'

'Then what?' Greger pressed.

'Then she said a lot of terrible things to me.'

'Such as?'

'Terrible things about how it wasn't her fault my daughters were dead, and she told me to stay away from her children.' Amina burst into tears.

She might be telling the truth, Charlie thought, but then again, she did lie about her alibi and now we're told she took another baby out of its pram.

'She was cold,' Amina repeated. 'The baby was cold, and no one came to the door. What was I supposed to do?' She looked at Jamal, who put a protective arm around her.

'Can we speak to you alone for a minute?' Charlie said.

Amina looked at her husband again and said something in Arabic. He said something back and shook his head.

'He doesn't want to leave me alone with you,' Amina explained.

'Then we're probably going to have to bring you down to the station,' Greger said.

That changed Jamal's mind. He put on his shoes and said he was going out for a walk.

'Amina,' Charlie said after they had once again sat down at the kitchen table. 'Have you really told us everything?'

Amina mumbled something inaudible. Tears dripped onto the table.

'What was that?' Charlie said. 'Talk to me.'

'My girls,' Amina whispered. 'My little girls.'

34

They hadn't been able to get anything else out of Amina. She had picked up her neighbour's baby because she was cold and crying and because no one had answered the door when she knocked. Amina had agreed to let them search her flat and there had been no signs of a baby anywhere.

They had gathered in the conference room. The team's growing frustration at their lack of progress was palpable.

'Let's bring her in,' Roy said. 'Oh, come on. She knows the family's routines, she lied about her alibi, and she took a neighbour's baby out of its pram. What more do we need?'

'A motive,' Charlie replied.

'Crazy people don't need motives.'

'She's not crazy,' Charlie said. 'She has been through a war, she's in shock, and she's scared, but she's not crazy.'

'Now you're a psychologist, too?' Roy said.

'No, but I have a lot of experience with crazy people.'

'OK, that's enough, let's not get side-tracked,' Stina said.

'Fine, let's just ignore how twisted it is that she took another person's baby out of its pram,' Roy said.

'It would be crazier not to bring it inside,' Greger countered. 'What's crazy is not contacting the authorities.'

'I don't think she has a lot of faith in authorities and the police,' Charlie said. 'And that could potentially be significant.'

'Besides, if Amina did take Beatrice, bringing her in could be dangerous. Better to put surveillance on her.'

'OK, let's do that,' Stina agreed and picked up her phone, which was ringing.

'Amina's husband is here,' she said after hanging up. 'Jamal's in the lobby, asking to talk to us.'

'I'll go,' Charlie said and, without waiting for an answer, she left the room and headed down the stairs. Greger followed her.

Jamal was standing just outside the barriers.

'Amina has been good to that family, it's not her fault Beatrice is missing,' he said.

'Then whose fault is it?' Charlie asked. She and Greger stepped through the barriers. Jamal backed up as though he were afraid of having them too close.

'I don't know,' Jamal said. 'I don't know whose fault it is, but it's not Amina's. She loves children.'

'Do you have reason to suspect anyone else?' Greger asked.

Jamal shook his head, but there was a tentativeness to his body language.

'Jamal,' Charlie said. 'If you know something, you have to tell us.'

'I don't know,' Jamal replied, 'but I saw something at Gustav and Frida's house, and ...'

He paused, as though whatever he had to say was painful.

'And what?' Charlie pressed.

'Someone has been digging in their garden. Someone has dug a hole and flattened the ground.'

'When did you notice this?' Charlie asked.

She could feel her pulse quickening.

'The day before ... I mean, the day before she disappeared.'

'Last Friday? And it wasn't there before?'

'I hadn't noticed it, anyway,' Jamal replied. 'I didn't give it any thought at the time, but then ... well ...'

'And did you or Amina see Beatrice that day?' Greger asked.

'I didn't see her, and Amina wasn't working that day.'

'Have you told Amina about this?' Charlie said.

'No, I'd forgotten about it,' Jamal replied. 'It was when Amina told you about Frida, that she ... The things she said to you, she hasn't mentioned that before. She's very ... She likes Frida very much. I don't know if ... but there had been digging.'

'Where in the garden was this?'

'Under the big tree, the one closest to the water.'

Gustav opened the front door before they had even turned into the driveway. He asked them to keep their voices down, said Frida was resting upstairs.

'We have no news,' Greger told him. 'But we've had information that you've recently been digging in the garden. Is that correct?'

Gustav said they had. They'd buried Frida's cat, which had been run over the day before Beatrice disappeared. He'd found it out on the road, pretty badly mangled, but he hadn't given it any thought since Beatrice disappeared.

'Makes sense,' Charlie said.

She looked at Greger.

'We're going to have to dig it up,' she said. 'Just to—'

'Oh my god!' Gustav exclaimed. 'How can you even think that's what happened?'

'It's not about what we think,' Charlie said. 'Our job is to know for sure. We would be remiss if we didn't verify your information.'

'Fine,' Gustav snapped. 'Go ahead. Waste time on that instead of finding my daughter. There are shovels out back. Go on, go and dig.'

'I understand that you're upset,' Greger said, 'but—'

'Stop talking and just get to your very important work,' Gustav said and slammed the door.

'We'll have to call the technicians,' Greger noted.

'We can do it ourselves,' Charlie said. 'I have gloves in the car.'

'I don't know,' Greger wavered.

'It's just that it's a whole to-do,' Charlie added. 'Do we really want to put them through that?' She nodded up towards the house.

'All right,' Greger said. 'Get the gloves.'

There was a three-foot long patch of bare soil next to a large oak tree at the bottom of the garden.

Deep hole for a cat, Charlie thought after they'd dug for a while without finding anything. Don't let her be in here, she thought next. Don't let it end that way.

'I just hit something,' Greger said. He tapped with his shovel. 'There's a wooden box here.'

It took them a few minutes to work the box free. Charlie inspected it and noted that it was big enough for a baby.

The box was held shut by two simple hooks. The lid creaked when Greger opened it.

The familiar smell Charlie could never get used to hit them.

Charlie breathed through her mouth and looked down into the box. Two yellow cat eyes stared blankly up at her.

Sara

Micke, the police officer, was in the pub, so I didn't want to drive to Vall's. He had been very patient with me and my driving, and I didn't want to push him now.

'That's fucking terrifying,' Lo said as we walked past GEA.

'It's just an old factory,' I said and caught her as she took a stumble.

She was pretty drunk. So was I.

'Why is it so goddamn dark everywhere?' Lo said. 'Why aren't the street lights on?'

'Because there's no point fixing them.'

'This hill is insane,' Lo panted as we climbed past Gullspång Electric and the electrical safety label factory. On our left was the river, the floodgates, and the spillway.

When we reached the bridge, Lo wanted to stop for a smoke.

We both lit cigarettes. Lo leaned out over the railing. 'The water is jet-black,' she said.

'Not just at night, either,' I told her. 'It's because it's so deep.'

'Am I just drunk, or is it swirling?'

'You're drunk,' I said, 'but it is swirling. The floodgates are open.'

I pointed over towards the spillway, where the contours of the floodgates could be made out in the moonlight.

'Does the lake end there?'

I nodded.

'So, what's beyond it?' Lo asked. 'What comes after the end?'

'A waterfall.'

'Can you even swim here?'

I said you could if the floodgates were closed, that we used to jump from the bridge and dive from the railing.

'That sounds really dangerous,' Lo said.

She was apparently staying a while longer on the bridge because she flicked her butt into the water and pulled out another cigarette.

I thought about the story of the poles we used to scare each other with. You couldn't see them from the surface, but they could split you down the middle if you jumped from the bridge.

Dad used to laugh at that. He'd heard the story of the poles in the river as a child, too. It seemed to be passed down from generation to generation, but it was all made-up. Think about it, where would the poles even have come from? The river was incredibly deep. When were they supposed to have been put there and how? And with all the children who had jumped off that bridge over the decades, wasn't it remarkable that none of them had been impaled by now?

He was right, of course, but I still hadn't been able to stop thinking about the poles every time I'd climbed up on the railing and thrown myself out.

And it was true what Dad had said, that no one had ever been impaled – but the river had taken lives in other ways.

Many a lonely fisherman and drunkard had been sucked down by the undertow.

I bummed another cigarette from Lo, gazed out at the water, and thought about Annabelle, about the summer when the whole town was in mourning.

'What a place,' Lo said once we'd climbed the last hill and could finally see the house. 'Like a fucking house of horrors.'

I looked up at the peeling white paint on the walls of the old village shop and the cobweb-like curtains in the windows. So much had happened there.

Lo was right. It was a house of horrors.

The thudding bassline from Svante's stereo could be heard all the way out to the street.

'Take your shoes off,' I said when we entered the hallway.

I led the way up the stairs and warned Lo about the missing step.

'Is your boyfriend already here?' Lo asked.

'I don't have a boyfriend.'

When we reached the first floor, we saw a girl lying prone on the floor.

'Is she alive?' Lo said.

I went closer and realised it was Rebecka Gahm. She didn't usually pass out, but this time, she evidently had. I put a hand over her mouth and felt her shallow breaths.

'She's breathing,' I replied. 'Help me move her a little so she doesn't get trampled.' We pushed her up against the wall.

'Wow, to what do we owe the honour?'

I looked up and saw Svante's mocking eyes. He made me regret coming.

'Sexy nightgowns,' he added.

'They're dresses,' Lo said.

'And who are you?' Svante asked.

'Who are you?' Lo countered.

'Svante,' he replied. 'I'm Svante Linder.' He said his name as though it were an insult that Lo didn't already know it.

'Do you live here?' Lo asked.

Svante chuckled. 'No.'

'Then who lives here?' Lo said.

'No one,' Svante replied. 'Everyone. And you?'

'I live in the same place as Sara.'

'So you've run away?' Svante said. 'You're little runaways?'

'Don't touch me,' I said when he put a hand on my shoulder.

'Always so angry these days,' Svante said. 'I don't understand what I ever did to you.'

I thought about all the things he'd done to me; the drinks he'd plied me with before I was even a teenager, all the times he'd used me, all the things he'd given me that I'd been better off without.

'Where are the others?' I asked.

'Some are in the kitchen or up in the attic,' Svante said. 'The rest are out in the yard. Benjamin shot a boar that he's trying to barbecue. Everything's wet, so they took a couple of chairs from the kitchen and drenched them in lighter fluid. I'm sure they've managed to get a blaze going by now.'

I brought Lo out through the back door. And in the garden, bathed in firelight, I found all my party friends standing around like I'd never left. There was Benjamin with his unkempt hair and flushed cheeks, Jonas who was trying to make everyone keep their distance from the fire, and a gaggle of teenage girls laughing hysterically.

I didn't know if I was happy or sad about seeing them again.

The whole thing reminded me about the world I'd left, the one that would never be the same. I didn't know if that made me feel relieved or miserable.

Lo wobbled down to join the others and I heard her tell Jonas he had to pour on more lighter fluid, otherwise the fire would go out any minute. Jonas did as he was told, and the flames climbed even higher towards the sky.

I don't know how long I stood there, but it was long enough for Rebecka to come to, because she came out and joined me. She didn't react to me being back, maybe she was too plastered to realise I'd been gone.

'Would you look at that?' she said. 'Sickest fire I've ever seen.'

I nodded. There wouldn't be any boar meat to eat, though, because its coat had caught fire and the whole animal was burning to a crisp.

'So tell me,' Jonas said when everyone was back inside, and we were sitting on the floor in the room off the living room. He almost had to shout because Svante had turned up the music. 'How are you doing?'

'I'm OK,' I replied. 'But I would prefer to be out on my own.'

'They'll let you out soon.'

Jonas had lit two cigarettes and handed me one. My eyes lingered on his hand. I thought about all the times it had gently caressed my body.

'I don't know,' I said and inhaled. 'I don't know if I have what it takes.'

'You do,' Jonas said. 'You're the strongest person I know.'

'But everyone else you know is pretty much an idiot,' I countered.

'True,' Jonas said with a smile. 'So, when are you coming back?'

'I'm not sure.'

'Well, give me a call, will you? When you get out, I mean.'

I nodded and felt I could do that.

Four hours later, we were done with Vall's. I told Lo neither of us was in a state to drive all the way back to Rödminnet, that we were too drunk. We were doomed. All Frans had to do was report us, and ...

'Frans won't report us, don't you get that?' Lo said. But why sleep in the car, she asked, when we could go back to Vall's.

I thought about all the things that had happened to me after falling asleep at Vall's and said I knew a better place.

35

They reburied the cat; put the wooden box back in the hole and shovelled the dirt on top of it.

'You didn't find anything, did you?' a familiar voice said from the terrace as they were walking back to the car.

Charlie looked up. It was David Jolander. He was standing next to Frida, holding a teacup that he now handed to her. Apparently, she was done resting.

'David,' Charlie said. 'We need to ask Frida some questions in private.'

David went back into the house and Charlie signalled for Greger to keep his distance.

'Frida ...' Charlie said. Then she broke off and pointed to a wicker sofa further down the terrace. 'Could we maybe sit down? I need to ask you a difficult question.'

They sat down and Frida pulled a blanket around her. Charlie braced herself and continued.

'Have you ever ... shaken Beatrice?'

Frida made no reply. She just stared out at the terrace from which her child had disappeared five days earlier. Or had she? Was she still here? In the water?

'Frida?' Charlie said. 'Talk to me.'

Frida dropped her teacup. It broke into several pieces on the stone pavers. She didn't even seem to notice.

'Frida?' Charlie said again. 'Are you OK?'

Frida shook her head. 'The pressure,' she said and touched her hand to her head and then her chest. 'It ... hurts so bad.'

'Try to take deep breaths,' Charlie suggested as Frida's breathing grew rapid and shallow.

'I can't,' Frida gasped. 'I'm not getting any air.'

Charlie called Greger over.

'Go and get Gustav. Hurry.'

Just then, Gustav and Charlotte stepped through the front door. Gustav started to say something about grave robbing but broke off when he realised Frida was struggling to breathe.

'What's going on?' he asked.

'I think we need to take her to the hospital,' Charlie said.

'I'm coming with you,' Charlotte said.

Charlie looked at Gustav, who seemed to think it was perfectly natural for Charlotte to go instead of him.

Frida's breathing was still laboured in the car. In the rear-view mirror, Charlie saw her put her head on Charlotte's shoulder and whisper something.

'What was that?' Charlotte asked.

'I didn't do anything to her,' Frida said. 'I love my daughter.'

Charlotte stroked her arm and whispered back that she knew that.

Charlie thought about their backgrounds, about Charlotte's scar and Frida's childhood. Maybe they had both journeyed out of darkness into ... well, into what?

*

The olfactory sense is most closely linked to memory, Charlie thought as they entered the psychiatric emergency ward and the smell of disinfectant triggered a slideshow of images of Johan in his hospital bed. *I'm afraid your friend's condition is very serious.*

They only had to wait a few minutes before a doctor came out into the waiting room.

Frida's breathing had slowed slightly, but she still looked very pale and was clutching her chest.

'Per,' she said when she saw the doctor. 'I can't breathe.'

Charlie looked up at the doctor, who wasn't wearing a name tag.

'She's been there before,' Charlie said after they'd left Frida and Charlotte and were walking towards the car.

'Yes,' Greger said. 'That much was obvious.'

'So maybe it's true what Madelene Svedin said, that Gustav has told her about Frida's problems.'

'What are you doing?' Greger asked when Charlie pulled out her phone.

'Calling Gustav. We don't have time for this anymore.'

She held her hand up when Greger looked like he was going to say something, because Gustav had picked up.

'How is she?' he asked, not bothering with pleasantries.

'Not great, but Charlotte stayed with her, and she's being seen by a doctor right now,' Charlie said.

'Good,' Gustav replied. 'She has been sleeping very poorly and all of this ... it's too much for her.'

'It's not the first time she's been in the psychiatric emergency ward,' Charlie said.

'What do you mean?' Gustav said.

'I mean it's not her first visit,' Charlie replied. 'Why didn't either of you tell us that when we asked how she has been feeling? The last time I brought that up with you, you said she had just been tired lately.'

Silence on the other end. Charlie waited.

'She has had a tough time,' Gustav said eventually. 'But that has nothing to do with this. Her parents were alcoholics, and it was ... really bloody tough. Those things leave their marks, and I haven't wanted to bring it up when everything is so difficult.'

Charlie thought that he didn't seem to have had reservations about discussing his wife's mental-health issues with his mistress.

'She would never hurt Beatrice,' Gustav went on. 'I swear. I know my wife well enough to know that.'

'Let me tell you something about mental illness,' Charlie said. 'It can change a person's personality.'

'Mentally ill people are primarily a danger to themselves,' Gustav retorted. 'I've talked to a few psychiatrists, so—'

'True,' Charlie said. 'But sometimes they do harm others, particularly when there is post-partum psychosis.'

'Frida would never hurt Beatrice,' Gustav repeated. 'I know it. You're simply going to have to believe me.'

And that's exactly the problem here, Charlie thought after ending the call. That Gustav had repeatedly asked them to take his word for things, to trust him, but that each time, it had turned out they shouldn't have.

36

Charlie didn't realise she'd had nothing to eat since breakfast until she saw the sandwiches in the conference room.

She checked her watch. It was almost eight.

It was clear they were all losing hope. Stina looked pale standing in front of them. She turned to Charlie and asked her to tell the rest of the team about Frida.

'Greger and I just drove her over to the psychiatric emergency ward,' Charlie said. 'It was after we dug up the cat in their garden, she was struggling to breathe and ... well, I guess it was a panic attack.'

'I don't understand why you were so gung-ho about digging,' Roy said. 'Did you really think you were going to find anything?'

'No, but we felt we needed to make sure,' Charlie replied.

Greger took over and said it had come to their attention that Frida had experienced similar episodes before.

'And why didn't they tell us that?' Roy asked.

'I assume one doesn't talk about such things,' Charlie said. 'And as far as Gustav's concerned, he seems to be keeping as much as he possibly can from us.'

'This puts Frida in a different light,' Stina commented. 'I

mean, a psychologically unstable mother who was alone with the child when she disappeared, a mother who has been known to shake her baby. And there are no signs of anyone else around the house …' She turned to Charlie. 'Do you think we can talk to her now? I mean, do you think she's well enough?'

'I think we have to,' Charlie said. 'And we need to officially make her a suspect.' She nodded towards the picture of Frida on the whiteboard. 'So we can access her medical records.'

'Agreed,' Stina said.

The conversation turned to Amina. Sebastian and Roy had talked to several of her neighbours and two of them had, independently of each other, said the woman in the flat next to Amina's often put her baby outside in her pram and let her cry. Charlie could understand why Amina had picked her up. She would have done the same thing with a sad and cold baby if no one had come to the door.

'I haven't been able to reach Kasim yet,' Stina said. 'So we haven't verified Amina's alibi. Our Danish colleagues will be in touch as soon as they find him.'

'It might be worth calling them again,' Charlie suggested. 'Sometimes things get lost in the transnational shuffle.' She asked Stina for the number of the officer she had talked to in Copenhagen.

'His name is Mikael Carsten,' Stina said while Charlie waited to be connected.

'Do you prefer Danish or English?' Mikael Carsten asked after Charlie had introduced herself and explained her reason for calling.

'Danish is fine,' Charlie replied. 'If you're OK with Swedish. We're working against the clock here, so I figured I'd call again.'

'We understand that it's an emergency,' Mikael said. 'In fact, I was just about to call you.'

He started to speak faster, and Charlie regretted not asking him to stick to English.

'So, if I understood you right just now, he's with his relatives in a flat in Copenhagen,' Charlie said.

'That's correct,' Mikael confirmed. Then he switched to English and told her that Kasim had confirmed everything Amina had told them. He had contacted her because he was in a bad way, and he had asked her to come to his house. The times she had given also tallied with Kasim's version. And no, there was no baby in the flat.

On her way back to the conference room, Charlie ran into Roy. 'The NFC just called,' he said.

'Do they have anything?'

'Well, first off, all the DNA found in the pram belonged to either Frida, Gustav, or Beatrice herself. And Gustav isn't the biological father.'

'OK,' Charlie said, thinking that Roy looked strangely excited about something they already knew.

'But they also discovered something interesting about Frida,' Roy went on.

'What about Frida?'

'She's not the biological mother.'

Sara

'Where are we going?' Lo asked as we left the town behind. 'We're in the middle of the woods.'

'Wait and see,' I said.

'Can you even drive here?' Lo said when I turned off the road.

'We're here,' I announced.

The house with its dark windows looked eerie in the moon-light.

The forest around us rustled as we walked towards the front door. Lo kept close to me and cursed every time her high heels sank into the soft ground.

'It's bloody dark out here,' Lo said. She pulled out her phone and turned on the flashlight. The tiny light made the atmosphere even eerier. 'What does it say?' Lo asked, gesturing towards the old wooden sign.

'Lyckebo,' I said.

'Is it your house?'

'No, it belongs to a ... friend.'

I told her about the police officer with the boy's name who had grown up in this house with her mother, Betty Lager. Loudmouth Betty whom my dad had always talked so wistfully about. *That woman sure knew how to have fun.* I told her about the parties in Lyckebo, the ones that had lasted for days and drawn people from all over Gullspång, and even as far away as Karlstad.

And I told her about the rumours that Betty haunted the house, that several of Dad's friends had seen her dancing in the garden long after she died. Lasse Smed had sat in our kitchen back home, swearing that he'd seen Betty Lager in her red dress among the trees outside Lyckebo. *I swear on my mother's grave that she was there, that Betty Lager was there and asked me to dance.*

'And this is where you think we should sleep tonight?' Lo said.

I told her it was fine, that I had spent both days and nights in the house without anything bad ever happening. We should be more afraid of the living than the dead.

'I'm afraid of both the living and the dead,' Lo replied. 'But all right, let's go. Should we break a window?'

'No need, there's a key.' We had reached the wooden pallets by the front door. I lifted up the flowerpot and grabbed the keys. 'Come in,' I said.

'Turn the lights on,' Lo said.

'There's no electricity.'

I found the matches in the spice rack above the old wood-burning stove and lit the candles still sitting in wine bottles on the kitchen table. There was firewood in the basket next to the fireplace in the living room.

I lit a fire and we huddled up next to each other in front of it.

'I could live here,' Lo said. She stroked my hair. 'I could live here with you.'

'What about the salon?' I asked. 'The salon and your mum?'

'She could come, too. People get haircuts around here, right? We could buy this house,' Lo went on. 'We could have the salon in the basement, and—'

'There's no basement,' I said.

'In some other room, then,' Lo said. 'Why don't you give me a tour?'

I showed her the downstairs bedroom, the one with the childish floral wallpaper and shelves full of books with damp pages.

'Was this where she lived?' Lo asked. 'The person you know?'

'Yes, I think so.'

Then Lo wanted to see the upstairs. Because there was an upstairs, right?

I told her there was, but I'd never been up there.

'Why not?'

'Because ... because they say that's where she died, Betty Lager.'

'Are you scared?'

I said I wasn't, but that it didn't feel right.

But Lo wanted to go up and see it. She said all my talk had made her curious.

We brought two candles and climbed the steep stairs to the first floor. Lo led the way, looking decidedly unsteady.

'A child lived here, too,' Lo said as we stepped into the room on the left side of the landing. 'Did she have more children?'

'Not that I know.'

'It's falling apart,' she said and shone the light on a couple of loose wooden boards.

'Or maybe someone was building something,' I said and went over to the window.

The sky outside was clear. I thought about all the times I'd stayed in this house when Dad was going through particularly bad periods. It had mostly been during the summers when the sun barely ever set. Everything was so different now, in the dark.

When I turned around, Lo was gone.

'Lo?' I called out.

No answer.

I went back out to the landing, closed my eyes, and listened, but the only thing I could hear was my own rapid breathing.

When I opened my eyes again, I saw her, Betty Lager, in her red dress. She was dancing towards me.

'What's the matter?' Lo called after me as I stumbled down the stairs. 'I was just kidding.'

'Cut it out,' I said when she followed me down and put her arm around me. 'It's not funny, Lo.' I suddenly felt completely sober.

'I'm sorry,' Lo said. 'But there's something about this dress. See how nicely it fits me?'

She twirled.

'Admit it fits me bloody perfectly.'

I told her there was nothing wrong with the fit, but that I didn't like that she'd taken Betty's dress, that it was offensive, that she had to take it off.

Lo sighed and pulled the dress off over her head.

'And put your own clothes back on,' I said. 'It's freezing in here.'

'They're still upstairs,' Lo said.

'Then go get them.'

'Will you come with me?'

While Lo changed, I looked around the room. The bookshelf below the slanted ceiling was filled with framed photographs.

I turned on the flashlight on my phone to have a closer look.

'Oh my god,' I whispered. 'Oh my fucking god.'

'What?' Lo said. 'What is it?'

'See for yourself,' I replied and handed her the photograph and my phone. 'Don't you see who it is?'

'Yes,' Lo said. 'I do see.'

It was insane, I thought, staring at the photograph of a young woman with a child in her arms and an overgrown garden in the background. The picture must have been taken at the same time as the one we'd found in the letter from her mother, the one she had wanted to return because it was too painful to look at.

Betty Lager was the daughter of the woman who had written those letters and that meant ... well, that meant the police officer I'd got to know that summer with Annabelle was ... she was that woman's grandchild.

'How did she die?' Lo asked. 'What happened to Betty Lager?'

We had put more logs on the fire, and she was lying with her head in my lap, holding her hands out towards the warmth.

I said I didn't know, that I'd heard everything from suicide to overdose.

'Aren't those the same thing?' Lo said and turned to me.

'I guess.'

'What about her daughter? What happened to her little girl?'

'She moved away. What's the matter?' I said when I realised she was crying.

'It's just horrible,' Lo sobbed. 'It's just all too horrible.'

I thought it was weird that she would cry like that over people she'd never met. I didn't know what to do, so I just stroked her hair until the fire died and she fell asleep.

37

The house on Hammarö was dark, but coming back in the morning wasn't an option.

Charlotte Jolander opened the door.

'What are you doing here so late?' she said, pulling her robe tighter around herself.

'We need to talk to Gustav,' Charlie replied.

'He's not here,' Charlotte said. 'It's just me and Frida. They gave her sedatives and discharged her, so I ... I'm here with her so she doesn't have to be alone.'

'And where's Gustav?' Greger asked, peering over Charlotte's shoulder as though he didn't quite believe her.

'He ... he and David are out looking for Beatrice.'

'Right now?'

'Yes.'

'Do you know where they went?' Charlie asked.

'No,' Charlotte replied. 'They told me they were going to look into a couple of things.'

'But no specifics?'

Charlotte shook her head.

It was odd, going out to look this late, Charlie mused. It would have been one thing if Beatrice were older and lost in the woods. What did they think they were going to accomplish at this hour?

'How is Frida doing?' Greger asked.

'Not well.'

'Can you wake her?'

'She just fell asleep. I really think we should leave her be. The doctor said sleep is the most important thing for her now, otherwise, her condition could get worse.'

Charlie took out her phone and called Gustav. It went straight to voicemail. Same thing when Greger tried to call David.

Charlie asked him to go into the living room and keep trying. Then she turned to Charlotte.

'Charlotte,' she said. 'We really do need to straighten some things out with Frida and Gustav, but since neither of them is available, maybe you could answer some of our questions.'

She could tell Charlotte was reluctant.

'Time is running out,' Charlie went on. 'Beatrice is out there somewhere. Don't let her down.'

'I don't know if I can help you,' Charlotte said.

'We've had the results of the DNA tests,' Charlie continued. 'They showed that Frida and Gustav are not Beatrice's biological parents. Did you know that?'

'You'll have to discuss that with them,' Charlotte said.

'But you lived in Moscow when they had Beatrice, right? And you spent a lot of time with them. Shouldn't you have noticed that Frida wasn't pregnant?'

'Like I said, I think you should discuss this with Frida and Gustav.'

'But since that's not possible at the moment,' Charlie pressed, 'and we're in a race against the clock. Clearly, things are not what they seem here, you all know more than you're telling us.'

Charlotte said nothing.

'What if it were your daughter,' Charlie said. 'What if it were Mika?'

'I'll call Gustav,' Charlotte replied. She pulled out her phone. And this time, Gustav answered. 'The police are here,' Charlotte said. 'They want to talk to you. Yes, right now.'

Fifteen minutes later, Gustav was back. He had swapped his suit for something that looked like hunting gear and his hair was dishevelled.

'We've been out looking,' he said. 'Has something happened?'

'We just found out that Frida isn't Beatrice's biological parent either,' Greger replied. 'Would you mind telling us what this is all about?'

Gustav looked at Charlotte as though she should be the one to answer the question. But instead of saying anything, she turned around and walked off towards the stairs.

'Do you mind if I sit down?' Gustav said.

They followed him into the living room. It wasn't quite as tidy anymore, Charlie noted. The blankets were no longer perfect squares over the arms of the sofa and the cushions were visibly rumpled.

'It was an egg donation,' Gustav said. 'An egg *and* sperm donation.'

He explained what that entailed, an anonymous egg donor who had been matched with an equally anonymous sperm donor. The fertilised egg had been implanted into Frida's uterus.

'This is getting increasingly incomprehensible,' Charlie said. 'Not the method,' she continued when Gustav launched into a more detailed explanation of the procedure. 'Why you and Frida have kept these key facts from us. I want to know why.'

'We didn't want it known,' Gustav said. 'By people around here or by Beatrice. We figured two anonymous donors couldn't possibly have anything to do with this, so ...'

'But didn't you realise we'd find out when we swabbed you?' Charlie asked. 'Why didn't you tell us then?'

'I don't know,' Gustav said. 'I guess neither one of us is thinking clearly right now.'

38

It was close to midnight when they got back to the hotel. Charlie had called Stina from the car to bring her up to date. She told her Gustav and David had been out looking by themselves in the dark, that Gustav must have thought that was a better way for him to spend his time than taking care of his wife, who was clearly not doing well. But maybe parents who had lost a child weren't paragons of rationality. Either way, they were going to have to talk to Gustav, Frida, David, and Charlotte again.

'I think I'll take the stairs today,' Charlie said as they approached the lifts.

'I'm not going to stop you this time,' Greger said with a smile. 'When do you want to meet tomorrow?'

'I told Stina we'd be there at seven unless there were new developments.'

'Great, then I guess we should try to get some kip now.'

'Yes,' Charlie said. 'I think that would be for the best.'

When she got to her room, Charlie took out her laptop and googled egg and sperm donations in Russia. Her search returned articles about happy parents who, after years of failed attempts in Sweden, had gone to try their luck in a country with less strict regulations. There were miracle children, mothers and fathers gushing about how they had finally been given the help they needed to become parents. Then followed critical voices pointing out the issues inherent in the idea of renting poor women's wombs, horror stories about deaths during pregnancy, children born with defects who were no longer wanted, lives ruined.

Charlie left the site and went to the Flashback thread about Beatrice.

There were a lot of new comments, although most seemed like empty gossip. But among the drivel, an anonymous user had written: *Of course you'll have problems if you choose your wife from the dregs of society.*

What do you mean? Justitia had asked, but there had been no answer.

Justitia again: *Source?*

Further down, another user had written: *If I were the police, I'd look into Charlotte Jolander's past. It's far from immaculate, believe me.*

That comment, too, was followed by unanswered questions about what the poster had meant.

Charlie googled Charlotte Jolander. The usual information about age, home address, and marital status came up, then her name on some petition to install speed bumps outside the local school, and a fact box about her as the wife of David Jolander in an article about him. There was nothing to indicate a murky history.

Charlie reread the comment on Flashback. *If I were the police, I'd look into Charlotte Jolander's past. It's far from immaculate, believe me.*

She thought about Charlotte, her beautiful house, her lovely family, and then, the scar on her wrist. Was it a leftover from a previous life?

But Flashback was a gossip forum, Charlie reminded herself, and people would write anything when they didn't have to sign their names to it. It could be made up or exaggerated. That said, some of the things on there were true. She closed her laptop. There was nothing more to be done tonight. The best thing she could do now was to let it all go and give her brain a rest.

Falling asleep turned out to be impossible. The case had kept the thoughts of the night she couldn't remember at bay, but now they came flooding back. Various scenarios played out in her head. The man, bigger now, pinning her naked body to the hallway floor. Or maybe he was just a guy who had helped a hammered woman home. Maybe he was just a regular guy?

There are no regular guys, Charline.

The dreams. They come more often now. I'm treading water, holding the child in arms numb from cold. She slips out of my grasp, sinks, disappears into the blackness. And even as I panic, it's as though I can finally relax. She's gone. There's nothing left to fight for. I let go and follow her. It's all over.

39

'We're still waiting for Roy,' Stina said as Charlie and Greger took their seats in the conference room, both holding a cup of coffee. She was wearing the same clothes as the night before and didn't seem to have looked in a mirror at any point. Her hair was wild and her blouse so rumpled that Charlie suspected she might have slept in it

'It's seven,' Charlie said. 'We'll have to start without him.'

Stina nodded, went over to the whiteboard, and picked up a marker. She held it in the air next to the picture of Beatrice for a moment, before writing a question mark and turning to them.

'As you already know, it has come to our attention that Beatrice isn't Gustav and Frida's biological child. According to their most recent information, Beatrice was conceived through an egg and sperm donation in Moscow. Both donors were anonymous. They had intended to keep this from everyone, including Beatrice.'

Charlie thought about the poem she'd read in Beatrice's room. *My laughing bundle with sun-bleached hair, what was life before you came?*

Roy joined them, whispering an apology.

'Yesterday,' Stina went on, 'we also found out that Frida Palmgren has been treated for mental-health issues on and off. And Charlie has new information about Charlotte Jolander.'

Stina nodded to Charlie.

'I wouldn't say I have any new information, I just came across a statement about how we should look into her past, that it's not as immaculate as it may seem. But she's not in any of our databases. Do any of you know anything about Charlotte?'

'I think she's originally from Stockholm,' Roy said. 'I don't know anything about her past.'

No one else did either.

'I happened to notice a self-harm scar,' Charlie said, 'on her forearm ... And I just had the feeling that there might be something to the rumours saying she has had a tough time.'

'I don't see what that has to do with the case, though?' Roy said.

'I never said it did,' Charlie retorted. 'But it can't hurt to talk to her. I'll do it.'

Charlotte suggested meeting at a café by the name of King Creole in the part of town called Haga. The place was, true to its name, dedicated to Elvis Presley.

Charlotte had bought coffee for them both. Charlie took a sip while she looked around the cluttered room. Every way she turned, her eyes met Elvis's sultry gaze.

'I like this place,' Charlotte said, 'and it's not usually crowded, so it's a good place to speak privately.' She took a sip of her coffee and let out a curse when a few drops spilled on her jumper.

Charlie watched her nervous movements. 'How are you holding up?' she asked.

'I'm shit, to be honest,' Charlotte said. 'The past few days have been awful and there's no end in sight. It feels like an eternity since she disappeared, like it's already ...' She lowered her eyes. 'It feels like it's already too late.'

'It's not,' Charlie said.

'How do you know?'

'I have to believe it. I could never forgive myself if I knew I hadn't done absolutely everything in my power to find her,' Charlie replied. She met Charlotte's eyes and tried to appeal to the same feeling in her.

'I've barely slept since she disappeared,' Charlotte said. 'My mind is racing but I'm not getting anywhere.'

Charlie nodded.

'You're from Stockholm originally, aren't you?' she asked and noticed Charlotte's expression changing.

'Yes, why do you ask?'

'I'm just trying to get a complete picture. Maybe you could tell me a little bit about your background.'

'I don't understand why,' Charlotte said. She leaned back as though she wanted to get as far away as possible from both Charlie and the subject. 'Who have you been talking to?'

'Does it matter?'

'I just feel like ... well, I suppose it's easy to feel paranoid.' Charlotte picked up a paper napkin from the table and folded it in half. 'I just want to forget my former life, but it's hard when people insist on digging it up.'

'No one is out to ruin your life, and everything you tell me will stay between you and the police,' Charlie said. So long as it has nothing to do with Beatrice, she added inwardly.

'I was a drug addict,' Charlotte said. She had lowered her voice and was looking around anxiously. 'I started using in my teens,' she went on, 'because ... it made me feel good. At first, it was just a little bit on the weekends, some weed and sometimes amphetamine. You always think you can keep it at that level, you know, that you're not like everyone else, and—'

She was interrupted by a bleached-blonde young woman who came over to their table and shrilly offered her condolences. How was Frida doing? Would Charlotte give them a hug from her? It was all just such a nightmare.

She reeled off cliché after cliché, but then, what else was there really to say? Charlie mused. What was there to do other than to offer condolences and lament the cruel world we live in and all the crazy people that inhabit it?

'Bloody hell,' Charlotte said once the woman had gone back to her table. 'Suddenly, everyone's their friend. But I guess that's what happens in situations like this. Where were we?'

'Drugs,' Charlie said. 'You thought you were different ...'

'Yes, and obviously I was wrong, because I was exactly like everyone else. The sad thing is that once you discover that, it's already too late, you're already hooked. And you keep pushing your own boundaries. At first, you think you'll never do anything stronger than weed, and then, never cocaine, and then, never heroin, and definitely never bloody syringes. But then one day, there you are, in a public bathroom, breaking every goddamn promise ...'

Charlie nodded. She knew everything about breaking promises to yourself.

'It's the addiction,' Charlotte said. 'It's stronger than love, than your will to live, than everything. I remember feeling sorry for people who didn't do drugs, they were stuck doing boring jobs and had boring families. Their lives seemed so

... empty.' She laughed mirthlessly. 'But I'm never going to become one of those smug ex-addicts, the kind that beat their chests and think they're better than the ones who didn't make it. A lot of the time, it's just luck. I don't think I'd be alive today if it weren't for Gustav.'

'Gustav?'

'Yes. He hired me as a receptionist for one of his companies. I had been clean for six months and was on the verge of relapsing because re-entering society was so hard. But then I met Gustav and he offered me a job.'

'Why did he do that? I mean, did you just run into each other on the street?'

'He was up in Stockholm and we met through ... common acquaintances. Does it matter how we met?'

Charlie shook her head and thought about how unlikely it was that a successful businessman and a young drug addict would have common acquaintances, unless it had something to do with drugs or sex.

'Anyway, I told him I was sick of Stockholm,' Charlotte went on, 'that I wanted to start over somewhere else, and that's when he offered me both a job and a place to live.'

'That was ... nice of him,' Charlie said.

'And that's how I met David.' She took another sip of coffee. 'So that's my story. Rags to riches, eh?'

Charlie nodded.

'I would prefer if you didn't mention this to David,' Charlotte said. 'He doesn't know. Very few people in my life do, and I would like to keep it that way.'

'David doesn't know?'

'He knows parts of it, but I've made it sound more like I ... just did some drugs at parties. Neither he nor Gustav knows how bad it was, but it seems you've managed to ferret it out somehow.'

'How do you think he would take it if he found out?' Charlie asked.

'Not well, I imagine. Appearances are important to him, and I ... I suppose I've tried to adapt and be what he wants me to be.'

'Sounds like hard work,' Charlie said.

Charlotte nodded.

'Do you think it's the same for Frida, with Gustav, I mean?'

'I don't want to discuss their marriage,' Charlotte said. She took another sip of her coffee. 'But there's a saying,' she went on, 'that a woman who marries for money is worth every penny. I believe both Frida and I would say that's true.'

'Would you mind expanding on that?' Charlie said.

'Well, it's common knowledge, I think, that men with money and power can't be trusted, especially if they're charming and used to getting their own way.'

'Charlotte,' Charlie said. 'Have you really told me everything you know about what might be behind Beatrice's disappearance?'

'You sound like you think I might have been involved,' Charlotte said. Then she lowered her voice. 'I may have done drugs, but that's hardly the same as kidnapping my friends' baby. I'm a mother myself. I don't enjoy being treated like a suspect.'

'I'm not accusing you of anything,' Charlie said. 'I just have a feeling you're not telling me everything you know. Maybe that's because you're trying to protect someone, or because you don't think it's important. Like with Amina, for example.

You gave her a false alibi because *you* had decided she was innocent.'

'She is innocent.'

There was a pause. Charlotte looked down at her wedding ring. Her nails were painted a pale shade of pink and there was a gold bracelet around her wrist. Charlie was no expert at jewellery, clothes, or handbags, but everything Charlotte wore looked expensive. She tried to imagine this woman in a dirty bathroom somewhere with a strap around her upper arm. It was difficult.

'I just don't want you to have regrets,' Charlie said. 'I don't want you to have to live with the knowledge that you could have saved a child but chose not to. I want you to say something now, before it's too late.'

Charlotte looked up from her hands.

'What if it's already too late,' she said.

Sara

Lo was naked in the garden. Running around like a crazy person between bushes, trees, and the headless angel. I hurried over to Nicki's room.

'It's Lo,' I said. 'She's … I think she's lost her mind.'

Nicki got up and ran over to the window. 'I see her,' she said when I pointed. 'What the fuck is going on?'

Lo disappeared behind a tree and it was a while before we spotted her again. She looked like the forest nymph in the story Dad used to read to me when I was little.

'We need to wake the staff,' Nicki said.

'They're already up,' I replied and pointed. Because now, Marianne, Frans, and several support staff came out and started to chase Lo. But Lo was too fast. She feinted her way past anyone who came near. If the scene hadn't been so disturbing, I would have laughed. 'We have to go out there,' I said.

Nicki grabbed my arm and said we probably shouldn't.

'But we need to find out what's wrong with her, come on.'

I thought Marianne would order us back inside, but instead she seemed relieved to see us.

'Nicki and Sara,' she said. 'Could you try to talk to her?'

'What happened?' Nicki asked.

'I'm afraid I can't—'

'If you want us to help, we need to know why she's running around like a wild animal,' Nicki said. 'What happened?'

'It's Donna,' Marianne said. 'Her mother. She's dead.'

Three days later, Lo disappeared. No one knew where she had gone. Marianne called the police, but they didn't seem to take it very seriously.

'Why haven't they found her?' I said when Lo had been missing for twenty-four hours. I was panicking. I felt like I wouldn't be able to go on living without Lo.

'She's not a priority,' Marianne said. 'The disappearance of a girl who is almost of age isn't considered very important. Besides, Lo has absconded before and she has always come back eventually.'

'But she's upset,' I said. 'She's in shock, did you tell the police that? Did you tell them her mother just died?'

'Yes,' Marianne replied. 'I told them all those things.'

'Well, where did she go the other times?' I asked.

Marianne said she didn't know, but that she thought Lo had mostly driven around looking for her mother.

'She didn't know where she lived?'

'No,' Marianne said. 'Her mother moved a lot.'

After dinner that night, I lay down on Lo's bed and breathed in the smell of hairspray in her pillow. When I turned to the wall, I noticed the edge of a book sticking up in the gap between the mattress and the bed frame, Lo's notebook. I shouldn't, I thought, holding it in my hands. But then I remembered Lo saying that if you wanted to keep something to yourself at Rödminnet, you had to lock it up. She must have wanted me to find it. I opened it to the first page and read: *A Sunshine Story*.

So, here it finally is, I thought as I turned the pages, my heart thumping in my chest. Lo's story.

On the next page was a photograph. It was Donna with a tiny, newborn baby that had to be Lo in her arms. The picture was taken in a hospital bed. I studied Donna's face. She was beautiful, but the teeth revealed by her smile looked like they belonged to a much older person. They reminded me of Dad.

I paused for a moment before turning the page. Shouldn't I just accept Lo's story about the misunderstanding that had separated the two of them, about all the things that could have been if it weren't for social services ruining their lives? But how could I, now that it was all here, right in front of me?

Mum, the next page read. *Mum is red lipstick, high heels, the smell of flowers, and soap. Mum is silky hair, soft skin, and laughter. I hear her heart beating when I sit on her lap, leaning against her chest.*

Then a line across the page and a different tone:

Mum is grief and betrayal. Mum is blue lips, screaming, and crying. Mum is I'm sorry I'm sorry I'm sorry. Mum is a body made of nothing but bones.

Confusing, I thought and read on. The text was full of weird rhyming poems and words I didn't quite understand. One page seemed like a regular diary, while the next was random memories and thoughts. Some pages about her mother were more coherent. Lo wrote about Donna, about how much she loved her, about how sad it made her that she always chose drugs over everything else, about the intervention I'd heard so much about. *They just came and took me for no reason.*

But in this version, it was there, the reason: the drugs

and the neglect. But it was still horrible to read about social services prying Lo and Donna's fingers apart and carrying Lo out of the flat. She had kicked, bit, fought, but she was just a little girl, and there were so many of them. Donna had run out onto the balcony. Lo and the social workers had watched her climb onto the railing, eight floors up, and scream that she was going to jump unless they gave her back her daughter, but not even that had helped. Donna had just tipped backwards onto the balcony, and it was several years before Lo saw her again.

Foster family number one, the next page said. And then followed a description of four foster children and foster parents who seemed to hate them. *We weren't allowed to speak without being spoken to, and we couldn't question anything. We learnt to make our beds like soldiers and not to cry when things hurt or went wrong. That was supposed to give us the most important thing a person can have: character. And maybe that character did come in handy when I moved to foster family number two.*

I read on about families that had at best been loveless and at worst violent. And then I reached the first residential care home Lo had been placed in.

They said everything would be better there, that I would be able to talk to experts who could help me. But I didn't meet a single expert. That's where things really started to go downhill for me. I felt so lonely, like there was no one who really loved me, no one who would catch me if I fell. I stopped participating in group activities, so they punished me, and when they punished me, I got angry, and when I got angry, there was RFA and restraints and then ... then it was like I stopped feeling.

I put the book down, climbed down from the bed and went over to the window. The sun was shining down on Rödminnet's shrubberies and the headless angel. I thought about what Nicki had said about her when I pointed out that her head was missing: *But she does have wings, for all the good it'll do her. I mean, what's the point of being able to fly if you can't see where you're going.*

I thought about all the times Lo had sat on the bench in front of the statue, waiting for her mum, who never came.

I didn't want to go back to Lo's bed and keep reading, because I could sense the worst was yet to come. I regretted opening the notebook in the first place, but since I had, I needed to finish it.

'What are you doing?'

I gave a start because I hadn't heard anyone coming in.

'It's her notebook, isn't it?' Nicki had stepped up onto my bed and was peering up at me in the top bunk.

'Get lost,' I said.

But Nicki didn't get lost. She heaved herself up, crawled in next to me and demanded to read too, because didn't she have a right to know Lo's story when she had turned herself inside out for her? Several times, too.

I sighed and Nicki lay down next to me on Lo's pillow. I flipped to the page where I had left off.

'Mum said enough of homes and foster families for me. She said I was going to go live with a good person, a person who loved her. This person wanted to take care of me now and I was going to go to live with her family. She would never treat me badly, because she was one of us. I would be safe with her.'

'Sounds nice,' Nicki said.

'I bet there's a catch,' I said. 'Why else would she have ended up here?'

'True,' Nicki replied. 'Keep going.'

'Close your eyes,' I said. Because I couldn't bear Nicki staring at Lo's book.

'I would be safe with her and maybe that's why everything was so scary later, because when you think you're safe, you let your guard down, and when you let your guard down, it takes you longer to realise something's wrong. I didn't notice when the flames started to lick my feet.'

The next paragraph didn't say anything about the flames, it was about the children: *'I loved the girl the most. She reminded me a little bit of me when I was little, or the way I imagine I would have been if Mum hadn't been sick.'*

'That's not the end, is it?' Nicki said. 'It can't stop now, it just got going!'

'No,' I said. 'It's in two parts. It says "Part Two" here.'

'So, read.'

I turned the page and read.

'Part Two: Hell.

I have come to lead you to the other shore, into eternal darkness.'

'What is she on about?' Nicki said.

I told her to be quiet and just listen to the story she'd apparently been dying to hear for so long.

Then I read about the big, glittering city, about illuminated streets and dark alleyways. About the language which had sounded so alien at first, but which had gradually become familiar.

Three pages later, I understood why Lo had named this part of the story *Hell*, because, one night, a door cracked open, eyes peered in.

'It was so sudden. I couldn't believe it. If I don't move, I thought. If I just lie still, nothing will happen. I thought about a foster brother I'd had once, about the live mice he used to put in his snake's

terrarium, the way they sat there, paralysed by fear. They knew the slightest movement would get them eaten. It was the same for me now. But shallow breaths and staying absolutely still didn't help. He flipped me onto my stomach, pushed up my nightgown, pulled aside my knickers and entered me.

'It didn't happen, I thought the next morning. This family man who gave his wife a good-morning kiss and wiped up his daughter's spilled milk ... he wasn't capable of pushing a girl down into her pillow and ... it was impossible.'

'What a fucking psycho,' Nicki said. She had sat up and was punching the mattress. 'Are you crying?'

'Don't touch me,' I said when she pulled the hair off my face.

'Then keep reading.'

'I need a minute,' I said and put the book down.

When I closed my eyes, I saw Svante's grinning face before me. *Relax, this feels good. Can't you feel it? Can't you feel how good this is?*

Nicki didn't want to wait, so she took over. Stutteringly, she read on. I listened with growing revulsion to the nightly visits in the home where Lo was supposed to be safe.

'I can't make the different pieces of him fit together. During the day, he's a successful family man, and then, after the sun goes down, a creature of darkness.'

40

Charlotte wanted to leave the café, so they went down to the canal and took a seat on a bench by the water.

'I still have one friend in Stockholm,' Charlotte said. 'I wanted to make a clean break when I moved here, but I couldn't cut her out completely because she saved my life once. I had overdosed. Deliberately, because I couldn't go on, but she broke into my flat and saved me. We got clean together after that, but, unfortunately, she relapsed.'

Charlie nodded. She didn't want to ask too much, just let Charlotte talk.

'Most people do,' Charlotte went on. 'Relapse, I mean. But those aren't the stories you hear. People who are down-and-out or dead don't have a voice. They're not the ones sitting on morning-show sofas or touring schools, talking to young people.'

Where is she going with this? Charlie wondered. Where is this story taking us?

'She had a child,' Charlotte continued. 'A daughter.' She gazed out at the canal. 'I don't even want to think about all the things that little girl went through. It was as though we all forgot there was a child in the flat. Me too. We just kept partying.'

'And then what happened?' Charlie asked when Charlotte didn't say anything else.

'The child was taken from her,' Charlotte said. 'I understand why, but it was still horrible. And the girl, the daughter, I kept an eye on her from afar. She was shuttled between foster families and care homes, and it didn't seem to be going very well for her. There was a lot of arguing about her, so I called social services and told her she could come stay with us. I figured things might work out for her if she could just be with someone who understood, someone who really cared. So ... we took her in, David and I. She was with us in Moscow.'

Charlotte's phone rang. She pulled it out, glanced at the screen and declined the call.

'And how did it go?' Charlie asked.

'It went well,' Charlotte said. 'It went well at first. The children loved her, and David and I did too. She was obviously scarred by her experiences. You need a lot of luck in the foster care system, and she had not been lucky.'

Charlie nodded and sent a grateful thought to the family she had ended up with, the safety, the boundaries, and the care they had provided.

'But we were able to talk about it,' Charlotte went on. 'We became very close.'

'And then?'

'There was trouble,' Charlotte said. 'She was pregnant and ... she didn't know who the father was. David and I tried to talk to her about ... getting rid of it. I mean, she was just sixteen and already so vulnerable and ...'

'So, what happened?'

'She kept it.'

'And ...?'

'Frida and Gustav had dreamt of having children for a long time, but it just wasn't happening for them. They had tried everything, even a surrogate, but she had a late-term miscarriage. They were both pretty distraught, so ... well, it was decided that they would adopt the baby. They adopted Beatrice.'

The series of lies they had been told played through Charlie's mind. Sperm donation, egg donation, anonymity. She felt her cheeks flush with anger.

'Why?' she said. 'Why didn't you say anything?'

'We promised Gustav and Frida we wouldn't. They really didn't want anyone to know Beatrice wasn't their biological child. They weren't even going to tell Beatrice.'

'Where is her biological mother?'

'In a home for wayward girls. It's called Rödminnet. Gustav and Frida didn't see the need to bring it up, since she ... well, she's in that place.'

'What's the girl's name?' Charlie asked.

'Lo,' Charlotte replied. 'Her name is Lo Moon.'

41

Charlie jogged back to her car. She called Rödminnet for the second time in less than three minutes. The answering machine again. This time, she left a message explaining who she was and asking someone from the management to call her back as soon as possible.

Charlie knew about Rödminnet, the old mental hospital. She remembered the stories she'd heard as a child in Gullspång. There had even been a rhyme:

If your mind is cracked and bent,
Rödminnet's where you'll be sent.

So that was where she was, Lo Moon, Beatrice's biological mother. For the first time in this investigation, they'd found someone with a real motive.

'The documents from Russia are fake,' Charlie said ten minutes later as she entered the conference room where Stina had called an emergency meeting.

'Beatrice wasn't conceived through insemination. She has a mother here in Sweden whose name is Lo Moon.'

'And where is she now?' Greger asked.

'At Rödminnet,' Charlie replied. 'A residential care home

for girls. It's just thirty miles from here. I've called them and left a message.'

'But how could Gustav and Frida have kept this from us,' Stina exclaimed. 'How could they think it's more important to keep this secret than to save their child?'

'Maybe because they're convinced Lo's locked up at Rödminnet and couldn't possibly have had anything to do with it,' Charlie said. 'Hold on,' she continued when her phone rang. 'It's from the home.'

She stepped out into the hallway to take the call.

The woman on the other end introduced herself as Marianne Rehn, manager of the Rödminnet Residential Care Home. Charlie told her she needed to speak to one of their residents, a girl named Lo Moon.

'She's not here,' Marianne said.

'Then where is she?'

'We don't know. She absconded over a week ago.'

'Has she been in contact since?' Charlie tried to keep her voice calm.

'No, we've tried her phone, but she's not picking up. We reported it to the police in Kristinehamn. May I ask what this is about?'

'It's about the missing baby,' Charlie said without explaining further. She assumed most people had heard about the case by now.

'But what does that have to do with Lo?' Marianne asked.

'She's the child's biological mother.'

There was a long pause.

'You're mistaken,' Marianne said. 'Lo doesn't have a child.'

'It turns out she does,' Charlie replied. 'And I need to come and talk to you.'

'I have a group therapy session in half an hour.'
'That's going to have to wait.'

42

Charlie had convinced Stina she could do the Rödminnet visit by herself. It was unnecessary, she'd argued, to send more people out there when they knew Lo wasn't there. Greger was going to take Roy with him out to Hammarö and confront the Palmgrens with the new information.

The woman who met Charlie at the main entrance made her think of a corpse. Maybe it was her livid, blueish skin tone, or maybe the pale lipstick. After seeing so many dead people, details like that were enough to trigger a chain of associations that turned the living into the dead.

'I haven't had any information to indicate that Lo ever gave birth,' Marianne Rehn said after showing Charlie into her office. An odd-looking dog whose appearance reminded Charlie of the inbred cats at Lyckebo sat by her feet.

'Lo gave birth to a daughter in Russia nine months ago,' Charlie explained. 'It's the little girl who is missing, it's Beatrice.'

'I don't understand,' Marianne said. 'We have her medical records and there's nothing in them about her having given birth.'

'It's not in her medical records,' Charlie said.

'But Lo has never said anything about a child. We've had many deep conversations and—'

'I'm not here to figure out why she didn't tell you,' Charlie said. 'It's imperative that we find her as soon as possible. Do you have any idea where she might have gone?'

Marianne shook her head. Her mother was dead and she knew of no other relatives. She had rung around the foster families she had contact details for, but no one had heard from Lo. A man had called a few days ago, asking for her, but when he was told she had absconded, he'd hung up.

'Did you save the number?'

'It was an unknown number.'

'Does Lo have any friends here?' Charlie asked. 'Someone she's close with?'

'Yes, she shares a room with Sara,' Marianne said. 'I've talked to her, too, but she says she has no idea, though that isn't necessarily true. The girls here are good at clamming up to protect one another.' She shook her head as though loyalty to one's friends was a character flaw. 'But you could try to talk to her,' Marianne went on. 'Maybe she'll understand the gravity of the situation if it's a police officer asking the questions.'

Framed black-and-white photographs lined the walls of the long corridor. Charlie glimpsed white coats and people in hats lined up as she passed.

Sara's room was on the third floor. On their way up the stairs, they passed a recessed window, where a girl with tousled dark hair had curled up.

'Get down from there, Nicki,' Marianne said. 'You know we don't sit in windows.'

The girl called Nicki jumped down. When Charlie turned

around a few seconds later, she was back in the window.

'This is it,' Marianne said when they reached the third floor. After two sharp knocks, she opened the door.

'Leave me alone,' a voice said.

'The police are here,' Marianne said. 'Come down from the bed and please put something on over that nightgown.'

'It's a dress.'

Charlie recognised the voice, but it wasn't until she saw the girl in the black negligée that she realised who was standing in front of her. Images of her smoking at the top of the diving tower in Gullspång, the house with Christmas decorations in the windows in the middle of summer, dark eyes that had grown ... darker, Charlie noted as she met Sara Larsson's gaze.

43

'Well, Dad died,' Sara said when Charlie asked how she had ended up at Rödminnet.

Charlie knew that. She knew Svenka Larsson's body had finally given out after years of alcoholism, but just having a dead parent didn't get you locked up in a place like this.

'I need to talk to you about Lo Moon,' Charlie said. 'Do you know where she is?'

Sara shook her head.

'I'm not just asking because I want to find *her*,' Charlie added.

'Is it the baby?'

'Yes, so if you know where she might be, it's really important that you tell me.'

'I don't know,' Sara said. 'I would tell you if I knew. But if you want to know her better, maybe you should read what she left behind.' She went over to the bed and pulled a notebook from under the pillow. 'Lo's going to kill me, but I'll just have to deal with that.'

'Is it a diary?'

'It's a sunshine story,' Sara said and handed her the book. 'And, unfortunately, I think it's true.'

Charlie started to skim the pages.

'The important things are in Part Two,' Sara said. 'The stuff about the baby.'

Charlie flipped past memories of miserable foster parents and care homes. *Part Two*, she read. *Hell*.

I have come to lead you to the other shore, into eternal darkness.

Lo described her love for the children, the fellowship she felt with Charlotte, her excitement at being abroad. *I want to learn the language. Imagine being able to speak fluent Russian.*

Charlie speed-read and noticed that the tone was changing. Now, it was nocturnal visits, encounters in the dark with a person who had turned into a monster.

She looked up at Sara. 'Is the husband of that family the father of Lo's child?'

'Yes,' Sara said. 'He is.'

Charlie stepped out into the corridor to call Stina. She studied a framed black-and-white photograph of women in white clothing staring vacantly into the camera.

'David Jolander is the father,' she said without preamble when Stina picked up.

'How do you know?' Stina asked.

'I'm looking at Lo's notes,' Charlie replied and read a passage about one of the nocturnal visits aloud. 'It's David,' she said. 'David abused her. He's the father.' She read another paragraph: *It'll be better for everyone and they're paying me. They're giving me enough money for Mum and me to start a salon and then, when we're all set up, I'm going to get her back.* Stina?' Charlie said. 'Are you still there?'

'Yes. It's just a lot to take in. It's ... horrifying.'

'We need to find Lo Moon,' Charlie said.

'I'll bring David in straight away,' Stina replied. 'And the other three, too.'

'I don't think they know where Beatrice is,' Charlie said. 'If they did, they would have found her already. But we do have to put the screws on them now, especially David.'

She had put Lo's notebook down on a windowsill and kept turning the pages as they talked. Suddenly, a word jumped out at her and made her stop dead.

She ended the call and went back into the room. 'Sara,' she said. 'Have the two of you been to Gullspång? Did you take her to Lyckebo?'

44

Gullspång town centre with its potholed high street looked as derelict as Charlie remembered. Boarded-up shops, ancient slips of paper flapping on the noticeboard, the ageing men on the drunk bench outside the supermarket. She thought about how they'd used to shout things after them when they passed by. *You look radiant today, Betty. And look at your little girl. More and more like her mother every day.*

She passed the pizzerias, both the one that had burnt down and the one that was still open, and tried to prepare herself for what might await her in Lyckebo. Was Lo Moon there with Beatrice? Was she going to be sitting there in Betty's spot on the porch, squinting at the spring sun with the baby in her arms?

Lyckebo, Charlie thought as she parked next to the sign from which time, weather, and wind had almost erased the name. Hasn't there been enough grief and loss here? Just this once, please give me a happy ending.

The tree swing on its rotting rope swayed slightly in the wind. Charlie looked up at the windows with their lace curtains. Nothing moved. She continued around to the back. The key was in its usual place under the terracotta pot next to the wooden pallets by the door. Just as she stuck it in the lock, she heard a noise behind her.

She spun around and stared straight into a pair of yellow cat eyes. For a few bizarre seconds, she thought it was the cat she had dug up in the Palmgrens' garden. But this one was feral, Charlie realised, because its fur was matted and its eyes ravenous. It was probably a descendant of the many cats she and Betty had kept once. The ones that had never been spayed and just kept multiplying.

When she opened the door, the cat slipped inside. Charlie shouted hello and listened, but the only sound was the deep creaking and cracking she remembered from her childhood.

Her phone rang. The sound made her jump. It was Greger. She pushed the 'Can I call back?' button and continued further into the house. Her house.

Everyone's welcome here, whether blind or lame, lost or drunk, human or animal.

Charlie recalled the partygoers and their confused dogs, remembered watching them roll around in the garden and mused that at times it had been hard to tell them apart, the humans and the animals.

She found the cat in the kitchen, drinking milk from an old sugar bowl.

Someone had given it milk. Someone had been here. She bent down and sniffed the milk. How old was it?

Charlie straightened back up and walked through the parlour, glancing over at the dusty piano. *Any song you'd like, so long as it's not in a minor key.*

The cat had followed her and now jumped up onto the moth-eaten sofa on which Betty had spent her dark periods. *Shut out the light, sweetheart. It's all the light that hurts.*

And there, on the table, lay something that didn't belong. Charlie moved closer. It was a dummy. Her hand trembled when she pulled a clean tissue out of her coat pocket and carefully wrapped it up.

'Hello!' she called again.

Silence.

She started to climb the stairs to the first floor. When she was halfway, she stopped and listened again. Nothing. The dust on the upstairs landing was illuminated by the rays of spring sun trickling in through the skylight. On her left was the room that would have been Johan's if he'd been allowed to come live with them. Charlie looked over at the half-finished bed Mattias had started to build, the cars Betty had painted on the walls, faded now.

She didn't want to go into Betty's room, but knew she had to. The door creaked when she pushed it open and stepped over the high threshold. She looked at the make-up table, the bed, and the window through which you could see part of the root cellar and the big oak tree.

Something was wrong. The clothes rack by the back wall under the slanted ceiling. Something was missing: Betty's red dress. She went up to the old fur coats and pushed them aside, but the dress was gone. She could have sworn it had been there the last time she was in the house. Could she be misremembering?

No. She had stood in this room and stared at it. She was sure of it.

After putting the key back under the flowerpot, she called Greger.

'But why would she have gone to your childhood home?'

he asked after she updated him on what she had found in the house.

'Sara, Lo's friend, is from Gullspång. I've met her before, and she used to stay at my house when things were bad at home. Apparently, she brought Lo there a couple of weeks ago.'

'And you think Lo went back there?' Greger said.

'Someone has definitely been here,' Charlie replied. 'Considering the dummy and that Lo has been here before and knows where the key is ...'

She reversed out from the grass road and glanced back at the house.

I haven't been getting enough sleep, she told herself when she suddenly thought she could see the contours of a face in one of the windows. She had checked every room. There was no one there.

'Have you brought David in?' she asked.

Greger said they had. Both the Jolanders and the Palmgrens were at the station.

'And what are they saying?'

'That a deal was made, a solution was found that worked for everyone involved and that at first they had been sure Lo couldn't have been the one who took her. They thought she was still at Rödminnet and didn't want us to start digging. Because the adoption wasn't exactly done by the book. But then, a few days ago, Gustav decided to make sure, so he called and was told she had absconded. Since then, they have been conducting their own search for her.'

'What in God's name were they thinking?' Charlie said.

'I don't understand it either,' Greger said. 'I mean, how were they going to explain it?'

'I guess they're used to looking out for themselves,' Charlie noted. 'Have you confronted David about the rapes, about him being the father?'

'Stina's with him now.'

'Don't let him go,' Charlie said. 'Hold on, Sara's calling. I need to take this.'

She ended the call with Greger.

'Sara?' she said. 'Did something happen?'

'It's Lo,' Sara replied. 'Lo's here.'

'And Beatrice?' Charlie asked. 'Is the baby with her? Sara?' But the call had cut out.

45

It felt like the cars in front of her were driving with their parking brakes on. Charlie cursed the winding road which didn't allow for overtaking. She wished she were in a car with lights and sirens. Greger and the team were on their way from Karlstad, but she would likely get there before them. She got a busy signal when she called Sara, so instead, she dialled the number to Rödminnet. Marianne, the manager, answered. She hadn't seen Lo, but she had just been told Sara was now missing, too.

'Look for them,' Charlie said.

'I'll tell the staff and the girls,' Marianne said.

'But be careful,' Charlie cautioned. 'I'll be there in thirty minutes.'

Soon after they hung up, Sara called back. She sounded out of breath and panicked.

'Lo met me out back to say goodbye,' she said. 'I tried to make her stay, but she ran off. Please, hurry.'

'Did she have the baby with her?' Charlie asked.

'Yes! She has the baby.'

It sounded like Sara was trying to say something else, but she was breathing so hard Charlie couldn't make out the words.

'Sara,' she said. 'It's important that you try to stay calm. Do you know where Lo is now?'

'She ran across the field and up into the woods and I fell and now I don't see her. She's gone.'

'Was it just now?'

'Yes! Just now.'

'Do you have any idea where she might be going?'

'I'm scared she might be going to the Cliff of Insanity,' Sara replied. 'It's this cliff that—'

'Run there as fast as you can,' Charlie said. 'Try to talk to her calmly if she's there. I'll be there very soon. Is there anyone at Rödminnet who can show me the way?'

'I'll make sure someone's there to take you,' Sara said. 'But don't bring anyone from the staff.'

Sara

Lo was standing at the edge of the cliff with the baby in her arms. Her dress, Betty Lager's red dress, was flapping in the wind.

'Stop,' she said when she saw me. 'Stop right there or I'll jump.'

'Lo,' I said. 'Please, Lo.' I reached out for her. My hand was shaking. My whole body was shaking. I felt sick. 'Lo,' I said again. 'What about our salon?'

'That's never going to happen,' Lo replied. 'How am I supposed to open a salon when all the money's gone. Mum spent it all on drugs.' She started to laugh. It was a loud, hysterical laugh that made the baby cry.

'You're making her sad,' I said. 'Lo?' Now I was crying, too.

'Mum's gone,' Lo said and adjusted her grip on the baby. 'There's nothing left.'

'Your daughter,' I said, pointing to the girl. 'Your daughter's still here, and you. We can start over.'

'No,' Lo replied. She shook her head. 'No, no, no. They're going to take her away from me. I'll never get her back.'

'But ...' I said. Then I didn't know how to go on, because Lo was probably right.

'Mum's dead,' Lo went on. 'The money's gone, and this world is rotten to the core. Don't you see that? Are you blind?'

'I know. But it can be lovely, too.'

'They're going to take her away,' Lo said. 'History's going to repeat itself. It has to end here.'

'She's so lovely,' I said with a nod to the baby. Her white lace hat was on the verge of blowing off. I inched forward.

'Don't move,' Lo said. She took a tiny step backward. She was dangerously close to the edge now. 'Don't come any closer.'

46

Nicki, the girl who had been curled up in the window, was waiting for Charlie outside Rödminnet.

'How fast are you?' she asked.

'Fast,' Charlie said.

'Good, because I don't think we have much time.'

Nicki broke into a run. Charlie followed her around the back of the main house and out into a field. The soft ground made her steps heavy, and Charlie felt panic growing inside her.

Finally, after what felt like an eternity, they reached the edge of the trees on the other side, and a narrow, slippery path led them up through the steep terrain.

Minutes later, Charlie saw them up ahead. The girl in Betty's red dress with the baby in her arms, swaying at the edge of the cliff. The wind snatching at the fabric and her hair. Sara was standing just a few feet away from them.

'Stop right there!' Lo shouted when she spotted Charlie. 'And you too, Nicki. Don't come any closer.'

Sara turned around. 'Charlie,' she called out. 'Help us, please help us.'

Charlie stood stock-still, her heart thumping from fear and effort, one mistake now and it would all be over.

'Lo,' she said. 'I know you're scared, but—'

'I'm not scared,' Lo said. 'I'm not scared of anything.'

'Could you just step away from the edge so we can talk?' Charlie said.

'There's nothing to talk about.'

'But the baby ...' Charlie began.

'She's mine,' Lo said. 'It's my baby.'

'I know that,' Charlie said. 'I know she is. And you've been treated very badly, Lo.'

'Stop talking to me like you know me. You know nothing about me.'

'I know you've had a really tough time,' Charlie replied. 'And I just want to help you and the baby.'

'You people always say that. I don't believe you.'

'I get that,' Charlie said. She thought to herself that this was a person that life had thrown far too much at, who'd had enough. *There's a limit and once it's reached there's no way back.*

But life couldn't be allowed to be over for this girl.

'You may not believe me,' Charlie continued. 'But I do promise. I'm going to make sure you get help.'

'It's true,' Sara said, tears streaming down her cheeks. 'Listen to her, Lo, she's one of us. She's the little girl who used to live in Lyckebo. She's a ... sunshine story.'

'There are no sunshine stories,' Lo replied. She wobbled precariously.

'Your daughter's life has barely begun,' Charlie said. 'Don't you want to give her a chance to—'

'To what?' Lo said. 'To let the whole world piss on her, so

she can be locked up in institutions and have her foster fathers fuck her?'

'It doesn't have to be like that,' Charlie said.

They heard dogs barking in the distance.

'Are there more people coming?' Lo asked.

'Yes,' Charlie said. 'But they don't want to hurt you, Lo. They want to help you.' She considered pulling her phone out and texting Greger to hang back, but she didn't dare to take her eyes off Lo.

'I don't believe you,' Lo said. 'I don't believe anything anymore.'

'Stop!' Charlie shouted at Sara, who suddenly dashed forward.

But Sara didn't listen. She reached Lo, who handed her the baby.

'Her name is Beatrice,' Lo said. 'Her name is Beatrice Lo Moon. Never forget her name.'

And then she jumped.

47

Gustav and Frida Palmgren looked out of place sitting on the green plastic chairs in the interview room. Beatrice was cooing happily in Frida's arms, with her bunny blanket in one hand and a small rubber giraffe in the other. She was the only one in the room who seemed unaffected by the events that had brought them all together at the police station.

Social services had made an expedited decision to temporarily reunite Beatrice with the Palmgrens, with reference to the best interest of the child. What the permanent solution would be, no one knew yet, but at the moment, Frida seemed unable to take in anything beyond the fact that Beatrice was back. She barely took her eyes off her.

Gustav was also completely focused on Beatrice. Charlie had to ask him to answer the question twice before he reacted.

'We wanted a child so badly,' he said. Then he told them about their longing, all the failed attempts, the broken dreams that had almost destroyed them. Maybe Charlie was supposed to understand and feel sympathy, but she couldn't, not when she knew a damaged young woman in a morgue had paid the price for their dream.

'She agreed,' Gustav said. 'Lo wanted to do it. She knew Beatrice would have a better life with us.'

'Then why didn't you go through the official adoption process? And why did you pay her?' Charlie asked.

'Because we wanted to,' Gustav replied. 'We wanted her to have the funds to open that salon she was always talking about. We just wanted to make her life better.'

'Or maybe you wanted to make your own life better? And keep the fact that Beatrice wasn't your biological child secret. You wanted it so badly you circumvented the law, and then, when Beatrice went missing, you withheld the truth from us. You wanted to take care of it yourselves, even though lives were at stake. There's no excuse for it.'

'You're right,' Frida said before Gustav could object. 'We were selfish.' She stroked Beatrice's head. 'We tried to keep it all secret so we could keep her, we—'

'Did you know David is her biological father? That he repeatedly raped the child who had been placed in his care and impregnated her?'

'What are you saying?' Frida exclaimed. She stared at Charlie as though she expected her to take it back, to say it wasn't true. Then she turned to Gustav. 'Tell me it's not true.'

'I don't know,' Gustav said. His face had gone from slightly sweaty to bright red and shiny. 'I don't know if it's true,' he continued, 'but I promise you I didn't know anything about it before this happened.'

'I don't believe you,' Frida said and hugged Beatrice closer. 'Your promises mean nothing.'

'Frida,' Gustav replied. 'I didn't know.'

'The girl,' Frida said. 'Lo ... it's so ... horrible ...' She shook her head.

Gustav seemed on the verge of tears now, but Charlie couldn't bring herself to say anything to make him feel better.

She kept seeing Lo throwing herself off the edge of the cliff, her mangled body on the rocks far below. She was the victim in this story.

'Maybe Stina and I should do the interview with David,' Greger suggested when Charlie came out to have a cup of coffee.

'Why?'

'Well, I think you know why. You just saw a girl jump to her death wearing your mother's old dress. You shouldn't even have talked to Gustav and Frida.'

'How did you know the dress was my mother's?'

'I talked to Sara,' Greger said.

'My mother died over twenty years ago,' Charlie said. 'And it was just a dress.'

'You've witnessed something horrific, Charlie,' Greger insisted. 'And you're as white as a sheet and ...'

'And what?'

'And you're shaking,' Greger said with a nod towards her hand holding the coffee cup.

'It's part of my job description,' Charlie said, 'witnessing horrific events. We vent later, when it's done.'

David sat down in front of Charlie and Greger in a tauntingly unwrinkled suit.

Charlie thought about Lo's description of him. *During the day, he's a successful family man, and then, after the sun goes down, a creature of darkness.*

Next to David sat his lawyer in an equally expensive suit. Not a lot of people could rustle up a lawyer on such short notice, but, of course, David belonged to the select few who could.

'How many of you am I supposed to talk to?' David said.

'You don't have to say a word,' his lawyer said.

'He agreed to talk to us,' Charlie reminded him. 'We just want to have a conversation.'

'What do you want to know that I haven't already told you?' David asked. 'I've already admitted I might be her father.'

'Yes, I suppose you figured we'd do a DNA test,' said Charlie. 'So there was no avoiding it.'

'It's not against the law to have an extramarital child,' the lawyer said.

'No one said it was,' replied Charlie. 'But your client has withheld important information from our investigation and obstructed our work.'

'I didn't want to destroy my family,' David said.

'But a child had been kidnapped,' Greger said. 'And if we had known the facts of the case from the start ...'

'Then maybe a young woman wouldn't have fallen to her death today,' Charlie finished.

She had crossed a line, she could tell from the look Greger shot her. But it was the truth. If David or any of the others who had known had talked to them, they might have been able to save Lo.

'It's not my fault she jumped,' David said. 'It's never anyone else's fault when a person chooses to ...'

Charlie met David's eyes and thought about what Betty used to say about her boss at the factory. *You can see it in his eyes. They're dead. He's a man without a soul.*

'Tell me what happened in Moscow,' Charlie said. 'Tell me what happened between you and Lo Moon.'

'What happened?'

David looked at his lawyer, who repeated that he didn't have to say a word.

'Sooner or later, you will have to talk,' Charlie said.

'I suppose we had some kind of relationship,' David said. 'That girl could be pretty—'

'Lo,' Charlie interrupted. 'Her name was Lo.'

'Yes,' David said. 'I know what her name was.'

'Go on,' Greger said.

'She could be pretty inviting,' David continued.

Charlie clenched her fists and thought about what Lo had written about her face in the pillow, gasping for air, about how David had shot his load inside her as though she weren't even a human being.

'We've been told differently,' she said.

'Is that right?' David said.

'We have Lo's diary. And she doesn't seem to be in agreement about what happened between the two of you.' Finally, she thought when she saw David's face twitch, finally something has broken through that cocksure façade.

'Well, the young woman in question is no longer alive,' the lawyer put in. He leaned back in his chair and adjusted his glasses.

'Lo,' Charlie said. 'Lo Moon.'

'I never said otherwise,' the lawyer countered.

'No, you never said her name at all,' Charlie retorted. 'So I just wanted to remind you and your client that she had a name, that she was a human being who ...' Her voice broke. She reached for her water glass and took a long sip. 'As I was saying, we have her diary,' she continued, well aware that Lo's words would be of little consequence. The lawyer knew this too, of course, and now he shot her a superior smile and said that it might be hard to assess the credibility of a confused

314

girl's diary. A girl who had a fondness for drugs and alcohol and had been in trouble with the law more than once.

'What happens now?' David asked. 'With Beatrice, I mean ...'

'That's not up to us,' Greger replied. 'What are you doing?' he said when Charlie got up from her chair.

'I'm leaving,' Charlie said. 'This conversation is over.'

A journalist stopped Charlie in the hotel lobby.

'How does it feel?' she asked. 'How does it feel to be the one who found Beatrice?'

'It feels good,' Charlie replied, 'but let's not forget that another life ended today.'

'Could you tell me more about that?' the journalist said and pushed her microphone so close to Charlie's face that it grazed her chin.

'No,' she said and pushed the microphone away. 'I can't.'

She went up to her room. In her bag lay a stack of letters Sara had given her with trembling hands before Charlie left Rödminnet. They're from your grandmother, she'd said. She lived here when this was a mental hospital.

Charlie had accepted the letters without correcting her, without explaining that she must be mistaken, that her grandmother had never lived at Rödminnet.

48

Dorothea was watering the geraniums in the stairwell. Charlie gave her a curt nod, but before she could make it past her, Dorothea pointed out it wasn't really her week to do the watering, it was Charlie's.

'I'm terribly sorry,' Charlie said, 'but I've been away for work. Maybe you've read about the missing baby?'

'Beatrice?' Dorothea put her watering can down. 'I didn't know you were there ... we've been following the case every day ... It's just amazing that you found her.'

Charlie nodded. 'I can water them later, just need to unpack first,' she said.

'No, no. I'll do it. I'm sure you need to ... rest. And no one takes care of them properly anyway. Mårbacka geraniums mustn't be overwatered, but I seem to be the only one who understands that.'

Charlie was just about to continue up the stairs when Dorothea spoke again.

'A man came here looking for you,' she said. 'He slunk in behind Annie from the first floor and rang your doorbell a bit longer than is usual. I just thought you might want to know.'

'What did he look like?' Charlie asked. 'Or, I mean, did you see what he looked like?' She did her best to appear calm, but she wasn't.

'Like a ...' Dorothea wrinkled her nose slightly. 'He was wearing a leather jacket,' she said, as though that said everything she needed to know about him. 'He said he wanted to check on you, that you had felt poorly last Friday, that he had helped you home. And then ...'

'What?' Charlie said.

'He said his name was Viktor, and he asked me to let you know that he hoped you were feeling better, so ... well, now I have.'

'Thank you,' Charlie said.

'Don't mention it,' Dorothea replied. 'It must be nice to have such thoughtful friends.' She smiled. Was it friendly this time, or just a new level of disguised scorn? Charlie didn't care.

Viktor, she thought and felt calm spread through her body. A nice, normal guy.

She stepped over the pile of advertisements and bills in the hallway, went straight to the sofa and lay down. She knew she should go to bed. Her brain was fried from stress, sleep deprivation, and the slideshow of Lo on the cliff playing on a loop. But then she remembered the letters Sara had given her. Why would she think they were from her grandmother?

Charlie got up, grabbed the stack of opened envelopes from her bag and picked up the first one.

The dreams are back. Last night, it was the three of us; you, me, and the little one, the way it should have been. We were walking down the path to the lake, autumn leaves and sunshine, past the house on the hill.

He wasn't there.

In all the world, it was just us – me and my daughters – and it was so real I never wanted to wake up.

Charlie turned the letter over to check the sender's name. But it just said *Mummy*. It was the same with the next one, and the one after that, they were all signed Mummy.

The girls, the daughters … could it have been … Cecilia Manner holding the pen? The woman who, according to Betty, *was an amazing person who dared to swim against the tide, who had just been unlucky.*

Why?

Because that's just how life is, unfair.

Betty hadn't said anything about Cecilia being sent to Rödminnet, but that didn't mean she hadn't been. Betty Lager had withheld bigger truths than that. *And don't blame me for it. Has the truth ever made you happier?*

Charlie pulled out the next letter and was transported back in time, to when Rödminnet was a mental hospital. She read about hot baths and monotonous chores, about other patients' visions, about the beetles under her skin and the snakes in her bed. It was like stepping into her own nightmare, the one about losing first her footing and then herself, losing her mind.

And then, an old photograph. Charlie needed no more than a quick glance to know Sara had been right. She recognised the young woman with the baby in her arms. She'd seen the picture in Lyckebo a thousand times. It was Betty. Betty and her.

Charlie put the photo down on her stomach and looked up at the ceiling. She had to pause to take it all in. It was dizzying to think that she had read her grandmother's words, that Cecilia Manner had been there, just a few miles away, without her knowing it. And so, here it was again, the horror story that had shaped her entire life. Betty's stillborn sister and the murder of the little boy whose dad had caused it, now told by her grandmother instead.

Charlie took a deep breath. She needed wine, but that would have to wait. She picked up the next letter.

We were sitting on the bench by the pavilion, and I said to Flora: here she comes. Here comes my daughter. And then ... I saw the child in your arms. You were carrying your sister. Your sister had come back.

And I didn't want to scare you. I didn't want to take the baby from you. I just wanted to hold her a while. I had dreamt about it for so long.

Charlie stayed on the sofa while dusk fell outside the windows. She lay there staring into space, thinking about how often Betty had lain just like that, moaning about sounds and light. But she wasn't Betty. Her thoughts circled back to Cecilia, the assault, the child that had come out dead, and seven-year-old Betty who had witnessed it all. Could Cecilia's and Betty's madness be blamed on terrible circumstances, or had there been a darkness in their natures? And if so, did that darkness exist inside her, too?

And what difference did it really make what had caused what? She was who she was regardless of what had made her that way and she could only do her best to avoid causing herself and others harm. So simple. So difficult.

She fell asleep. In her dreams, a girl in a red dress was dancing to Betty's favourite song. Her face shifted with every twirl: Betty, Annabelle, Francesca, Lo. They laughed, became one, fell, were crushed, got back up, and fell again.

*

When Charlie woke up, the room was dark, and she was sweating as though she had a fever. She had to eat something, shower, and go to bed.

In the butler's pantry next to the kitchen, she turned on the overhead lights and stared at Susanne's painting. The flowering cherry grove. Lyckebo. Betty and her on the porch. Her eyes went to the little children in the grass, the baby girl and the boy wrapped in each other and the grass. They lay with their faces pressed together and now she thought she could make out something she hadn't noticed before, a hint of a smile on their faces.

Sara

Did I seriously think I was going to become a moustache plucker at a salon? Did I think Lo, me, and her mother were going to run a business together and live happily ever after?

Had I become a girl who believed in sunshine stories?

Maybe not, but as I walked up the gravel path and past the headless angel with Lo's doll styling head under my arm, I felt hopeful for the first time in forever. Social services in Gullspång had set me up with a flat. If I behaved myself and didn't break their rules, I would be allowed to live by myself, like I'd wanted to from the start.

I looked over at the bench where Lo used to wait for Donna and wished more than ever that there was a life after death, a place where they could be together and their dreams would come true. And I thought about little Beatrice. I hoped life would be kinder to her than it had been to her mother.

Jonas was standing in the car park, smoking. When he saw me, he raised his arm and waved.

Just as I was about to close the iron gate behind me, Picco came running across the forecourt. I squatted down in the grass and let her lick my face. Then I grabbed her deformed little ears and pressed my nose against hers.

'Bye,' I whispered. 'Bye, my little sunshine story.'

Credits

Orion Fiction would like to thank everyone at Orion who worked on the publication of *For the Lost* in the UK.

Editorial
Francesca Pathak
Lucy Brem

Copyeditor
Rebecca Wilcock

Proofreader
Jade Craddock

Audio
Paul Stark
Jake Alderson

Contracts
Anne Goddard
Humayra Ahmed
Ellie Bowker

Design
Debbie Holmes
Joanna Ridley
Nick May

Editorial Management
Charlie Panayiotou
Jane Hughes
Bartley Shaw
Tamara Morriss

Finance
Jasdip Nandra
Afeera Ahmed
Elizabeth Beaumont
Sue Baker

323

Marketing
Tanjiah Islam

Production
Ruth Sharvell

Publicity
Patricia Deveer

Sales
Jen Wilson

Esther Waters
Victoria Laws
Rachael Hum
Anna Egelstaff
Frances Doyle
Georgina Cutler

Operations
Jo Jacobs
Sharon Willis

If you loved *For The Lost*, don't miss Lina's first novel featuring DI Charlie Lager . . .

For The Missing

And check out the thrilling second novel in
the DI Charlie Lager series . . .

For The Dead